I0726812

# THE HOUSEWIFE ASSASSIN'S GREATEST HITS

JOSIE BROWN

A BOOK BY

SIGNAL PRESS

Library of Congress Cataloging-in-Publication Data is available upon request

Cover Design by Andrew Brown, ClickTwiceDesign.com

Trade Paperback ISBN: 978-1-942052-78-4

V022319

and humorous from the start, and that continued throughout, I was pleased to discover that this is the first of a series and look forward to getting my hands on Book Two so I can see where life takes Donna and her family next!"

—*Me, My Books, and I*


"The two halves of Donna's life make sense. As you follow her story, there's no point where you think of her as "Assassin Donna" vs. "Mummy Donna', her attitude to life is even throughout. I really like how well this is done. And as for Jack. I'll have one of those, please?"

—*The Northern Witch's Book Blog*

# Novels in The Housewife Assassin Series

*The Housewife Assassin's Handbook* (Book 1)

*The Housewife Assassin's Guide to Gracious Killing* (Book 2)

*The Housewife Assassin's Killer Christmas Tips* (Book 3)

*The Housewife Assassin's Relationship Survival Guide* (Book 4)

*The Housewife Assassin's Vacation to Die For* (Book 5)

*The Housewife Assassin's Recipes for Disaster* (Book 6)

*The Housewife Assassin's Hollywood Scream Play* (Book 7)

*The Housewife Assassin's Killer App* (Book 8)

*The Housewife Assassin's Hostage Hosting Tips* (Book 9)

*The Housewife Assassin's Garden of Deadly Delights* (Book 10)

*The Housewife Assassin's Tips for Weddings, Weapons, and Warfare* (Book 11)

*The Housewife Assassin's Husband Hunting Hints* (Book 12)

*The Housewife Assassin's Ghost Protocol* (Book 13)

*The Housewife Assassin's Terrorist TV Guide* (Book 14)

*The Housewife Assassin's Deadly Dossier* (Book 15: The Series Prequel)

*The Housewife Assassin's Greatest Hits* (Book 16)

*The Housewife Assassin's Fourth Estate Sale* (Book 17)

*The Housewife Assassin's Horrorscope* (Book 18)

---

1

# That'll Be the Day (That I Die)

RECORDED BY BUDDY HOLLY AND THE CRICKETS. RELEASED MAY 1957, the song spent one week on the greatest hits chart at Number One.

*You find a man's body in a ditch. It is face down and seems to be unconscious—or worse yet, dead. How can you tell if he is still alive?*

*First, check for a pulse. You do this by placing two fingers on the man's wrist. If a few minutes go by and you haven't felt a heartbeat, time to face up to the fact that you've been holding hands with a dead man. Drop it before someone sees you and thinks you have some sick fetish.*

*Next, hold up a mirror under his nose to discern if any vapor is exhaled. If indeed some condensation collects, well then huzzah, you've got a live one! (Tip: Do wait a bit after he gains consciousness before suggesting he clip any nose hairs you found particularly disgusting.)*

*A final suggestion: give him mouth-to-mouth resuscitation. If he doesn't come to, restrain the urge to tell any future blind dates that you kissed a stiff. Seriously, you don't want a corpse's kiss to be your last.*

THE HOWLS FROM THE RUSSIAN HACKER WHOSE SPINE I'M CRUSHING with my knee could easily pass for Chewbacca's signature wail.

Despite this, no one else on this floor of the San Diego Marriott seems a bit concerned. In fact, applause can be heard coming from up and down the hall. It is, after all, the middle of Comic-Con.

I'm dressed in a replica of the iconic Slave Girl outfit: perfect for luring my Star Wars-obsessed target into my ad hoc torture chamber. In fact, Russian Hacker is dressed as Darth Vader—or was, until I convinced him that stripping naked except for his helmet was a much better look for a princess with daddy issues.

Darth's costume is apropos since he and a few of his tech team in Russia's intelligence agency, the GRU, successfully hacked the cell phones of every member of the United States Congress and the U.S. Senate. (Really? Would our elected officials believe POTUS would send a personal email invitation to his wife's book launch party with her name misspelled? But I digress...)

My Leia-kini may not leave much to the imagination, but hidden within the links of my fifteen-foot-long slave girl chain are all sorts of goodies that will give any man nightmares he'll never forget. Whereas a few twists of the nipple clamps got Darth to follow me anywhere—even to the bed, where he now lies, spread-eagled—he has yet to give up the intel I need: his phone's pass-word. Through the device, the CIA can release an undetectable virus that will allow it to peruse all the GRU's dirty little secrets—

Especially as they pertain to all that Putin and company know about us. One good hack deserves another, right?

It should be interesting to see how their dictator—*COUGH*—president reacts when he learns that *he's* lost Russia's next election.

Darth's hacking mission was so successful that he and the rest of his tech team—for now, let's just call the other two guys Han and Luke—were rewarded with a trip to anywhere in the world they wanted to go. Where did they choose? You guessed it: Disneyland!

So, off they went in a private plane formerly belonging to a Russian oil oligarch who disappeared after refusing to allow Putin's cousin to buy his company for a few shekels on the ruble. However, the moment the plane landed in Orange County, Darth, Han, and Luke ditched their GRU babysitters and hightailed it to Comic-Con instead.

I intercepted Darth at a Star Wars Cosplay meet-up sponsored by Tinder. His English is good enough that he understands the words sex, drugs, and nipple clamps. Who'd have figured that our revered statesmen's texts could serve as the perfect S&M language primer for our enemies?

What Darth didn't understand is that he'd be wearing the nipple clamps—not me.

And because this interrogation is taking much longer than I anticipated, it's time to bring out the heavy artillery.

So that he can see the full extent of what I have planned, I yank the slave chain that is now wrapped around his neck, gagging him unless he follows his tether that insists he flip over onto his back. His eyes bulge as I pick up Leia's weapon of choice: the laser sword. When switched on, it becomes a glowing green beacon—

Of truth.

*His.*

I stab the bed a few inches from his right foot. The sound of the sword searing a perfect slit into eighteen-hundred-thread count Egyptian cotton bed sheets is nothing compared to the pungent smell it makes when it hits the Duxiana mattress's goose-down layer while making its way through memory foam.

"It's a real laser?" he screams.

"You betcha," I assure him. "Cool, huh?" My black-ops mission team's tech operative, Arnie Locklear, had a blast designing this adorable little gadget.

To squash Darth's doubts to the contrary, I trace the inside of his leg—ankle, calf, knee, and thigh—with the beaming blade. When it gets within an inch of the appendage he'll miss the most; I allow it to hover there. "Ah! Little Darth has never been circumcised."

I click my tongue as a way of pointing out the obvious: how, with a flick of my wrist, I can remedy this dilemma, perhaps by an inch or two.

Darth is sobbing so loudly that, at first, I don't hear the trill of my cell phone.

Annoyed, I sigh loudly. "Hold that thought," I command him as I glance down at the phone.

It's the baker who's making the cake I ordered for tonight's intimate gathering—

To which Darth is certainly not invited.

The baker is talking a mile a minute. Unfortunately, between Darth's whimpers and all the shouts and murmurs from the cosplay out in the hall, all I can make out is, "—concerned that this record heat wave we're having will melt the seven-minute egg-white icing on the cake before being delivered to the hotel! Would you prefer we switch to buttercream, or marzipan?"

"Wait…what? Look, hold on a moment, please. It's a bit noisy here," I explain calmly before muting my cell phone.

So that Darth gets the hint to shut the hell up, I stab the bed with the sword just an inch from his ear. As it sizzles through the foam, I growl, "If you make one more sound, I'll give you the closest shave of your life. Get me?"

He stifles a groan and then nods his head vigorously.

Much better.

Back to the baker: "Here's a thought: bring it in a refrigerated van."

The baker pauses before asking, "Well, okay…but you do know it will quadruple your cost, right?"

"Doesn't matter. In fact, I don't mind renting the hearse—I mean, the 'van' for the whole night. I'll get it back to you in the morning, all spick and span"—I mute the phone again, but Darth doesn't know it—"from any blood or DNA."

My declaration brings tears to his eyes. Darth finally gets the picture:

The Force is not with him.

"Sure." The baker sighs with relief. "Then egg-white icing it is."

I hang up before she can hear Darth, who is now blubbering incoherently.

Okay, time for me to play good cop. "Look, handsome, I know what you're thinking. On the one hand, all it takes is one little oopsie and you're a eunuch—or worse still, a dead man. On the other, is that any worse than what's bound to happen when one of your buddies is eventually given the task of tracing the virus to your cell?" I click my tongue at his dilemma. "Vlad and his GRU Impalers will toss you into a Chernobyl cell so deep that the only way anyone will be able to find you is that you'll be glowing in the dark from all that radiation."

His patented Chewbacca howl echoes off the walls.

Enough of this crap. I've got places to go, and a very special someone to see. Tonight, I'm hosting a very important soiree:

A surprise birthday party for my husband, Jack.

I should never have allowed Ryan Clancy—my boss at Acme Industries—to talk me into this assignment, and today of all days! I only agreed to this mission when Ryan promised that I could keep any and all swag I picked up. My fourteen-year-old son, Jeff, will be beside himself when he sees that I scored autographs from Felicity Jones (*Star Wars*), Ryan Reynolds (*Deadpool*), Benedict Cumberbatch (*Dr. Strange*), and Scarlett Johanssen (*Black Widow*).

(To be honest, Darth collected those goodies. Well, too bad. They fall under the category of spoils of war.)

With my sword, I cut figure eights in the air. "It's your lucky day, Darth. Now, if you can shut your pie hole, you'll hear an offer that I'm sure you'll find hard to refuse."

He purses his lips to keep them zipped.

"Much better. Now, here's what you'll do." I hold up his cell phone. "You give me your password, and then redial your GRU babysitters. Heck, they're probably so frantic by now that they've already got the Kremlin in a tizzy! Better to get a jump on this thing before they figure out on their own how and why you ditched them, right? It's the only way to save your manhood." I aim the sword within an inch of little Darth. "And for that matter, your life."

No need to ask twice.

I hold up his cell phone. "What's the passcode?"

"R2D2…twice," he sighs.

Duh. Gee, I could have guessed it.

After I punch in the code, I dial Arnie Locklear, my tech-op at Acme. When he picks up, he chortles, "One-two-three…Mother McGee!"

It's his way of signaling me that he's ready to release the virus without a trace of its originating source.

Next, I re-enter the number of Darth's Russian babysitters, who've left a message every minute on the minute. The second they pick up, the virus will be released.

Darth is still cuffed, so I have to hold it up to his mouth. Another twist of the chain around his neck lets him know that I'm monitoring every word—and that the wrong one will kill him.

My handler, Abu Nagashahi has had eyes and ears on me since the start of this mission. Fluent in Russian, he also listens in. A few minutes later, he murmurs into my ear: "They're pissed, but they're buying his story. All's well that ends well."

"Good, because I need closure on this anecdote."

"I hear yah." Of course, he knows what I mean:

I've got a pressing engagement, one that cannot be missed.

With that in mind, I end the connection.

Before Darth can protest, I've stabbed him with a needle filled with Kickapoo joy juice—as it turns out, of Russian origins.

Known as SP-117, it works as a truth serum and also erases any memory of events that took place before taking the drug.

In other words, Darth's torture at the hands of Princess Leia will soon be just a pleasant fantasy, if he remembers it at all.

"Better get hopping. The GRU is already en route, and Darth's buds are banging on doors, looking for him and 'Princess Leia with 'zee hoot bood…'"

I snort. "'Hot bod?' Gee, I guess I should feel flattered."

Well, of course I am. Perhaps I'll hold onto this costume if only to see if Jack finds it alluring. Not that he needs any cosplay to get in the mood. He's got a pretty impressive laser sword, and it's EverReady.

Thank goodness it doesn't glow in the dark.

By the time Acme's helicopter lands back in Orange County, Abu has already briefed Ryan on my mission's success. As I drive home, he calls to congratulate me.

"All in a day's work," I respond glibly. "Ryan, I presume you'll keep Jack busy so I have the afternoon to take care of business?"

"Not to worry. Something major has come up that should have us tied up for at least a couple of hours: a conference call with Marcus Branham." Ryan is referring to the United States Director of Intelligence who replaced Carl Stone, my ex, who blackmailed the United States president, Lee Chiffray for the position before his terrorist activities were once again exposed by Acme.

And, yes, we took Carl down.

Ryan adds, "MI6 will also be on the call, along with the *Bundesnachrichtendienst*, and the D.I.H."

"Sounds like an important powwow," I murmur. The fact that Branham's counterparts in Great Britain, Germany, and Japan are included indicates something big is going down, and it won't be pretty.

Well, here's hoping it doesn't happen before the evening is out. Otherwise, Jack's party will have to be postponed—

Leaving me with a cake that's dripping seven-minute egg white icing in this Godforsaken heat wave.

"I'm sure Jack will fill you in on it when you see him." By Ryan's wistful tone, I can tell he's hoping that I'll suggest joining them.

Ain't happening. The night belongs to Jack.

With that in mind, I remind Ryan, "Remember, mum's the word."

Ryan sighs. "Don't worry your pretty little noggin. Hell, if he finds out about this shindig you're planning, my head will be on the chopping block along with yours."

"Seriously, Ryan, unless the world blows up, try not to hold him any later than seven o'clock, okay? And if you permit the rest of my party guests to clear out of the office by six, all the better."

By that, I mean everyone on Jack's and my mission team—not just Ryan and Abu, but Arnie too, along with Emma Honeycutt, who is Arnie's wife as well as our team's COMINT supervisor.

"Speaking of POTUS—"

"Who? I never brought him up." My heart lurches.

"Oh…I thought you had." It's wishful thinking on Ryan's part. President Chiffray's infatuation with me has worked out well for Acme, but it's put a strain on my marriage. As much as I appreciate Lee's trust and respect him as a friend, I've made it very clear to him:

I'm a one-man woman.

I think he gets this now. But the way in which his wife, Babette, unsheathes her claws whenever I'm within scratching distance, tells me she has her doubts about it too.

That's okay. Whenever Lee's name is mentioned, Jack growls, which is just as disconcerting.

"In any event, Lee will also be on the call. In fact"—Ryan

pauses—"he's in town. Babette is due to go into labor any day now."

"I know. And from what I hear, she insists on having the child at Lion's Lair." I try to keep my annoyance out of my voice. The Chiffrays' monster mansion is in my hometown: Hilldale, California.

I'm doubly pissed when Ryan declares, "I hope you don't mind, but I took the liberty of inviting the Chiffrays to Jack's surprise party tonight."

"Mind?" I mutter. "It's the cherry on the cake of my day."

I don't even wait for Ryan to say goodbye. Instead, I slam down the phone.

"Tell me again why you won't be on this call?" Jack asks me before he heads out the door.

I find it easier to lie if I don't have to look him in the eye. Scrutinizing my lip gloss in my compact mirror, I murmur, "Ryan assured me that I'm not needed. Frankly, I'm glad. Otherwise, I wouldn't have time to run into Beverly Hills and pick up Mary's dress for her prom tomorrow night." As if annoyed by the time crunch caused to run my errand, I glance at my watch and frown. "If I leave now, I'll just barely make it back before traffic on the 405 backs up."

Jack laughs. "Yeah, well, good luck with that." We both know I'm kidding myself, since Los Angeles' I-405 is at a standstill almost night and day, especially in evening traffic.

I snap my fingers as if a thought has just occurred to me. "Hey, I've got a great idea! Since you'll be leaving the office by seven, why don't we meet up in Beverly Hills for a drink? That way, we can hang out there until traffic lightens up."

His brow arches, proof that my offer tantalizes him. "You

mean, have drinks and then maybe dinner out, like two carefree adults?"

If only he knew.

"Sure, why not? Aunt Phyllis is already on her way. Her Rumba class is on this side of the city." It's true, so why not use it as a convenient excuse for her imminent arrival? "I'm sure she won't want to fight the traffic to get back to her place. And she won't mind chaperoning the kids until we get home. She can warm up Tuesday's leftover casserole for the kids. They'll be glad to have a break from us too—if only to watch *Game of Thrones* without us hounding them about their homework."

Ha! In truth, Mary, Jeff, and Trisha are beside themselves about surprising Jack, as is our ward, Evan. (He is the son of the deceased president-elect Catherine Martin, who was implicated in the murder of her husband, Robert, which was carried out by my ex-Carl. Yes, I know—even a messy divorce pales by comparison!)

"Well, then, count me in." He draws me in for a kiss.

I linger in his arms, but only for a moment. As much as I'd prefer to stay in them forever, if I'm to pull off this charade, I must leave now. Reluctantly, I pull away.

But Jack is not ready to let me go. "I miss you already," he says.

His words put a smile on my face, but from the look in his eye, he's not teasing.

Egad, now I feel guilty.

To cover up my feelings, I whistle as I walk out the door to my real destination—the Hotel Bel-Air—I don't look back. Otherwise, he'll see the blush on my face and know something isn't right.

Within twenty-four hours, he'll thank me for what I'm doing.

At least, that's what I tell myself so that I'm not tempted to call the whole thing off.

"MRS. SMITH? IT'S A PLEASURE TO HAVE YOU WITH US." THE TONE OF the front desk clerk is deferential even as his eyes sweep over me curiously.

He's wondering if I'm a celebrity incognito, but he can't easily place me. My hair is upswept into a wide-brimmed hat with netting that scrims my profile. My large sunglasses also obscure my face. My black leather jacket and fitted jeans over beige Gianvito Rossi leather V-neck peep-toe booties give me the polished look of a moneyed socialite. Even my perfume, Joy by Jean Patou, is the ultimate scent: equal parts old wealth and anonymity.

With a few clicks, the desk clerk confirms the room I've reserved—the Swan Lake suite—is ready for occupancy. He snaps his fingers. "One of our bellmen will escort you to your suite."

As if by magic, a broad-shouldered blond Adonis appears by my side.

With a demure smile, I wave him away. Other than my purse, all I have with me is a small suitcase. "Thank you, but no need. I'll just take my key."

The desk clerk nods. "Your cottage is out the back terrace, the last one on the far side of the pool."

Our eyes meet as he hands me a key card. Yes, I'm annoyed by the derision I see there. He has me pegged as a call girl.

Considering what I have planned, he's not that far off.

My heels tap sharply on the tiles as I saunter out the terrace door.

THE ROOM IS PERFECT FOR WHAT I HAVE IN MIND.

Its ten-foot high walls, adorned with excellent replicas of a Klee, a Jackson, and a few other modern artists, are textured and creamy beige: a gentle contrast to the stark white overstuffed sofa facing the fireplace and deep hues of the lush intricately designed antique Persian rugs.

Colorful glass chips, heated by the gas flame burning beneath them, flicker in the marble fireplace.

A large sterling silver tray on the sideboard makes for a fitting bar. It holds cut-glass decanters filled with expensive liquors: Macallan Whiskey, Hendrick's gin, Henri IV cognac, Diva vodka, and Wray and Nephew Jamaican rum.

Sheer curtains, hung over the full-length paned windows, give the room a hazy glow.

A full-length mirror runs the length of the hallway leading to the en-suite bedroom. The doorways into every room are arched. The marble friezes that run a foot below the suite's ceilings curve upward before creating a ledge for the suite's recessed lighting.

Yes, this is the perfect setting for my purposes: unadulterated sex.

My preparation for the role of sex kitten lover is always exacting. This time, though, the adrenaline rush is different.

I'm doing it for Jack.

Metallic sandals, clasp my ankles like bracelets: a fitting reminder to us both since tonight I am his slave.

My nails, oxblood red, are the same hue as the gloss on my lips.

My hair, now swept to one side, can be released from its clasp with a mere flick. He'll enjoy doing so, but his hands won't stop there.

My gown is simple: Versace, gold sleeveless, ruched dupione silk that hugs me like a second skin. A slim spaghetti strap is bejeweled with tiny diamonds. A princess neckline crosses my chest diagonally, from over one shoulder to the far side of the backless dress.

Another spray of diamonds will beckon his eyes downward to a slit in the gown, high enough to reveal my left thigh. I've no doubt it will taunt his hand to wander through it. There, he'll discover nothing beneath it to hinder his probing fingers.

They will find me moist and wanting.

In anticipation, I wait for him.

HE TEXTS ME:

*Coming your way. It's been a hell of an afternoon. Our next assignment is a doozy. Cyberattacks all over U.S. public utilities, hospitals, etc.*

I sigh to myself. Tonight, I don't want to hear about it. My subtle way of moving him off the subject of work is to text back with the ultimate tease:

*Hotel Bel-Air, Cottage Suite 15.*

He responds:

*Interesting choice.*

I remind him:

*The anniversary of your birth is an occasion that deserves a little TLC, wouldn't you agree, Mr. Smith? Park in the alley out back of the cottage.*

I can't have him running into any guests who may arrive early. Knowing Aunt Phyllis's lousy sense of time, it could be her and the kids.

He texts back a happy face, followed by:

*And all this time, I thought you'd forgotten! Be there in 40 minutes.*

Which means he'll be at least an hour earlier than expected. Perfect! We'll have much more time for fun and games.

Afterward, I'll have to rouse him from the bed. I'll claim to be famished, and then I'll shrug off his inevitable suggestion that we order room service on the pretense that I want to listen to the jazz combo playing in the lounge while we enjoy the hotel's excellent filet mignon.

Instead, we are to be guided into one of the lounge's alcoves, where our friends and family have gathered and are waiting to shout happy birthday to him.

Jack will be shocked, annoyed, and then resigned to my covert plan. Having made love first will have put him in an amenable mood.

Even when we're surrounded by those closest to us, I'll be

thinking of the next time we can be alone again wrapped in each other's arms.

I know he'll be doing the same.

JACK HAS YET TO ARRIVE. WHAT THE HELL IS KEEPING HIM?

No doubt, it's the godforsaken Los Angeles traffic.

Every tick of the clock on the mantel has me jumping out of my skin. I'm freshening my lipstick by the mirror over the fireplace when, finally, I hear a gentle rap on the door.

It's about time! As late as it is, if we're interrupted—

Well, I don't even want to think about the look on Jack's face.

I'm disappointed to see that it's only Adonis the Bellman. He stands next to a rolling cart bearing a bucket of champagne, flutes, and a caviar service. "Compliments of the hotel," he assures me.

For what I'm spending here tonight, it damn well better be.

I open the door so that he can wheel it in. "Please set it up there, by the bar."

He nods. As he rolls the cart in that direction, he adds, "The front desk asked me to relay the message that, as you requested, you and Mr. Smith will not be disturbed by any other guest who may ask for you."

Good, because Jack would not appreciate that. Not on his birthday.

And certainly not when he thinks we're spending a quiet night, just the two of us.

Relieved that all is going as planned, I smile sweetly at the bellman. "Thank you! Please wait. I have something for you…" I walk back toward the mantel to grab my purse for a tip.

Through the mantel's mirror, I see the bellman's sleight of hand: a gun is pulled from under a shelf hidden below the cart's tablecloth.

By the time he turns around to take aim, I've lifted the marble-based clock off the mantle and heaved it in his direction.

He yelps in pain when it hits his shoulder. Still, his first shot just barely misses me as I drop behind one of the two facing sofas.

He too crouches low so that I can't see him. He doesn't realize I can watch him through the hallway's mirrored wall.

Silently and slowly, he makes his way to the left of the sofa, thinking he'll flank me. "Mrs. Smith—or should I call you Mrs. Craig? In any event, let's not play games, shall we?"

While keeping my eyes on him, I reach behind me and grab the ash shovel beside the fireplace. By nudging the mesh fire screen to one side, I'm able to slide it under some hot glass crystals.

Just then, Adonis spots me. He aims—

But not before I fling the crystals at him.

As they hit his face, he curses. Blinded and burned, he takes a step back.

Quickly, I grab the fireplace poker. Grasping it in both fists, I run at him—

And stab him with all my might: low, but with the poker angled up, so that it enters between his ribs and to the left of his sternum—

Piercing his heart.

But by then he's got off one last shot. My eyes follow its trajectory: wild and upward. It ricochets off the curved lip on one of the wall's marble frieze moldings—

Before tearing into me with a thump.

I gasp in agony as it rips open my abdomen. When I look down, I notice that the gold of my gown instantly deepens to bright red. Awed, I touch it. What I feel is damp and warm, whereas the rest of me is suddenly ice-cold.

I seem to have shed my body like an unwanted coat. As its falls to the floor, I think, *so, this is how I look when I'm asleep.*

My body is as loose as a marionette whose strings have been cut. My hair, clasped to one side, fans out from behind my head, which now rests on the rug closest to the hearth. My brow has lost the tiny wrinkles I've earned while battling life's tribulations. My skin is the color of pearls.

And yet, I smile slyly, as if I hold dear to a secret.

Somehow, my essence—my very being—is left hovering above my body. The presence of my assailant is hanging in mid-air as well. I float to him. I put my hands around his throat and hiss, "Who are you? Who sent you to do this to me?"

He whispers back, "It's payback…"

I then watch, astonished, as his soul blackens like a rain cloud.

A moment later, it dissipates into thin air.

His mournful howl reverberates long after the rest of him is gone.

But I'm still here.

Or am I?

# 2

# Every Breath You Take

RECORDED BY THE POLICE. RELEASED MAY 1983, THE SONG SPENT twenty-two weeks on *Billboard*'s Greatest Hits chart, reaching Number One.

*She takes his breath away—*

*Literally. Here's how:*

*Way #1: A plastic bag over his head. The long ones taken from the dry-cleaning of one of your little black dresses are perfect!*

*Start by binding his hands and feet to the bedposts. (Yes, you can let him think this is your favorite form of foreplay.) Then, very quickly, put a plastic bag over his head, pull it tight, and twist it so that it's devoid of air. It shouldn't take long: say, two minutes, max.*

*Feel free to file your nails. By the time you're finished, he will be too.*

*Way #2: Tape his mouth—and nose shut. Again, the foreplay ploy will make this easy to believe. Once again, start by tying his hands behind his back. Duct tape is suggested, since it's wide, thick, and sticks.*

*It may take a while for him to expire, so feel free to polish your nails. He—and they—should be done around the same time.*

*Way #3: Shove him into the refrigerator and lock the door behind him. Try drugging him first, since he probably won't believe you're playing "Naked Hide-and-Seek."*

*If need be, use a bungee cord to hold the fridge door shut.*

*Considering how much pure oxygen he needs per minute and how much a fridge holds after he's stuffed into it, he should expire within an hour and forty minutes.*

*This is enough time for you to put on your makeup, do your hair, and put on that cute little black dress before you sashay out to pick up your next victim.*

TIME HAS STOPPED STILL—AND YET, IT STILL MOVES AT WARP SPEED.

The hands of the clock on the mantle move so slowly that if I didn't know better, I'd guess it was broken. At the same time, a dragonfly zips by the window. She stares at me, nods, and then zooms away.

Not even a minute has passed when I hear a knock on the back door. It is playful: to the tune of *Shave and a Haircut, Two Bits.*

When I don't answer, it opens anyway with a click.

Jack stands there, grinning with lusty anticipation. His eyes scan the room in search of me.

Instead, he sees Adonis's limp and bloody corpse.

His eyes narrow when they come across Adonis's gun just a few feet away from it. Jack pulls out his gun. Ducking warily, he circles the room. He takes the risk of breaking the silence by shouting frantically: "Donna!"

Finally, he sees my body on the far side of the couch, crumpled on the floor. He rushes over.

Usually, when Jack kneels beside me, it's to murmur sweet nothings or a naughty innuendo into my ear—

Unlike now, as his whispered prayers alternate with anguished swears.

Usually, his touch is much gentler than the two-palm press he now applies to my abdomen in a desperate attempt to stop the blood flowing out of me.

When he realizes he can't, he grabs a pillow from the couch and places it over my wound. Whipping off his belt, he tightens it around me, so that the pillow stays in place while he grabs for his phone.

I know the number he calls: Ryan's. When the line goes live, he doesn't wait for Ryan's voice. Instead, he says, "It's Donna! She's been shot! I'm taking her to UCLA Med Center… Yes, Hotel Bel-Air! How did you know?" Awed by Ryan's response, he stares down at me. "Oh? I see."

*Worst birthday surprise ever.*

Knowing my boss and our company's procedures in such matters, Arnie will soon hack into the hotel's security feed in order to loop benign video to cover Jack's and Adonis's paths to the cottage.

Abu will soon be here: lugging a laundry cart containing everything needed to clean the suite of any evidence of Adonis's visit, and mine too. Afterward, it will be used to wheel Adonis to a dock. There, a boat awaits. It's his one-way ticket to his final resting place: somewhere deep in the Pacific.

What exactly is my condition? Am I alive, or dead?

I guess I'll soon know.

JACK CLICKS OFF AND THEN PICKS ME UP. HOLDING ME TIGHT, HE heads for the cottage's back door.

He doesn't feel my arms around him, or the dampness of my existential tears when my face touches his.

*I love you, Jack.*

IF THERE IS NO TRAFFIC, UCLA MEDICAL CENTER IS ONLY A SEVEN-minute drive from the Hotel Bel-Air. Unfortunately for us, it's rush hour.

That doesn't deter Jack from driving like a mad man: careening around the drivers too stubborn to hug the curb when they hear his blaring horn. At least Hilgard Avenue is two lanes in both directions, giving him the access he needs to zip down the hill—

In the hope that there is still time to save me.

Jack has placed my body in the front passenger seat, which reclines all the way back. While steering with his left hand, he presses his right palm against the pillow.

Jack's prayer is silent, but I hear it anyway:

*Please, dear Lord, I need her here, by my side. Don't take her away from me.*

THE TRIAGE TEAM SECURED BY RYAN IS WAITING FOR US AS JACK PULLS into the UCLA Medical Center's emergency entrance.

They place me on a gurney gently but also at lightning speed. Jack watches as they swarm over my comatose body. "Her pulse is faint. GSW perforated the abdomen. Large caliber, but the angle is odd: down into the left upper quadrant"—With the utmost care, the lanky bearded ER doctor rolls me over—"but no exit wound. She's in hypovolemic shock."

A grimace darkens Jack's lips when, without a second thought, a male nurse strips off my gown with a pair of trauma shears. And, yes, Jack winces when a female RN staunches the blood flowing out of my abdomen with antiseptic packing and adhesive. Agonized, he watches as they hook me up to an IV line of antibiotics and cover my nose and mouth with an oxygen mask.

He runs alongside them as they ferry the gurney down a hall to a surgical suite, answering all of their questions to the best of his ability. He knows my blood type is A-positive, that I have no allergies to antibiotics, and that I don't take any medications; that I was conscious to receive his text an hour before he arrived at the hotel; and yes, he is my next-of-kin.

He is my husband.

He is the love of my life.

By now, they're vaulting into the surgical suite. Barred by the male nurse from crossing the threshold, Jack slumps against the wall.

At that moment, my husband realizes that his hands are covered in my blood.

A tear rolls down his cheek.

*I love you too, Jack.*

I HOVER HIGH ABOVE MY SURGICAL TEAM AS DR. MCLANKY LEADS them in what seems to be a frantic ballet. Applause comes only when and if they save my life.

From what he shouts at them, and what they yell back, this is shaping up to be a very big if.

I've lost so much blood that I look as if I've been carved from alabaster.

In other words, I already look as if I've died.

I try hard not to stare at my exposed body—not out of any false sense of modesty but because it's tremendously disheartening.

"Giving up already?" I don't recognize the voice, and I certainly don't appreciate its hopeful tone. I look around to see who's talking.

A black cloud has formed on the opposite side of the ceiling. As it deepens, I can make out the shape of a person (Man? Woman? At this point, it's hard to tell) who stays aloft thanks to wings that span the full-width of the room.

"Who are you?" I ask.

"Want to take a guess?" It asks. The voice is deep but friendly.

It's a trite concept, but I'll ask anyway: "Angel of Death?"

"Bingo!"

I can hear the apparition's chuckle ring through the room, but it has little effect on the surgical team other than to make one of the RNs attempt to scratch the wax from his left ear.

I've got to be dreaming, I think.

"No," the apparition assures me. "You're in the here and now—for whatever that's worth."

"So, you can read my mind." I'm dismayed at what is now obvious to me.

"True. And you can read mine too." To prove it, he shares the one bit of information I've been dreading:

My body is failing me.

This is validated by what is happening below us: Dr. McLanky is shouting directives to the others.

"Look at it this way," the Angel of Death suggests. "You've had a longer life than others you know. Say, Catherine Martin—"

"Not necessarily. She was a few years older than me to begin with," I point out.

He chuckles. "Okay, then. Your old friend and neighbor, Nola Janoff."

Adamantly, I shake my head. "I'm a few years younger than her as well."

Death pulls out a well-worn notebook from deep inside his wings. "It says here that your age is thirty—"

"Something. Thirty-*something*," I insist.

Death rolls his eyes. "Okay, yeah, have it your way. Bottom line: considering your line of work, you've had a good run. Why not go out on a high note..."

He stops short when he notices something. Slowly, he extends a gnarled talon toward my face—

No, under my neck.

I freeze. What's he going to do, I wonder—slash it?

Having read my mind, he chuckles. Instead, he taps the soft flesh under my chin. "As I was saying—"

I slap the talon away. "It's not my time," I growl.

"Oh, yeah? Well, it says so, right here." Death points to the page he's turned to in his little notebook so that I can read it for myself.

In a medieval script, it reads:

*DONNA SHIVES STONE CRAIG dies on—*

Below us, the trauma team is panicking. They shout at each other over the screeching monitors. I hear "losing her" and "crashing" and other phrases that give credence to Death's declaration.

As my life force seeps away, what should be soon-to-be-made memories appear in my mind's eye like a film on fast-forward. When it stops, I am with Mary on the last leg of a road trip in which the plusses and minuses of six colleges are being discussed. She and I laugh when it becomes apparent that, no matter which path she takes, her future is filled with promise.

A moment later, I watch as my Aunt Phyllis graduates from college—righting a regret she once divulged to me as we shared a bottle of wine. "It's never too late," I implored her.

"I wasted my youth on foolishness, and I'm too old now," she insists.

"Pshaw, missy!" I retorted. She laughed at my audacity to use her favorite expression to shove her beyond doubt. I now know why she's always busy on Tuesdays and Thursdays. She took up the challenge, even if she hasn't yet admitted this to me.

I swerve further down into the world of What Could Have Been—this time to watch Trisha give the valedictory address at her high school graduation. My baby has grown into a tall willowy beauty. As her name is called, the thunderous applause of her classmates attests to their love of her sweetness and infectious smile.

Time leaps forward again. This time I find myself gazing at Jeff.

His eyes are filled with joy as he watches his beautiful bride walk down a church aisle toward him.

The next time I find myself at the precise moment in which Mary puts my first grandchild in my arms. Jack, his hair now grayer and his fine wrinkles now deeper, looks on in awe.

Mary watches us with pride, her husband at her side. (Is it Evan? He stands too far away for me to make out his features…)

The faces of those near and dear to me flash before my eyes: Emma and Arnie; Abu and Dominic—

And, of course, Ryan.

When Lee's face appears in my mind, his confident smile turns wistful at the thought of me.

Even as I die, I realize they will survive. Their lives will go on.

Without me.

I get that. But for it to take place now, like this—

*No.*

I have some unfinished business. I've got to find the son of a bitch who did this to me.

"Let's make a deal," I declare. My tone is devoid of any fear.

Death rubs his chin as if weighing the offer. But the fact that I can now take deep breaths proves that he is intrigued.

Finally, he asks, "What kind of deal?"

# 3

# Don't Fear the Reaper

Recorded by Blue Öyster Cult. Released July 1976, the song spent fourteen weeks on the *Billboard* Greatest Hits chart, reaching Number Twelve.

*Your worst blind date ever? Trust me—you haven't had it yet.*

*Here's the scenario:*

*He shows up early—or even worse, unexpectedly.*

*He's tall, dark, and brooding. You like your dates to have an air of mystery, but his vibe is sooooo dark.*

*He declares he's taking you someplace new and exciting. But when you get there, it's a living hell. All you can think of is how to ditch him and get home.*

*Aye, there's the rub: you're stuck there—thank goodness, not necessarily with him, but it's not as if anyone else there is someone you'd want to hang with.*

*In other words, he's made your life a living hell.*

*I mean for you to take that literally because he is the Angel of Death.*

*You know—the Grim Reaper.*

*Should he appear on your Tinder or Bumble feeds, swipe left.*

"AH! SO, YOU WANT TO MAKE A PACT WITH THE REAPER!" GLEEFULLY, Death rubs his hands until he notices that I'm wincing. "What? Too stereotypical?"

I sigh. "Let's just say it doesn't surprise me." I roll my eyes.

"So, what exactly are you proposing, milady?"

"Some tit-for-tat. You give me back my life, and I do you a solid as well—say, take out a few of your harder cases."

He snorts. "You've got it all wrong. I don't decide fates. I'm just in the delivery business." He points up, and then down. "Think of me as the UPS for Departed Souls."

"Gotcha! So pitch my offer to the Powers that Be."

Death nods grudgingly. "All I can do is try. Wait here."

I look down at the surgical team trying to resuscitate me. "Yeah, well, I'll do my best…"

He's already gone—

But not for long. A moment later, he's back. He gives me a thumbs-up. "Huzzah! What you're proposing just got a green light from the Prince of Darkness. Good for you!"

"Satan? But…" Maybe I haven't thought this through properly. "Why not the Good Guy?"

"Because the Man Upstairs goes strictly by the book." He cups my ear in order to whisper: "Free will, yada yada. Those who commit a mortal sin"—he tosses a thumb backward—"are outta there."

"Of course." I frown. "Why exactly would Satan be interested in the deal?"

"Because of your chosen line of work. It'll make things interesting."

"I'm not following you. I mean, sure, I kill, but my hits are only those who are evil enough to deserve it."

"Says who?" he snorts. "Pray tell, who died and made you God?"

I wince. "You're right. I'm the last person who should pass judgment."

My declaration makes him smile. "Contrition? Now you're getting the hang of things."

"Okay, so the Devil it is." Maybe I should have kept my mouth shut. "How will he use me? Like for the assassination of someone who somehow keeps slipping your noose? Of course, there will be caveats. For example, no one who is innocent. It's got to be a *really, really bad guy*—"

Death snickers. "Silly girl! '*A*' bad guy, as in singular? One lousy trial won't buy you five minutes, let alone the rest of your life!"

I look down at my crash team scrambling to resuscitate me. "Okay then, what will?"

"You know your Dante. Purgatory has seven circles—"

"Or toll houses," I interject.

"A rose by any other name—yadda, yadda. In any regard, to get back to the living, you'll have to face seven demons."

*"Demons? Seven?"*

"More akin to a few reunions with some old friends." Death winks. "To tell you the truth, they won't be any happier to see you than you are to see them. A few of them may be downright ticked." He shrugs. "Who can blame them? I mean, let's face it, they owe their untimely demises to you. And what a lineup!" He raises a hand skyward as if pointing to a marquee. "*Donna... Stone... Craig's... Greatest... Hits!*" Each word comes with a thrust of his palm.

"That's ridiculous!" I point below. "Look! I don't have time to fight seven dead assassins!"

"*Au contraire, ma chére.* You'll have all the time in the world—if they stabilize you in time." He gazes down at the triage team.

Just then, my body flatlines.

"The Devil's deal is seven trials," Death snarls. "Take it or leave it—but tell me now."

McLanky shouts, "Code Blue!"

"*Yes! Okay*! It's a deal!" What else could I say?

Suddenly, the monitors spring to life again.

"Thank God," a nurse murmurs. "It's a miracle!"

"'La-dee-dah, it's a miracle!'" Death mimics, and then grumbles, "I never get any credit for the work I do."

"You would if you let a few deaths slide every now and then," I point out.

"You're not my first, you know." His grin widens. "But if you succeed at this little bet, you'll be plowing virgin territory. Let's see, who's jonesing for a rematch?" He flips open his little notebook and peruses the list. "Ha! Well, what do you know! Practically everyone you've killed curses your name. It looks like Satan will have to hold an auction."

"Tell him to go for it." I'm proud that my voice doesn't tremble.

"You say that now, but you may regret it," he retorts ominously. "Eternal damnation has a way of making one ornery."

"Duly noted."

He fades into nothingness.

Below me, my saviors are hugging and high-fiving. I float down among them. When I place a kiss on Dr. McLanky's cheek, unconsciously, he rubs the spot. A trace of a smile rises on his lips.

It doesn't stay there long. A nurse pokes her head through the operating suite door. "The husband is throwing a fit. He wants to know—"

"Tell him I'll be right out," Dr. McLanky says.

"Can I at least give him the news that she survived?"

"If you can call it that." McLanky glances over at my pale body. The thick tubes connecting me to the life support machines bleeping out their dire warnings are crisscrossed with the thin catheters that feed me the sustenance of life: plasma, saline, and hope. "I'll go with you. Her husband should hear the worst directly from me."

He doesn't know the half of it.

Seven assassinated beings wanting retribution. They may not be able to go home, but if I don't beat them yet again, neither will I.

And yet, I'm hopeful. Whoever the Grim Reaper has in mind, the good news is that I've beaten them once. I can do it again.

I hope. I pray.

Because my future life depends on it.

I follow Dr. McLanky out into the hall. It's worth hearing my plight from his perspective.

MY FRIENDS AND FAMILY ARE THE BEST-DRESSED VISITORS IN THE trauma floor's waiting room. If I weren't already on life support, the looks of shock and dread on their faces would indeed break my heart.

It must be wearing on Dr. McLanky too because his explanation starts off with the good news first. "We removed the bullet," he explains. "Luckily, it hit soft tissue as opposed to any major arteries or organs, although, a few millimeters lower and to the right and it would have torn through her stomach."

He pauses in order to accommodate their collective sighs. "However, she's not out of the woods by any means. In fact, she's far from it. Mrs. Craig went into cardiopulmonary arrest. It helped that her husband came quickly enough to give her CPR, but the subsequent lack of oxygen has left her comatose"—he pauses before adding—"and possibly brain-damaged. We're monitoring her brain activity."

Mary's lips tremble. "But—she won't stay like that forever—will she?"

"It's too early to tell. The medical term is anoxic encephalopathy," McLanky explains. "Right now her heart is beating, but to be honest, it almost gave out."

My loved ones are silent as they contemplate my reality.

Finally, Jack asks, "What can we do?"

"Talk to her," McLanky suggests. "And touch her. Coma patients respond to voices and to tactile motion as well as heat and cold. But not all of the patient's movements are voluntary," he warns them. "I'm not saying for you to take it with a grain of salt. I'm just asking you to…well, not get your hopes up."

Aunt Phyllis's knees buckle. Ryan catches her right before she falls to the floor.

Trisha turns in order to bury her head in Mary's chest so that the others don't see her crying.

The sound of sobs comes from behind me too—

From the Grim Reaper. He wipes away a crocodile tear before blowing his nose in the sleeve of his monk's robe. "So sorry! This is the part that always gets to me—all that false hope folderol."

"But I'm coming back!" I retort fiercely.

"Sure—if you win *all seven fights*." Suddenly, his robe changes its texture. It's no longer sackcloth but satin. When he lifts his arms through his sleeves, I can see that his hands are in boxing gloves. He holds them out to me, flat-knuckled, so that I can read what is written on them:

Right hand: NUCLEAR Left hand: BOMBSHELL

He smiles. "Great fighter's name for you, don't ya think? My gift to you, along with these." He takes off the gloves and tosses them to me. "Go ahead, try them on."

I put my hand in the right glove—

Only to pull out a skeletal hand.

I'm proud that I don't scream. Instead, I toss it back at him. "I think you'll need this."

"Nah. Believe me, there are plenty where that came from."

Suddenly, there is a dark hole that has opened up in the floor. Flames flare from this smoky abyss. The hand of the Reaper, now floating, beckons me down.

His toothless grin sends a shiver through my soul. "Shall we?"

4

# Stayin' Alive

Written and performed by Robin Gibb, Barry Gibb, and Maurice Gibb. Released November 1977, this disco song was the second single from the *Saturday Night Fever* soundtrack. It spent twenty-seven weeks at Number One on *Billboard*'s "Hot 100 Chart."

The Gibbs had originally named the song "Night Fever," but the movie producers wanted the word "Saturday" added, to match the movie's original title, *Saturday Night*. Apparently, it wasn't original enough for the Gibbses, who felt there were already too many songs with the name "Saturday" in them. The movie's title was changed instead.

*Life is about the survival of the fittest, right?*

*Not everyone can be king of the jungle. Even if your sights are set lower—say, somewhere below the mighty Simba but above the lowly slug, here's how to increase your chances of stayin' alive:*

*First, start out swinging: either to catch your opponent unawares, or vine-to-vine if you want to cut your losses and run (before you get cut instead).*

33

*Next, not everyone is your friend. Even if they gush compliments while in your presence, the real test of trust comes when you and they come face-to-face with wildebeests that show their fangs. If said friends turn tail, drop them as quickly as possible (which would be if and when you survive this primal dressing down). However, if your beastie-besties snarl back at this brat pack, chances are you'll stay BFFs for life.*

*Finally, don't presume anything. No circumstance is black or white. The gradient shades of life, love, and loss are etched firmly with each year and every tear.*

*Hey, I'm not being poetic here! I'm just telling it like it is. You don't have to believe me. But if you're smart, you'll take what I have to say to heart—*

*Before yours stops beating.*

TIME STOPS WHEN YOU'RE IN A HELLHOLE.

Even as you're dropping at the rate of a runaway freight train, it is a feast for the eyes, albeit less than palatable for those who never hunger for the punishment doled out to the Damned.

I look away at the cages that line the walls around me, where the inhabitants cry out as they are beaten raw, gurgle one last gasp while being disemboweled by a sword, or scream out the names of their mothers as they are burned alive. Each torture is as ingenious as it is unforgiving.

Death, now my constant companion, chuckles. "You're taking note, I assume?"

Doing my best to keep things light, I reply, "Hey, you never know when a new technique will come in handy."

"You'll have to be cunning if you're to survive here," Death warns me.

This is a nightmare. To awaken, I must do my best to be the worst—not something I'd ever say to my children.

But that's just it: I want to be able to tell them something, anything, face to face as I hold them in my arms.

I want them to hear me and see me, not just dream that they have.

"No time to dawdle," Death warns me. "He's waiting for us."

I've hit bottom.

AT FIRST I DON'T SEE SATAN. THAT'S PAR FOR THE COURSE WHEN you're dropped in the middle of an ancient coliseum filled with the Unliving who see you as much-needed entertainment for their abysmal afterlives.

They're chanting, "Kill Donna, Kill Donna, Kill Donna…" They don't even know me! If only I'd been given a day or two to win them over.

I'm so taken with the sights and sounds of ecstasy and agony that I barely feel the tap on my shoulder. Since Death is standing right beside me, I know it can't be him.

I steel myself for the worst—

At least, I think I have until I realize that Satan has used his forked tongue to do the honors. Ugly can be mesmerizing. Dread can be paralyzing. If Hell is your worst nightmare, a face-to-face with its demon regent is even worse.

He is taller than the stadium. When he spreads his wings, we are enveloped in complete darkness. The cacophony of epithets being shouted by the sinners gored on his horns silences the stadium throng.

Try as I might, I can't look into Satan's eyes. The darkness of too many souls is reflected in them, mine included.

I'm still staring at him when I feel a presence beside me. I turn to find an extremely handsome man beside me: dark hair with light eyes above sharp cheekbones and a strong nose. His well-cut tux seems molded to his fine firm physique: broad shoulders, trim abdomen, thighs that are thick and strong.

His smile is an invitation to trouble.

"Ignore the man behind the curtain," I say as a way of introducing myself to Satan's alter ego.

His booming laugh confirms this. "Can't fool a smart woman!" His head tilts inquisitively. "How did you know this wasn't me?" He jabs a clawed talon toward the Jumbotron-sized mythologized version of himself.

"Bread and circuses, right?" I toss a hand in the direction of the crowd. "Got to keep the asses in the seats."

He takes this as an invitation to stare at my ass. "The human form is such a delicious temptation." He points up. "I thank Him for that."

"We all do," I assure him. "It's why we do our best to hold onto it as long as possible." I lean in. "Level with me. Why would you accept this deal?"

Satan flicks the tail that has suddenly appeared, as have two tiny horns on either side of his head. "Because it's a win-win for me, sweet Donna. If you lose, you join these huddled masses yearning for anything other than eternal damnation."

"And if I win?"

Satan nods in the direction of the crowd. "The rabble's dreams of some get-out-of-Hell-free card go up in flames, once and for all. Death may have talked me into this spectacle once, but you will have broken the mold, Doll." He looks pointedly at Death. "Don't you have a few souls to take?" To make his point, he glances down at the very expensive Patek Philippe watch on his wrist.

I don't know how he can tell time with it, considering that its face is shattered and covered in blood. Gee, I wonder what happened to its owner! I glance up at his horns. Ah, yes, one of those gored is missing a hand and wrist. Finders, keepers. Losers, weep tears for eternity.

Death takes Satan's hint. Nudging me, he says, "If I don't see you again—"

"Oh, but you will," I assure him.

I wish I were as confident as I sound.

Death dissolves into nothingness.

A single clap of Satan's claws summons a beautiful woman, naked from the waist up. Frankly, there are four of her: identical quadruplets, conjoined on a single hip.

Three of the sisters' eyes have been plucked out. The fourth has lost just one eye.

I think I've found the missing orbs: in the snakeskin basket One-Eyed Jane holds in her hand.

"Seven eyes for seven challengers!" Satan shouts.

His much scarier illusion amplifies his silken baritone into a guttural growl that shakes the coliseum's ancient pillars. He continues, "Each one will reunite her with a lucky challenger eager for a rematch with the lovely housewife assassin in the hope of a chance for upward mobility: Purgatory!"

The mob howls its approval.

"However, should our guest win, her opponent will burn in the Seventh Circle—for eternity."

This dire thought subdues the crowd.

"And if our guest wins all seven events, she will go back to her mortal life."

The crowd wails in envy. Can't say that I blame them.

Satan strides around the arena like a motivational speaker working an auditorium packed with devotees. "Our guest will choose her weapon from three that are available to her. Once she has done so, her opponent will name the weapon of his or her choice."

"But if I don't know what my opponent will ask for, how will I know if I chose something that can stop him or her?"

"Aye, girlie, but there's the rub." A talon strokes my cheek. "A word to the wise: Nothing is probable, and anything is possible."

Whatever the heck *that* means.

"You've stacked the deck. We both know it," I counter. "Here's a thought: if I win the round, shouldn't I be granted some sort of reward?"

The mob grows silent. I have no knowledge of Satan's wrath. Apparently, they do.

The talon on my face pauses for a moment. His eyes have darkened. I can't read them, but I assume this is not a good thing. I may find myself carved up even before my personal Hunger Games have begun.

I steel myself to stand perfectly still. One quick move may cause an eighth eye to plop into the basket: mine.

"Fair enough," Satan finally mutters. "I offer you this: there are a few you know in Purgatory. They've been angsting over Life—yours. With each match you win, you'll be allowed a reunion with one of them. I'll even let you ask them a question that might be useful to you—that is, if you ever get out of here."

"You're very generous. Thank you." Maybe one of them will know who ordered the hit on me. It's certainly worth asking.

"First things first, then!" Satan claps his claws. "The weapons!"

Like magic, three items appear: a sharpened wooden pole, a flame-thrower, and a grenade.

I'll pass on the pole because I doubt my opponent will get close enough for me to kill him with it. Besides, how can you kill someone who's already dead? And considering the torture that goes on down here, poking someone with a stick will feel like a tickle. As for the flame-thrower, the odds of getting singed in Hell are very high, so why even bother?

That leaves the grenade.

I reach for it and hold it up for the crowd to see. Might as well try to win a few hearts and minds while I'm at it…

*What? They're booing?* The nerve!

The blind girls hold out the eyeball basket.

"Reach in, my darling. Don't be shy." Satan's voice is as smooth as silk.

Yuck. Okay, here goes.

My hand hovers over the squishy little orbs. I must be taking too long because suddenly a snake's head pops up. I duck just in time before it tags me with its venom.

"Not fair," I mutter.

"Get used to it," Satan suggests. "Nothing is as it seems."

Duly noted. I reach in quickly, plucking one. As I stare down at it, Gunter—the dearly departed aid-de-camp of the Quorum's leader, Eric Weber—glares back at me.

In a flash of lightning, Gunter appears at my side. He comes nose-to-nose to snarl, "You stole my life! Now I'm taking yours! You'll never go back! Do you hear me? Never!"

I stare innocently at him. "*Sprechen sie Deutch?*"

I'm sure that what spews from him is not fit for the ears of *vornehme frauen*.

I am fascinated with his most distinguishing feature: the bullet hole I put in this sadistic little oaf's forehead. I had the honor of doing so after the Quorum kidnapped Jack on the eve of our wedding to coerce me into assassinating Ryan, among other devious tasks that would have put me on the International Terrorist Watch List if I hadn't let Ryan in on my dilemma. Eric made sure that Ryan's extermination was left for last. Only the promise of Jack's release from a Mexican drug lord's private prison would have made me agree to the hit, although I had no way of warning Ryan of it. Both Ryan and Jack survived.

And the bullet that now allows access to Gunter's brain came from my gun.

I'm tempted to stick my finger into that hole to see if there was anything in there to begin with, but a gong sounds, so I guess it's battle stations.

I look around. Gunter has disappeared. What's his weapon, an invisibility cloak?

Apparently not. It's an armored tank: a German Puma infantry vehicle.

And it's headed my way.

Gunter is gunning it. He doesn't care how many of the dazed souls staggering through Hell he runs over to get to me.

My initial instinct is to flee into the stands. But what's the use? To get out of Hell, I'll have to stand and fight. Ideally, I'll be close enough to use the grenade—

Not that it can penetrate cold hard steel.

Hey, you only die once, right? These folks may be here for Eternity, but I've got a shot at a new lease on life if I remember…

How did Satan put it? Oh yes: Nothing is probable, and anything is possible.

I estimate the seconds before the tank reaches me. When it's just a few feet away, I leap up—

And grab onto one of the many holds mounted on the tank. Quickly, I crawl, crab-like, toward the gun's long turret. Finally, straddling it, I make my way to its head.

By now, Gunter is driving around in circles, trying to toss me off. When he realizes I'm climbing the gun, he swings the turret skyward.

He's too late. I pull the grenade's pin and toss it down the barrel before leaping as far away as I can.

The tank's armor panels are first-rate for shielding the tank's crew from shelling. Likewise, an explosion inside the tank makes it shake, rattle, and roll,

But it doesn't explode.

Instead, it implodes.

The mob is awed. When the shock wears off, the crowd's banshee-scream fills the air.

I dust myself off. One trial down, six more to go.

~

"I've got a treat for you," Satan informs me. "Guess who's come for a visit?"

I could use a friendly face. Sarcastically, I clap my hands like a child on Christmas morn. "Whom?" I ask.

Another minion of Eric Weber's, Varick Velasco, materializes in front of me.

Oh, just great.

The square-jawed, dimpled-chin pretty boy is dressed in a kimono. His face is painted white, like a kabuki. He flutters his pale blue eyes over a paper fan. "Sakura, sugar!"

Needless to say, I'm disappointed. "You said I'd see a friendly face," I scold Satan.

"You didn't mind seeing it when his head was delivered to you in a box tied up with a pretty bow," Satan counters.

"I was concerned I was going to find Jack's head in there instead, so yes, I was relieved to see who it was as opposed to who it wasn't," I explain.

"Semantics," Satan counters. "He's here, so obviously he has something to say. Ask away." He disappears in a puff of gloom.

Satan is right. If Varick was so eager to come here, it's to give me some guidance I can use if I return to the living.

No—make that *when* I return.

I know better than to waste my question on a yes-or-no answer, so I ask: "Varick, tell me—who's causing the cyber attacks that are taking place all over the country?"

Varick pulls a hand mirror from a pocket deep within his kimono in order to admire himself. Sheesh! Same old Varick. "We have a mutual friend," he purrs.

"You're talking about Eric, aren't you? But he's still in jail!" Eric is in Magic Mountain, a Federal maximum-security prison located high on a sheer mountaintop in Utah.

Varick sighs impatiently. Pointing to a blemish on his nose, he mutters, "I'm breaking out!"

"You're making no sense at all." I roll my eyes. "Even if he were behind it. He's got to have outside help. Is it Russia? China? North Korea?"

Instead of answering me, Varick giggles as he sings:

*"Three little maids in attendance come*
    *To one little maid is a bride, Yum-Yum*
    *Nobody's safe, for ONE cares for none*
    *Three little maids from —"*

"I know that tune! Gilbert and Sullivan, right? From…let me see—*The Mikado*!"

He ignores me—perhaps because he is growing smaller and smaller until he disappears.

No, I'm wrong. He's not disappearing—

I am.

# 5

# It's a Sin

Written by the techno-pop duo of Neil Tennant and Chris Lowe, also known as the Pet Shop Boys. When the single was released in 1987, it reached number one on the *UK Singles Chart* for three weeks in 1987, and was their third Top 10 single in the US when it reached #9 on the *Billboard's* "Hot 100."

According to Tennant, the song aptly describes his Catholic upbringing and education, where he felt the message was that every pleasurable act in life was to be regarded as sinful. One would hope that he has since proven his instructors wrong.

~

*What is a sin, exactly?*

*The simple definition is that it's "a willful or deliberate violation of divine law or moral principle."*

*With that in mind, take this pop quiz! True or false: which of these seven acts should be considered sins?*

1. *Setting your neighbor on fire, no matter how well deserved...
   and then insisting it was an accident.*

2. *Lying to cover your tracks or those of someone you wish to protect.*
3. *Taking anything that is not rightfully yours.*
4. *Thinking that in the world there is no one person more wonderful than you.*
5. *Following orders in the performance of a government-sanctioned execution.*
6. *Taking a second helping of pie before everyone else has had their first piece.*
7. *Telling the disheveled homeless person that you have no money when there's spare change in your pocket that could be put to no better use.*

*If you answered true to all of the above, consider yourself a pious person. Should you be considered for sainthood? That's up to a higher authority.*

*If you answered true to four or less, consider yourself human! All of life's choices are nuanced by the situations we find ourselves in.*

*Now, if you answered false to every scenario, then obviously you lack a moral compass! So, go ahead and have fun in this life because the next one could be sheer Hell.*

"—TOOK SO DAMN LONG. THE ONLY PLACE OPEN THIS LATE AT NIGHT was The Carving Board on Wilshire," Abu is saying. "Let's see here... Ryan, you're the Sweet November, right?" He takes one of the foil-wrapped sandwich bags out of the box in his arms and tosses it to our boss, who sits in one of the chairs now circling my hospital bed. The aroma of roasted turkey fills the room.

Does anyone on my mission team see the tear at the corner of my eye? No, not yet. That's okay. At the moment, it is the only way I have to show my appreciation for their efforts to include me in their lives in the hope that it will induce me to wake from my coma, just as the doctor suggested.

Here's hoping he was right.

Abu reaches into the box again. "Ah! Here's your Bentley, Dominic."

Our British operative catches his foil-wrapped steak sandwich with one hand.

"Emma, you ordered the Roughage, right, with a kale pasta salad? Reach in and grab it, will you? Oh, and take the Grilled Cheese for Nicky too."

Emma shifts her toddler from one hip to another before grabbing her bounty. As she leans in, Nicky pats Abu's cheek and giggles.

When Abu pretends to bite off one of Nicky's fingers and chew on it, Nicky shrieks at the joke.

"Shhhh…" Emma admonishes him. Guiltily, her eyes move toward me.

"No, it's okay," Jack tells her. "Maybe Donna…" His hesitation comes with a catch in his throat—"Maybe she hears him too."

Hearing my name, Nicky looks over at me. "Don-Dah! Sweepy!" he reaches out to me. Emma bends so that he can pat my hand.

With all my might, I strain to touch him. If only.

Suddenly, his eyes open wide. He slaps my hand. "Wake! Wake! Don-Dah, wake!"

He knows I'm here! Listen to the little sweetie!

As Emma pulls him away from me, she coos, "No, honey! Donna is still sleeping. See? Her eyes are closed."

I try as hard as I can to open them, to no avail. Darn it! If I could, I'd wiggle my nose…

"And Arnie, here's your Big Kahuna." Even Abu's gentle underhanded toss is too much for our fumble-fingered tech-op.

Thankfully, Jack's catch saves it from hitting the floor.

"Jack, I know you said you didn't want anything, but I got you a Clydesdale, just in case." Abu's tone is gentle, but his point is made: You've got to eat something.

Jack shrugs off his concern. "Now that Abu's back, we can get on with the discussion of the cyber attacks." He turns to Arnie. "How many have taken place, and who got hit?"

Arnie wipes his hands on a napkin before swiping his iPad screen. Through a mouthful of ahi tuna, he mumbles, "Right now, several public utilities have been hit, in various states: Florida, Virginia, Oregon, and Maryland. Also the databanks of a few hospitals."

"Odd choice," Dominic murmurs.

"Not really," Arnie assures him. "They keep great records on patient financials, and they're known to pay off quickly."

"Is it ransomware, or the first stages of a terrorist attack?" Dominic asks.

Before answering, Emma lowers Nicky onto the floor. He's too busy gnawing on his grilled cheese sandwich to notice that he's no longer on his mother's lap. "Despite asking for money, the NSA is getting the vibe that it may be a cover for the latter."

Jack leans in. "Why is that?"

"During the same time period, a couple of U.S. defense contractors were also hit. A day after, they noted hacking activity on some governmental installations. NASA, the Nuclear Regulatory Commission's Cyber Command, a couple of federal maximum security prisons, even the White House's servers were affected."

Maximum security prisons…

Eric.

*Breaking out.* Varick's words float into my consciousness.

So, that's what Varick was trying to tell me!

I have to let Jack and the others know about it.

The conversation shifts to the digital platforms breached—firewalls, antivirus programs, and other state-of-the-art security protections. The hackers deleted data files and destroyed hundreds of computers.

Even as I listen, I float next to Nicky. Now sated by his

mozzarella and cheddar feast, he busies himself with alphabet blocks that topple from his toddler gear bag.

He sees me too. I know, because he reaches out for me. Excitedly, he squeaks, "Don-Dah!"

I murmur, "Yes, Nicky! I see you too! And I want to play with you."

I point to the block stamped with the letter E.

"E," I say. "Can you say it too? E!"

"Eeeee!" he shouts. He picks it up.

"Good!" I say. "Put it on the chair by your Mom, okay?"

Emma is too caught up in Arnie's analysis to notice, but that's okay—for now.

I now point to the letter R. "Are!" I say. "Like a tiger! Arrrrrrrr!"

"RRRR!" he copies.

"Perfect! Now, pick it up and put it next to your mommy, again, in the chair."

He grabs the block and toddles over to the chair, dropping it next to the other one before scurrying back to the blocks.

"Now this one." I point to the block stamped I. "Eye! Can you say it?" I point to my eye as well. "Eye!"

"Eye!" he shouts, and then he picks up the right block and puts it by the others on the chair before plopping back down on the floor with me.

"Okay, now, C! See!" I place my hand on the C block.

When he picks it up, he shivers and squeaks.

He feels me.

If only I could feel him, too: warm, soft, oh so gentle.

He takes the block to complete the name we're building: ERIC.

I say it out loud. "Eric. You see that, Nicky? You spelled Eric! Can you say Eric?"

"EEE-Wick!" he shouts. "*Ear*-Wick!"

"Yes! Yes! You win!" I shout back.

Emma is in the middle of saying, "I can understand going after the utilities, and certainly Cyber Command. But the federal pens? That's certainly—"

Nicky giggles hysterically and runs to his mother. "Earwick! Earwick!" he shouts, pointing to the blocks beside her.

She picks him up to shush him again, but he's not having it. He takes her hand points with it! "Earwick!"

"Nicky, please… What?" Instinctively, she glances down.

But a second later all the lights in the room go out.

No lights anywhere. The whole hospital is dropped into darkness.

My monitors suddenly go wild.

"What the… Nurse!" Jack jumps up. "Please! Nurse!"

A light goes on near Ryan: it's the flashlight app on his iPhone.

A moment later, the hospital lights go on again. My monitor calms down, thank goodness.

But when Jack went to get the nurse, he knocked over the chair with the blocks. They are now spread all over the floor.

Nicky staggers over to Jack. Hitting him hard on the thigh, he shouts, "Bad!" He points to the fallen blocks. "Bad Jack! Earwick!"

Yes, Nicky! Yes! Thank you!

Surprised and amused, Jack picks up the toddler. "What does he mean—'Earwick'?"

Ryan's cell phone buzzes. "It's a text from DOI Branham! There was a cyber attack at Magic Mountain. It allowed for a jail break." He reads more, then sighs. "Eric Weber has escaped."

"EARWICK!" Nicky shouts triumphantly.

"I think he just said 'Eric,'" Arnie mutters uncertainly.

"He did," Emma confirms. "And he spelled it, too. At least, I think he did. It was on the chair…" Her eyes shift to the upturned chair. "Was that what you meant, Nicky?"

He nods. "Dondah! Dondah!" And then he points to me.

Not the Me lying on the bed, but the Me who stands beside Jack with my arms wrapped around his waist, squeezing him in the hope that he'll feel me too.

Like Nicky, I'm frustrated that he sees me but they can't.

Ryan is staring at my face—or at least the face of the Me in the bed. "Hey, is that a tear on Donna's cheek?"

He notices my tear of joy.

It isn't anymore because it's too late. Despite my team now at least open to the concept that Nicky had intel for them, it's too late.

Eric is already on the outside.

I FLOAT OVER JACK AS HE SLEEPS IN THE CHAIR BESIDE MY BED. WHEN I kiss his lips, he smiles.

And when I nuzzle his neck, he mumbles my name.

His dreams are made sweeter still when my hands roam over his chest.

I lay my hand on his chest to feel his heart beating.

His arm moves up so that he can place his hand over mine.

"I love you," I whisper.

He murmurs something, but I can't understand him.

"He says he loves you too," Death tells me.

I sigh. "What are you doing here?"

He pulls an hourglass from a pocket in his cape. The sand is almost gone. "Time for your second trial."

"Can't it wait until morning?" I plead.

"The sooner you get it over with… Nah, I shouldn't say that since it can go either way." He stares down at Jack. "Hey, do you know what percentage of people die in their sleep? Just twelve or so. Why do you think that is?"

"Heck, I don't know. But just leave Jack out of it, okay?"

Death shrugs. "For now, I will. You know, it's not such a bad way to go."

Still…

He points to a door in my hospital room that I've never seen before. "After you."

"So happy to see you again!" Satan, dressed in white tails (better to show off his red one?) waves gaily at me from the front row of this Victorian-era theatre.

I'd wave back except for the fact that my hands are tied—literally, both over my head and on opposite sides of a wooden wheel. My legs are also shackled so that I'm spread-eagled.

"Let me guess. I'm the entertainment," I retort.

"The primo spot," he assures me. "Third on tonight's bill!"

"Oh, yeah? What did I miss?"

"In the first act, the Fat Lady sang." He rolls his eyes. "Wagner's *Brünnhilda*—my guest of honor's favorite." He points to the man beside him: Hitler, sporting his signature 'stache as well as a bullet hole in his temple. What is left of his skin is in crispy red tatters.

Germany's infamously disgraced dictator attempts a salute, to no avail. Someone has cut his right hand off at the wrist. Since his body was incinerated by the time the Red Army got to the *Füherbunker*, I presume it happened here in Hell. An apt punishment.

The Devil continues, "Unfortunately, our soprano's high notes were so offensive to the second act—prancing dogs—that they tore her apart."

"That is truly a hard act to follow," I mutter.

"No need to worry about an encore of that one"—Satan hesitates, but then adds—"albeit, I have promised the audience that whoever loses this act will meet the same fate." He points to the sinners in the millions of rows behind him.

"Well, now, that ought to keep them in their seats and up popcorn sales!" I retort.

To that end, he realizes it's time to introduce me to my next challenger. "Mrs. Craig, I'm sure you remember Ratko Zoran?"

Ratko appears stage right. He's also in a tux and sporting a tall hat.

I guess I'm to be his magic trick. Does that mean his attempt on my death will be an illusion? Hardly! He'll consider it payback for when I choked him. The car he was driving skidded off a bridge. Miraculously, I survived. Otherwise, I'd have been fodder for the swine in his pig farm.

I bat my eyes at Satan since my head is the only part of me that can move. "Certainly, I know the appropriately named Ratko! As a henchman in Yugoslavian dictator Slobodan Miloševich's ethnic cleansing war, he was responsible for the deaths of millions of people. Unfortunately, he escaped and became a plastic surgeon in Los Angeles—"

"We're not here for a history lesson," Ratko growls.

"Indeed, we're not," Satan nods. "And since Ratko is a crack surgeon, a little surgical knife throwing should be right up his alley, eh?" He winks at Ratko.

"Precisely." Ratko smiles confidently. "A wonderful pastime, and I had lots of practice."

"*Wünderbar!*" The Devil beams supremely. "Now, listen up, lady and gent! The rules are as follows. The wheel turns. Ratko is allowed no more than four knives. If he misses, you switch positions."

"I won't," Ratko declares firmly.

"Superb!" Satan claps his hands gleefully. "Then around and around we go! Where she stops, nobody knows—if she survives!"

Magically, the wheel spins. It is moving so fast that I can't see anything at first—

But I can certainly feel the first surgical knife whiz by. It lodges itself just inches from my right hand.

By now, Ratko has figured out he moved much too quickly. He waits for the wheel to slow down to a crawl for another throw—

Which whizzes by my cheek before hitting the board. Yikes!

The wheel speeds up for a second dizzying spin. All the while, I work to loosen the rope around my left hand. At the same time, I inch my right hand toward the knife—

And grab it. By scooting my wrist above the restraint, I'm able to grasp it. I nudge it looser, but I'm not able to dislodge it.

However, I am able to slip my left hand out of its restraint. My left arm crosses over to reach for the knife—

Just in time, too. The wheel is slowing down and everyone can guess my game plan, including Ratko, since my body is twisted into something akin to an Egyptian hieroglyphic.

By the time he aims his third knife, I've yanked out the one above my head with both hands—

And duck just as his throw finds the perfect bulls-eye: where my heart used to be.

I'm upside down, and I've got only one shot. I've got to make it before the wheel speeds up.

I aim and let the knife fly—

And watch as my hit pierces his chest.

Ratko looks down. As the blood seeps slowly from his body, the hounds from Act Two bound onto the stage and tear into him.

The grisly sounds of canines attacking fresh meat are no worse than his pained screams. But just in case they view him as the appetizer, I jerk another knife from the board and brandish it at any hound headed my way. They get the hint pretty quickly, and keep their distance, allowing me to cut the bindings on my feet and fall to the floor.

"You never cease to amaze me," Satan exclaims admiringly.

A puff of smoke envelops me. When it dissipates, there is someone standing in front of me:

Edwina Doyle.

She was the illegitimate daughter of one of the evilest men I'd ever met: the international industrialist, Jonah Breck. He was also one of the twelve original members of the Quorum. Without knowing Edwina's true parentage, Jonah hired the shy, mousy woman as his personal assistant. It allowed her to get close enough to him to try to kill him to avenge her mother, whom he sold into slavery.

He killed Edwina first. I tried to stop it. Instead he blamed her death on me and escaped to his private island, where the United States could not extradite him.

Ironically, Babette Chiffray was Jonah's widow before meeting and marrying Lee. Had he never purchased Breck Industries, his life path would have taken a different journey. I doubt mine would have ever crossed it—but who's to say? I'll be more inclined to believe in Divine intervention if I ever get out of this coma.

"Edwina," I whisper, "I have to know: what is Eric Weber's plan?"

Out of thin air, a football appears in her hands. As she runs away from me, she throws it my way, shouting, "Donna please— *don't drop the ball!*"

But I do.

It explodes and I'm blown high into the smoke and fury.

When I open my eyes, I'm back in my hospital bed.

Jack is gone, damn it.

If I could, I'd cry.

---

6

Only in my Dreams

---

Written and performed by Debbie Gibson. Released on her 1986 album by the same name, the song reached #4 on *Billboard*'s "Top 100 Hits." It was also voted #95 in VH1's "100 Greatest Songs of the 1980s."

*How do you know when you're dreaming?*

*Here are three telltale signs. By heeding them, you can give yourself a much-needed wakeup call when your subconscious is working overtime:*

- *Sign #1: You can't see yourself. And if you do, it was you at your very best. (In other words, it ain't you now.)*
- *Sign #2: As in Tevya's dream in* Fiddler on the Roof, *everyone you know is there. Make that, everyone you knew. And since* This is Your Life *is off the air and you're not renowned enough to have your very own celebrity roast, either you're in a wonderful dream, or you're in one awful nightmare. (Look down: are you naked? Then totally the latter...)*

- *Sign #3: People talk, talk, talk, but they say nothing, nothing, nothing. You do a lot of activities, but nothing gets done. It seems as if you're running in place—*

*Oh, wait—it's exactly the same as when you're awake.*
   *Go back to sleep.*

"Your mom looks dead," Cheever murmurs.

Trisha's punch has him doubled over and groaning.

That's my girl.

Jeff high-fives her above his so-called friend's head.

"Why are you here, again?" Trisha asks.

"To…pay…my…respects," Cheever explains during gasps.

"No," Mary corrects him. "You're only here because it was Mom's day to carpool. But because junior varsity basketball practice ran so late, we couldn't take you home first. Otherwise, we'd have gotten to the hospital after visiting hours were over."

"We should have made him walk home," Trisha growls.

Evan rolls his eyes. "The idiot doesn't have his house key and his parents are duking it out in divorce court today."

Jeff nods at Cheever. "Which unlucky parent gets custody of you?"

Cheever shoves him. "They both want me, doofus! I'm worth my weight in dough."

Trisha's eyes open wide. "One of them is going to be very, very rich!"

Cheever glowers at her.

"Are you talking about child support?" Mary asks. "Wow! Talk about an undue burden."

"You mean, to the parent who has to pay out?" Evan asks.

Mary snickers. "No! For the one who has to live with this Neanderthal." She pokes a thumb in Cheever's direction.

"Why are we talking about Cheever in front of Mommy?" Trisha asks. "She probably hates it!"

Actually, I enjoy watching the rest of you beat up on Cheever, Little One, so no worries. I've taught you well, grasshoppers…

"She's right," Jeff acknowledges. "Let's each tell Mom at least one good thing that happened today."

Trisha nods fervently to that suggestion. "Okay! I'll start!" Her brow furrows as she contemplates her offering. "Oh, I know!" She takes hold of my hand. "Mommy, guess what?"

"She can't, you moron. She's in a coma," Cheever mutters.

This time, both Mary and Jeff pummel him.

Trisha crosses her arms at her chest until they stop. Good for her! She refuses to be upstaged by the little jerk. When he's finally and deservedly chastised, she continues: "Mommy, I got an A on my Geography test! AND I tried out to be Clara in my ballet school's Nutcracker—and I got the role! AND Daddy took me to sign up for soccer!"

I would love to hug my youngest child for her great grade; watching Trisha try out for the Nutcracker would have been wonderful! I feel like shedding a tear because I couldn't be the one to sign her up for her very first sport.

Thank God they have Jack. He's always been great at tag-teaming our family duties, but…

Should I fail at the rest of my trials, can he handle them alone?

My heartbeat monitor pings a tick faster, reflecting my dread.

*I will win because I must win.*

One of the nurses, Nancy Carr, comes in to check the monitor. After making an adjustment, she turns to the children in the room. "Did any of you touch this?"

Collectively, they shake their heads.

"Good—don't," she warns them.

This time they nod adamantly in agreement.

She leaves the room.

A tear rolls down Trisha's cheek. "I guess Mommy wasn't happy about my news."

Mary put her arm around her. "No, Trisha! I think Mom was very happy! Those were good beeps, not bad."

Evan nudges Mary. "Your turn. But, watch what you say."

Mary nods as she takes hold of my other hand. "Hi, Mom. Hey, I just wanted you to know that I got accepted to the debate team. And I got a B+ in Trig."

Again, my heart swells with my oldest child's great news.

"And Mom," says Jeff, "The coach says I can start on Saturday—"

"—and me too, Mrs. Craig," Cheever butts in.

Jeff shoves him aside. "Hey! She's my mom, not yours!"

"What difference does that make? When she wakes up, she may not remember any of you," Cheever retorts.

As if!

Before Jeff, Mary, and Trisha can pummel Cheever again, Evan steps in front of them. "Okay, enough! Look, why don't I take you girls to grab some sandwiches in the hospital cafeteria? We can bring them back up here for the boys."

Mary and Trisha nod reluctantly.

As Evan passes Jeff, he whispers, "Don't let him get Mom upset, okay?"

"Got it," Jeff assures him.

By the time the door closes behind them, Cheever has moved toward my bed. "Hey, do you think she can feel anything?"

"We hope so. The doctors think she can. They want us to touch her a lot—"

"Duly noted." Cheever gives him a thumbs-up.

The next thing I know, his grubby paws are a mere inch from my breasts—

But Jeff grabs him before they reach their targets.

My son is pummeling his frenemy so hard that even I have to wonder if he'll kill the kid.

Not that I'd blame him.

As Jeff's hands become a vice around Cheever's neck, his captive gasps, "Uncle! Please! Uncle!"

"I'm only telling you this once," Jeff warns him. "If you dare touch my mother—worse yet, if you say that you did to anyone—I'll hunt you down like a dog."

Like mother, like son.

Cheever nods slowly while he stumbles to his feet.

By the time Evan gets back with my girls, both boys are sitting quietly in their chairs. No one says anything about Cheever's bruised fat lip.

And when Cheever begs to leave, no one encourages him to stay.

Evan offers to take Cheever home. "I'll come back for you guys before they want to kick us out," he promises.

I love my kids.

THE GIRLS HAVE BROUGHT MY HAIRBRUSH AND PERFUME. AFTER brushing out my hair and spritzing behind my ear, they each take a foot and paint my nails bright red while Jeff reads out loud from the *L.A. Times*. Apparently, the press has gotten wind of the terrorist attacks.

"What are 'rolling blackouts'?" Trisha asks Jeff.

"It's when the electricity goes off throughout the city. You know —like it did yesterday while we were in school."

"Will it happen again?" she wonders.

"Maybe. The government thinks it's an act of terrorism," Mary explains.

Trisha frowns. "How do they know?"

"Because it's happening all over the country, and the disruptions are hitting things that are important, like power plants, and all the things that make us safe. Even hospitals," Jeff explains.

Trisha looks around the room. "But won't that hurt the patients? What about Mommy? What if it happens here?"

"Yes to the first question," Mary replies. "And we will always be here to protect Mom."

Trisha yawns as she nods. It's late for her: nine-twenty. Nurse Nancy has given them a reprieve to stay until ten o'clock, an hour past visiting hours. If they could, they'd sleep over.

I see their love and concern for me in their eyes. I can also feel their touches: their soft pats, their tender kisses. Jeff is kissing me now—

And then I am gone.

DARKNESS.

Did it happen? Am I dead?

Did my children watch me die?

I feel Satan beside me. My instincts are confirmed when I feel his noxious breath on my neck. "Miss me?"

"To be honest, your timing was less than desirable."

"Too bad," he growls. "The show must go on. Your old friend has been waiting impatiently for his reunion with you."

"I can't wait to see who it is," I retort. "Speaking of which: why can't I see?"

"Ah, you've noticed!" Satan crows gleefully. "It's part of your trial. To be honest, it was Salem Rahmin al-Sadah's idea. He felt that a game of Blind Woman's Bluff would be jolly fun. I now see his point!" I feel his claw on my breast.

It takes all my might to resist slapping it away. "My competitor is Salem?" Dread charges through me. The sadistic Saudi prince was one of the Quorum's money launderers. He was also Babette's lover and the father of the child she will soon deliver.

It's a small Netherworld after all.

I killed him on the eve of my wedding to Jack. I had good reason: he attempted to rape me.

"I've dreamt of this moment since you broke my heart—with a bullet." Salem's voice grates on me: fury leavened with lust. Then I feel it— his tongue rolling down my spine.

Satan laughs uproariously. "With what Salem has planned for you, not having to watch will be a blessing"—he pauses in thought —"which is non-existent here, as you can imagine."

"When I break her, Dark Emperor, you're invited to do more than just watch," Salem declares magnanimously.

"A generous offer, but I don't do sloppy seconds." Satan's tone could make Hell freeze over. "Should she fail, I have my own plans for the sumptuous Mrs. Craig. As your endgame is Purgatory, I suggest you keep your mindset in 'slam, bam, thank you, ma'am" mode and move onto it as quickly as possible—"

"Excuse me, gentlemen," I interrupt, "And I use that term lightly. If indeed this is to be a fair fight—rape, whatever—I find it most unfair that I'm to be blindfolded. For example, how will I choose my weapon?"

"Aye, and this is where you'll have an advantage, Delicious Donna," Satan assures me. "When you feel the time is right, just think of the proper accouterment and, *voila*! It will magically appear!" He leans in and whispers, "Fair warning—you only get one. And if your timing is off, Salem may benefit from it instead."

"Duly noted," I mutter.

"Then, let the games begin!" Satan declares.

I run—

But I don't get far. I feel Salem's hand go around my waist. He's dragging me off to who knows where.

Since I certainly don't want to find out, I lift both legs and kick behind me—

Into his gut. He grunts as he falls backward.

Unfortunately, I fall too, face down. I scramble to my knees—

Which is, apparently, the wrong position when a horny creep is after you. He crawls close enough to grab both my legs and pulls me toward him. But before he can straddle me, I twist around so that I'm facing him. My fist goes up, connecting with his jaw. He howls as he tumbles backward.

I leap up and run. But where does one go when one is blind?

Apparently, in the wrong direction because I bump right into Salem—

Whose fifth appendage is extended even beyond what I remember.

Salem laughs. "You're making this much too easy for me, Donna!"

He throws me to the ground. In a second, he's straddling me again. He's already naked, so no need to unzip—proof positive that we're in Hell.

I'm thinking…

Chainsaw.

*Voila* is right. I rev it up and swing it upward, in an arch.

Salem's scream reverberates through hell.

"The bitch—she neutered me!" he howls. "Why you—"

This time when I swing the chainsaw it cuts through something thicker:

Satan's sash falls from my eyes in time for me to see Salem's torso and head hit the ground. His guts fall out. His angry eyes stare up at me.

His legs are running in circles, like a chicken whose head has been cut off.

"Here, enjoy this souvenir!" Satan picks up the object of my first successful chop and tosses it my way.

I let it fly past me. "Thanks but…no thanks."

Laughter comes from behind me. It's been a while but I still recognize him.

I turn to see Bobby Martin. He was my first crush—but the boyfriend of an older girl: CeeCee Connelly. When she found out about it, she ruined my reputation when, as a pre-teen, I needed friends most: as my mother was dying of breast cancer.

After college, Bobby and CeeCee married. By then they were going by their given names: Robert and Catherine. He became a successful tech entrepreneur. She became a senator, and more recently a presidential candidate. When I became her bodyguard, I found out that Robert had never forgiven her for her cruelty toward me. And when Catherine discovered he still had feelings toward me, it made it easier for her to order a hit on Robert in the hope that a wave public sympathy would carry her all the way to the White House.

The extermination was carried out by my ex-husband, Carl, courtesy of the Quorum.

Yes, Catherine was elected president. And, yes, it made her indebted to the terrorist organization. But before she could take office, I exposed the plot.

Robert puts his hands on my shoulders. "Thank you for all you're doing for Evan," he says.

"He is so much like you," I reply. Then, shyly, I add, "I miss you."

Robert places a hand over my heart. "I'll always be right here."

An orchestra of violins plays around us. I recognize the tune: Tchaikovsky's *Violin Concerto in D major, Op. 35.*

*"Wah, wah, wah!"* Satan pretends to wipe away a tear. "Very touching. But hey, I've got a lot happening here"—when he cups his ears, sinners' screams of agony drown out the lush string symphony—"so let's get this show on the road. *Una pregunta, por favor.*"

I lean into Robert and whisper, "How will Eric carry out his act of terror?"

Robert points to his left—high above the arena, to a clock tower. "The clock struck one—"

The top half of Salem chimes in: "And Lee was done!"

Startled, I stare at him, and then back to Robert. "What do you mean? And…what does *he* mean about Lee?"

Robert starts to reply, but I can't hear him—

Because he's no longer there. Off he goes in a white light—

And off I go, back into darkness.

~

MY CHILDREN ARE SLEEPING.

My kiss on Mary's cheek brings a smile to her lips.

When I nuzzle Jeff with my lips, he actually touches his cheek and sighs.

I stroke Trisha's cheek before leaning in. When her eyes open, I hesitate.

"Mommy, please—don't stop," she begs.

"I'll never stop—either loving you or kissing you," I assure her. To prove it, I kiss her again, very gently.

"I miss you," she murmurs. "Please don't die!"

"I won't," I promise. "You must never give up on me. Promise!"

"Cross my heart," she mumbles. "Mommy…is this a dream?"

I shake my head. "No! I'm right here!"

She sighs mightily. "Will you be with us…you know, permanently, soon?"

"I'm trying my best," I admit sadly. "I wish you could always be with me too." Suddenly, an idea comes to me. "I know what! The next time you visit, bring Birthday Bear." On the day of Trisha's birth, Carl gave her a tiny white Steiff stuffed bear from Germany. He then went on the run. "If you leave him in my arms, I'll always have you next to me."

"I will," she promises, but she is already nodding off again.

I place my cheek next to hers. My tear floats on her cheek for a moment before dissolving into nothingness.

Like me.

# 7

# Don't Rock the Boat

Sung by American trio The Hues Corporation, and written by Wally Holmes. The song was first featured on their 1973 debut studio album *Freedom for the Stallion* and hit #1 on both *Billboard*'s "Hot 100" and *Cashbox*'s Top 100" lists.

Some music historians consider "Don't Rock the Boat" one of the earliest disco songs. (That honor may actually belong to "Love's Theme" by Love Unlimited Orchestra, which was a chart-topper from earlier in 1974.) Others say no, but acknowledge the claim may have been made because "Don't Rock the Boat" was the first *disco* song to hit #1 on the charts.

In any event, the song is still a favorite of wedding singers all over the world.

*Everyone has committed at least one act of self-sabotage.*

*It might have been while going through the emotional turmoil of a relationship break-up. Or maybe it was a "Take This Job and Shove It" moment.*

*At the very least, your mother can attest to a few of the hissy fits you threw while in your Terrible Twos.*

*Should you now find yourself tempted to rock the boat in the placid pond of your lovely life, do this instead:*

1. *Take a walk around the block. It's one way to cool off. (And if you're still tempted to burn down the house, you can at least scope out someone else's—perhaps one with less curb appeal.)*
2. *Talk it through with a friend. Your bestie may give you some sage advice—or at the very least a different perspective on the situation. (Tip: Do not take her advice while either of you is intoxicated! She may not remember giving it, and you may regret taking it.)*
3. *Never flip a coin! By tossing that piece of silver in the air, you might just be throwing your life away. Don't be your own Judas!*

ONE EXPECTS HELL TO BE HOT.

Not wet.

When I walk through the door, I'm immediately immersed in water. Of course, I panic! First, I look behind me for Death—

But the coward is nowhere to be found.

I then take a second look—over my head, where water rises forever— and toward my feet, which have yet to touch bottom. Which way is up?

The fish swimming languidly around me are no help—

Until they scatter, panicked. Their flurry of activity has created a cloud of bubbles that makes it hard for me to see what has scared them away.

Then I see it: a large motor yacht above my head.

I kick my feet up so that I can meet it—

Only to have to duck again below its wake as it zooms right over me.

That's okay. From what I saw, I don't like what's above the surface anyway: The sky is pitch-black except when etched by lightning.

The yacht, at least eighty feet in length, has Satan at the wheel. He looks quite jaunty in his double-breasted blazer and white slacks. A blood red cravat adorns his neck.

His horns, however, cannot be hidden by his jauntily tilted captain's hat.

By the time it comes back around to me, he's slowed to a crawl and I notice he's not alone. A bevy of bathing beauties—all breathtakingly gorgeous, from what I see of their bathing attire from different time eras—coo in awe of his nautical skills.

They're faking it. There's certainly no joy in their laughter.

There is also no plastic surgery in Hell. Everyone still carries scars from their mortal lives. One of his chippies has a hole where her heart should be. Another has a mangled neck. A third has a bullet between her eyes, emphasizing the deep sadness in her gaze.

"Ah, Donna, there you are!" Satan waves gaily. "I've got your weapons." He reaches down into the hull and pulls out an ancient treasure chest—

Which he then promptly tosses overboard.

"Um…thanks," I mutter.

He revs the yacht's engine. "Remember, choose just one. Leave the rest in the box. I'll pick them up later." He waves as he zooms away.

I dive after it.

I FIND THE CHEST DIRECTLY UNDER ME.

It is protected by a lock. When I take a rock and slam it against the lock, it breaks into pieces.

Quickly, I open the chest.

*Hmmm…*

I've been given a flare gun and a harpoon. The rest of the chest is filled with gold doubloons.

As I try to sift through them with my fingers, I discover that it's really a filmy gown covered in the coins—

Nothing else. Where is the third weapon? Damn Satan! He shorted me!

*Calm. Down.*

I'm still deciding which of these two weapons to go with when suddenly a school of fish flurry over the chest and me. I can't see anything—

But I can feel something—

Ominous.

And I see its shadow on the ocean floor—

A shark is just over my shoulder.

I turn to it—

Only it's not a shark. It is Sebastian Gillingham, a screenwriter who was also a Quorum operative. He passed intel to the terrorist organization through the dialogue in the scripts of his movies and internationally syndicated television shows. While we were on a movie set, he tried to kill me in the middle of a tumultuous coastal storm. Instead, he got washed out to sea.

No wonder the fish are frightened of him! Death has not been kind to Sebastian. The saltwater has peeled off several layers of skin. What is left is pink and puffy, like a flatulent balloon filled with gooey puss and water. His eyes, too, are bulging from their sockets. His appendages are twice the size of a normal human's, and his fingers and toes are webbed. What little hair he has left is intertwined with long flowing waterweeds. All sorts of parasites cling to it. Those who feed on such critters swim in and out of it too.

When Sebastian sees me, he grins, revealing teeth as sharp as a shark's. He dips down and around me. I figure that my best weapon against him is the harpoon, but I'm too late. He butts the chest's lid closed. The lock's pieces fly back together, snapping it shut again.

I'm left holding the coin-encrusted gown. A lot of good that will do me!

"How truly marvelous! The opportunity to take the Housewife Assassin to Hell is something one lives—or in my case *dies* for!" Sebastian's purr is garbled by the bubbles blown out with each word.

I glance around. The bottom of the ocean is rough terrain. Should I head for a cave, or just hide between the peaks and valleys of jutting rocks?

Better to make my plan of attack on the run. "You'll have to catch me first!" I shout. I kick off hard, heading for a ledge off to my right. I turn the corner—

And find myself face-to-face with a giant electric eel. Yikes!

I dodge its forked tongue, ducking into a cavern. The eel ends up electrocuting an errant clown fish instead. RIP Nemo!

I can barely catch my breath before I see Sebastian coming my way. He too seems keen on dodging the eel. Good to know he's afraid of something.

As he looks around for me, I back into the cavern. It seems fairly deep, so maybe I'll have time to think of a course of action before running into him again—

As opposed to Mama Eel and her nest of babies. Ah, so that must have been Papa Eel keeping guard!

Thinking her little ones are under attack, she strikes at me. I dodge out of the way just in time.

A sinister chuckle echoes off the cavern's walls. "Which will it be, sweet Donna—electrocution, or a shredding by me?" He taps his forehead with a webbed finger. "Ah, but one must play by the rules." He shrugs. "I'm sure Mama won't mind if I slice and dice her babies' next meal for them."

He's wrong. She slithers and hisses even closer, ready to do battle.

Sebastian darts in my direction, jaws open wide.

I have nothing to stop him except for the coin-laced gown—

So I cram it deep into his mouth—

And then I duck.

He's either gasping at my audacity or choking on the cloth and coins.

Mama Eel's forked tongue goes into his jaws as well. When her electric current hits the coins, Sebastian lights up like the winning jackpot screen on a one-armed bandit—an apt analogy, now that what's left of him is fried. His body dissipates in a hazy cloud.

I, on the other hand, find myself being pulled out of the cavern and up through the water—

I pop up—soggy, shivering, and gasping for air—in the center of the Devil's ocean.

"Bravo! Bravo!" he chortles. He stands on the yacht's deck, clapping enthusiastically.

Behind him, off in the distance, someone is sailing our way: Nola Janoff.

This dearly departed Acme operative was one of the organization's most notorious swallows. Carl killed her. Thanks to her dog, Rin Tin Tin, Jack and I located her body in the spare freezer in her garage. I hadn't known until that moment that her mission was to watch over my children and me. I adopted Rin Tin Tin in homage to her.

She waves when she sees me and pulls me onboard with her.

I hug her tightly, even as I shed tears of joy. "I want to thank you for all you did for my family and me," I say.

Nola's husky chuckle warms my heart. "It was the best assignment I ever had," she replies. "Tell me: how many of the neighborhood DILFs attended my funeral?"

I can't help but laugh. "All of them! In fact, they fought to see who would carry your casket."

Nola sighs. "I left them with some wonderful memories."

Satan sighs loudly. "Enough with the girl talk already! Don't you have something to ask your BFF?"

Nola nods sadly. "He's right. The sun is already setting in the west."

I look around. She's right, but does it matter? We're in Hell where the days are endless as are the afterlives. Still, the sooner I ask, the sooner I can get back to my life. "Nola, can you tell me where Eric's act of terrorism will take place?"

Something flies over our heads. It's a carrier pigeon. It carries a metal briefcase in its beak.

Suddenly, the bird makes a crash landing beside me. The case breaks open, revealing tiny gold coins. As Nola coos gently at it, the bird hops closer to us. "Ah, look—its wing is broken!" she exclaims.

I stretch out my arm toward it, only to get nipped.

"*Lee! Lee!*" it caws.

The bird is right. Lee is in my hospital room.

But before I have a chance to ask Nola what she means, I'm there too.

THE PRESIDENT OF THE UNITED STATES STARES DOWN AT MY unconscious body.

Inch by inch, his eyes move over me, taking in the severity of my condition: my stillness; my slackened face; the alabaster pallor of my skin; the way in which my eyelids tremble, oh so slightly.

This dismays me, but only because I hate for anyone to see me like this. Thank goodness he's left his Secret Service detail outside the closed door.

He pulls the closest chair as near to my bed as possible. Gently, he takes my wrist to measure my pulse rate. His lips turn down at the corners because he doesn't like what he's feeling:

Despair.

*Don't give up on me, Lee.*

As if hearing me, he leans in and murmurs, "And I want you to know I'll always be here for you, for as long as we both are alive."

*Thank you, Lee.*

"I also need to tell you, Donna, that…I love you. Your honesty and your strength and your loyalty…" His voice trails off.

*I love you too, Lee. For all those same reasons.*

"And should you wake up from this terrible nightmare, I hope you'll marry me."

*What? But—Lee—*

He strokes my cheek. And then his lips brush mine.

"What the hell?" Jack exclaims. He grabs Lee's shoulders and shoves him away from me.

Poised with his fist within punching distance to Lee's nose, he asks, "Did you just ask my wife to marry you?"

To Lee's credit, he doesn't flinch when he declares, "Yes. If you want to punch me for doing so, go for it."

Jack's fist hovers for a long moment. Finally, it drops to his side. "Why, so that the Secret Service can tackle me and put me in prison for the rest of my life? You'd love that, wouldn't you?"

"No, not really. I'd prefer to wait and ask Donna when she regains consciousness—and for that matter, when she comes to her senses about you."

Jack's eyes narrow in anger. He strains to keep from going at Lee again.

Heck, I'm straining to keep Jack from throwing a right hook.

Jack's body finally goes limp, but not his tongue: "I wonder how Babette would feel if she knew what you just did?"

"Probably like you," Lee retorts, "Helpless."

Jack keeps his cool for a full three minutes after Lee walks out the door.

But when he slams a chair to the floor, three nurses rush in to check on the commotion.

He smiles apologetically. "Sorry. It slipped out from under me."

They nod uncertainly and back out cautiously, closing the door behind them.

It takes a while for Jack to fall into a fitful sleep.

As he tosses and turns, I crawl into his lap and whisper again and again, "I am yours forever."

All night long, he swats away my kisses.

---

8

# Rip Her to Shreds

---

PERFORMED BY BLONDIE, ON THE BAND'S 1977 DEBUT ALBUM BY THE
same name. Written by band members Deborah Harry and Chris
Stein.

Though it was released in the UK, it never charted there. Harry
claims that the song poked fun at the tabloids' take on celebrity.

*It's not nice to gossip. However, should others try to draw you in on their
catty chatter, here are two things you should do:*

*First, if they go low, you go high. (I'm talking about your aim here.
Talk doesn't hurt half as much as bullets—trust me.)*

*Second, remember what your mother taught you: if you can't say
something nice about someone, don't say anything at all…*

*Wait—your mother never said that. Oh, well, then, never mind. Feel
free to rip your frenemy to shreds.*

"WHAT DOES HE SEE IN HER?" MUTTERS NARCISSA BELMONT, Babette's Chief of Staff.

"Beats me. She's so…I dunno. *Ordinary*." Chantal Desmarais, Babette's personal aide, shivers, as if my looks are a disease. "Maybe she's a great lay, because, seriously, he could have anyone. When Jack Craig comes within twenty-feet of me, I'm so wet I have to wring out my thong—"

"No, silly! I mean…" Narcissa puts a finger to her lips and then jerks her thumb toward the closed bathroom door as if wondering if their very pregnant boss can hear through particleboard. Finally, she hisses, "*POTUS*. He's crushed on Donna since forever!"

"And Babette knows about this?"

I don't recognize the woman's voice coming from behind them. Whoever it is, she finally walks toward the bed to take a closer look.

She is taller than the others. A few auburn tendrils have escaped her loose bun. Her large glasses can't conceal the steeliness in her wide slate gray eyes. Her sheer blouse is buttoned primly to the neck, but her language is anything but modest.

"Damn it, Scarlett, I forgot you were still in the room!" Narcissa's frown is accompanied by an eye roll. "I thought you even went with her into the bathroom because you shadow the First Lady everywhere."

Chantal snickers. Obviously, she was under the same assumption.

"You're not jealous of the time I spend with Babette, are you?" Scarlett's honeyed tone contrasts with the derisive look in her eyes.

"Not at all," Narcissa retorts coldly. "As her biographer, I realize having you underfoot is a necessary evil."

"How long will you be with us, anyway?" Chantal's pleasant smile does little to smooth the edginess in her voice.

Scarlett shrugs. "That depends on the First Lady, of course. But considering her youth, this may be an ongoing project." She leans in to add, "So you might as well get used to me being around."

Duly warned, Chantal backs away—fast.

"Oh? You know Babette's age?" Narcissa asks innocently. Her wink at Chantal is anything but.

"It's whatever she claims," Scarlett growls. Then, nodding in my direction, she adds, "She's certainly a few years younger than this cadaver."

How dare this bitch call me a cadaver!

Wait…she thinks Babette is younger than me? That is so not true!

"Despite your attempt to change the subject, I'd still like an answer to my question," Scarlett retorts to Narcissa. "Is Babette aware that Lee has a thing for this woman?"

"It's nothing. Drop it." Hearing Babette's voice, Chantal swallows a yelp and Narcissa turns white.

On the other hand, a sly grin rises on Scarlett's plumped lips.

Babette is now at my bedside too. She glares down at me disdainfully. "Besides, you're writing my biography, not his."

"And it will be a tome for the ages!" Chantal exclaims. "The only style icon to grace the White House since Jackie Kennedy—"

"And with such a big heart, too!" Narcissa butts in. "Readers will be going, 'Um…Mother Teresa? Who?'"

"You both are much too kind," Babette murmurs, "At least, while I'm in the room." She puts her arm around Scarlett's waist. "However, Ms. Packard has expressed her concern with your candidness regarding Lee and my lives, and that greatly concerns me. In fact, I'd consider it cause for dismissal—"

"But…you told us to tell her everything, no holds barred!" Chantal protests.

"Now, now, Babette." Scarlett scolds her employer in the gentlest of tones. "In truth, that was before you discovered how much more comfortable our little chats make the process of getting your story down from your own perspective. Please, don't take it out on the staff."

Narcissa bristles when she hears herself reduced to something so impersonal.

My giggle is felt in one interesting way. Babette frowns as she clutches her now very extended baby bump. "My goodness, the little man sure is kicking today."

"Can I feel him, Mummy?" Janie stands in the doorway. Trisha and Jack are there too. As promised, Trisha has brought Birthday Bear too.

Babette waves her daughter off. "Not now, darling. I hate it when you're all touchy-feely."

Noting Janie's frown, Trisha pats her friend's hand.

"On the way to the gift store, did you see any newborn infants?" Scarlett asks.

The girls shook their heads. "All the mommies and babies are asleep with their doors closed so we couldn't peek in." Janie was truly disappointed.

"I miss the days when they let the moms sleep by themselves the first night," Chantal says brightly. "Back when my little brother was born, they put all the newborns in one long room. You could look at them as if they were on sale or something. I imagined you could pick out the perfect one and take it home with you! Like that song, 'How Much Is that Doggie in the Window'!"

"But wouldn't that be kidnapping?" Trisha asks.

Chantal glowers at her.

Jack's smile is forced. "Babette, it's really kind of you to spend a few moments with Donna. At this late stage of your pregnancy, I imagine it's not an easy task to be out and about."

"Nonsense! What are friends for?" Babette purrs. "Besides, when I discovered Lee had already paid his respects, I came as soon as I could. I would have hated to have missed the opportunity to say goodbye…"

Her voice dies off when she sees the anger in Jack's eyes.

Trisha, horrified, declares, "My mommy isn't going anywhere! She told me herself!"

"Of course she did, darling," Narcissa's patronizing murmur is too familiar to Janie. In a show of solidarity, she sticks out her tongue at her mother's aide-de-camp.

"Janie, that's enough," Babette warns. "If you mimic Trisha's rude behavior, I won't let you play with her anymore."

Janie's scowl withers under her mother's threat. Our daughters' friendship is near and dear to both of them. Janie is smart enough to change the subject. "Mummy, you should have your baby here. The newborns all seem so happy, and—"

"Not in a million years," Babette sniffs. "The First Baby—the First Son—deserves better!"

"But I was born in a hospital," Janie counters. "And I'm the First Daughter."

"At the time, you weren't 'First' anything," Babette reminds her. Seeing her daughter's face fall into despair, she quickly adds, "Except first in my heart, darling. And besides, it's already been decided: Benjamin Harrison Chiffray will be born in the White House."

"What?" Chantal exclaims. "But...I've already made the arrangements for your doctor and his nurses to set up in Lion's Lair, like you always said you wanted!"

Babette dismisses her dismay with a flick of her wrist. "I'm sure they won't argue about the change of venue."

"A birth has never taken place in the White House," Scarlett points out. "It'll be a historical first. Such a wonderful anecdote for the First Lady's biography!"

"Her idea, I'll bet," Narcissa murmurs just loud enough for Chantal to hear her.

"By the way, Scarlett, I've decided it's to be an *autobiography*," Babette informs her. "You'll only be ghosting the book. No credit line."

Scarlett's smile fades. "Oh, I see. Sorry, not my usual thing. If you'd prefer to work with someone else—"

"I'm sure we can work something out. Trust me, you'll love

being my ghost." Babette's tone could cut ice.

Scarlett is smart enough to keep her mouth shut.

Babette smiles prettily at Jack. "It's late and I'm tiring, but Jack and I must have a little 'we time' before I go. Ladies, will you excuse Jack and me?"

Narcissa nudges Chantal knowingly. But when Chantal tries to hustle Trisha out with them, Trisha shakes her head firmly. "I'm staying with my daddy!"

Babette sighs. Bending down so that she's face-to-face with Trisha, she says, "Little one, I must express my condolences to your father in private. Your mother would have wanted that."

Trisha's eyes shift from Babette to Jack.

Her back stiffens when she sees his slight nod. Reluctantly, my daughter follows the others out the door, slamming it behind her.

"Way to lose friends and create enemies, Babette," Jack murmurs dryly.

"You'd hate me even more if I kept my mouth shut about what I know about Donna and Lee."

Jack's face hardens. "Are you referring to the way he pants after her like a dog in heat?"

Babette retorts, "Do you honestly believe she hasn't led him on? Or that she doesn't love his attention?"

"If you're asking if my wife has been anything less than faithful to me, my answer is an unequivocal no." Jack sounds convincing, even to me—until he coughs. It's his poker tell.

He's never trusted Lee. And, distressingly, yesterday, Lee gave him no reason to change his opinion.

"Don't lie, Jack. We're both in the same boat." Her lower lip trembles. Tears haze her eyes. "I get it. Your wife's rapidly failing situation has you upset. I just want you to know that…well, I'll always be there to comfort you."

His face is close enough for her to kiss him.

At first, he doesn't pull away.

Is this because he's shocked, or because he enjoys it too much?

Angered, I fly out of my body to pound him on the back.

He feels nothing…

Oh, no, I take that back: he must feel her hand cupping his crotch because he grabs her wrist and jerks it away.

Babette chuckles raucously. "Why did you stop me? We both know you enjoyed it."

Firmly, with both hands, he forces her down into a chair. "You're wrong, Babette, on all counts. I don't like it when desperate women cling to me—even if it is the First Lady of the United States."

"You're right. It's much too soon for consolation. Better to wait until after a decent mourning period," she purrs as she rises gracefully and then walks out the door.

He keeps his head bowed as she walks out.

It stays that way until Trisha peeks in. "She took way too long! Visiting hours are almost over!" My daughter walks over to my bed. Her kiss on my lips reminds me of sunshine, flowers, and laughter. As she tucks Birthday Bear under my arm, she whispers, "Just like I promised, Mommy! Now come back to us, like *you* promised."

Jack watches. I've never seen him look this sad. Is he concerned that Babette is right—that I won't pull through?

I put my arms around my daughter. She smiles as if she sees me, but of course, she doesn't.

It's great to know that at least she feels me.

She beckons her father to her side. This gives me the opportunity to put my arms around both of them—

And then I'm gone.

"Your timing sucks," I yell at the Devil.

"You'll thank me," he retorts. He rises from the chaise lounge onto which he's flopped. "I'm going to make this one easy for you!

Three doors. Two have a tiger. One has a lady. You have a two-to-one chance to choose the right one—the lady—who will give you your tip." He winks at me. "However, if you choose one of the tigers…well, you know her too."

"I know a tiger? How is that even possible?"

"Down here, we don't turn up our noses up at those who choose alternative lifestyles—in this case, shape-shifting. Your next challenger loves donning fangs, furs, and claws." He sighs ecstatically. "You've got to admit; it's a bold fashion statement."

"Indubitably," I murmur.

"I thought so too!" He beams like a child at Christmas. "So, are you ready?"

I shrug. "Sure, what the hey?"

Not.

～

THE CURTAINS RISE HIGH BEFORE DISAPPEARING INTO THIN AIR, revealing three sets of large double-doors.

Over the frenzy of sinners' moans and cries, Satan's voice booms, "Alright, Donna Stone Craig—the decision is yours! Which door holds the one thing you seek? Is it Door Number One?"

A deafening drumroll follows his pause.

"Or is it Door Number Two?"

Again, I have to wait for the damn drumroll to stop.

"Or is it Door Number Three?"

He had me at, "Okay, Donna Stone Craig," but since I'm only a guest on this game show, I wait until the theatrics are over before shouting out, "Number Three!"

The Devil appears beside me. He has a microphone in his hand. With a serious tone, he asks, "Donna, tell the studio audience why you chose that number."

Okay, I'll play along. "Well, Satan, in hindsight, maybe I was too obvious."

He nods, as if seriously considering my concern.

"I mean, I do have three children," I continue. "Then again, I could have chosen two—you know, for two husbands; or one—since I only have one life to live." I crook my finger at him. "But if you ask me what I think, my guess is that it wouldn't have made a hill of beans which door I chose because this is Hell, and I'm in a lose-lose situation."

Bells chime and whistles blare. Confetti falls from the sky.

"Donna—you are *CORRECT!*"

My heart skips a beat. "You mean…I chose the right door?"

Satan nods and laughs. "No, of course not, silly woman! But you did guess right about your chances of choosing the wrong door."

"You mean the right one."

He clicks his tongue. "Nope, sorry. The *wrong* door—but for all the right reasons. You see, the lady *is* a tiger!"

Door Number three now rises skyward, revealing a tiger the size of a Mac truck. Its roar reverberates through Hell.

But the most unusual thing about it isn't its size or its sound, but its face.

It looks like the rogue Chinese assassin Liang Xia.

"Hello, Donna," she purrs. In the wink of an eye, her claw reaches out—

And I barely have time to duck out of its way.

Xia and I had a hate-hate relationship—appropriate, considering that she is just as skilled and as fearless an assassin as me. But the biggest difference between us is that she worked for hire, whereas I must believe in my cause.

I have no doubt she has a cause now: kill me and leave Hell for the much more desirable Purgatory.

I've ducked into the thick velvet folds of the stage curtains, but it is certainly not a permanent solution. She shreds them as if they are toilet paper, all the while taunting, "Come out, come out, wherever you are…"

The only thing good about the shredded curtains is now I can use them to climb up—

And just in time, too, because Xia is angry that her handiwork has been for naught. When I'm halfway to the catwalk, she snarls, "Right behind you, love! Watch your back, because my claws are sharp and the smell of blood makes me hungry!"

She only needs to leap once to reach my height. She hangs from a curtain, batting at the catwalk with her paw as if it's a ball of yarn that needs unraveling. The catwalk creaks loudly as it swings side-to-side. Bolts ping as they pop off from the strain of her slaps.

The next thing I know, the catwalk crashes to the concrete floor below, collapsing into a jagged heap of metal.

My only hope now is to grab one of the sandbags tied to the dark cloud above, and swing out of her reach—

Caught one! I climb as high as I can.

Xia roars with laughter. "Silly fool! I've got you now!" She climbs the rope after me—

But I have other plans that don't include her. Now that I'm at the top, I loosen the knot holding the rope to the cloud. Under Xia's weight, the rope swings and frays.

I'm just about to reach for another rope when it breaks!

Xia roars as she falls backward—

And is speared by one of the rails of the catwalk.

I land on my feet beside the dead cat.

"And Xia thought *she* had nine lives!" Satan guffaws. "What are you up to now—six circles?"

If only.

"Five," I mutter.

He shrugs. "I've always been bad with numbers. A lesser person would have lied about that."

"If that's the case, pretend I agreed with you."

"Nice try—but no." He scrutinizes the scene before him. "Ideally, you'd be naked on a cat rug."

I shake my head. "Ideally, I'd be waking up from a coma."

"Only when you complete our little wager successfully. Still, as promised." He snaps his fingers.

Catherine Martin appears in a puff of smoke.

I wince. Purgatory has not treated her well. Holes are burned into her inaugural suit, exposing welts all over her body. Her skin is translucent, revealing raw bones. I shudder when a worm slithers from her ear.

Reading my mind, she scoffs, "It's better than the alternative."

She's right.

"Considering you were responsible for Robert's death, I'm surprised about your reprieve," I admit.

"Evan prays for me every night," she murmurs. "If you make it back, thank him for me." She stares down at Xia's dead body. "And thanks for killing the bitch a second time."

"My pleasure." Satan is tapping his foot. I don't have much time. "Catherine, tell me: Where will we find Eric?"

She stares off into the darkness beyond the stage. "Do you hear that?" she asks.

I shake my head impatiently.

"Spooks. Ghosts. The building is filled with them," she murmurs. "Carl knows that better than anyone."

"What does Carl have to do with anything?" I look around cautiously. He's nowhere to be found. Breathing easier, I add, "Look, I hate to rush you but—"

"Lee is clueless about the power that is wielded in Washington," she declares bluntly. "I mean, let's face it: He's no Eisenhower. That man knew how to dodge a bullet, literally and figuratively…"

"What is this, sour milk because he got what you always wanted?" I throw up my hands in disgust. "I didn't come here for your pity party, Catherine! I need to know—"

Where the heck did she go?

But no, it's not her that's gone—

It's me.

9

# Runnin' with the Devil

RELEASED MAY 6, 1978, BY THE BAND VAN HALEN. WRITTEN AND performed by David Lee Roth and Eddie Van Halen. Other writers on the song were Michael Anthony and Alex Van Halen. The song was released from the band's 1978 debut album that took the name of the band.

Although only hitting *Billboard*'s "Hot 100" chart at #84 and the *UK Singles Chart* at #52, VH1 still calls it the ninth greatest hard rock song of all time.

As for its "satanic" lyrics, the band insists they are metaphors for the ups and downs of the band's life on the road. (Must have been one hell of a tour…)

*Don't you hate it when you give in to your worst instincts and do all those naughty things that get you in trouble?*

*Because you'd much rather play the saint than to be called out as a sinner, here are three golden rules to follow:*

87

- *Rule #1: Do unto others as you'd have them do unto you. (Caveat: This rule never applies to knife fights or shoot-outs; otherwise, you'd both be dead.)*
- *Rule #2: Blasphemies be damned! (Okay, admittedly, this declaration defeats the purpose, but you get the point.)*
- *Rule #3: Always play the Good Samaritan. If you see someone bleeding on the side of the road, call for help. (Then again, if they're bleeding because of a bullet from your gun, you may want to consider a different act of kindness: putting them out of their misery.)*

My neighbor, Tiffy Swift, stares down at my comatose body and sighs. "If there were any chance she'd come out of this, if I were Jack, I'd request that she have a few nip-tucks while she's still out cold. I mean, she wouldn't feel it anyway." She shrugs. "I know my hubby, Rex, would consider it."

Yeah, well, Rex wants to turn you into his own personal Barbie doll, I want to yell at her. Let's see: how many times have you gone under the knife? Six? Seven? But who's counting...

The fact that I'm still breathing doesn't stop another neighbor—the unfortunately named Hayley Coxhead—from predicting so matter-of-factly: "Jack will do well as a widower."

"That's an understatement!" exclaims Tiffy. "Every divorcee in Hilldale will be knocking on his door with condolence casseroles—"

"Among other things," Hayley giggles. "Now that Peter Bing has moved to Beverly Hills, Jack will be the most desirable DILF in town!"

"What's that you say about Peter?" Hearing Penelope's growl, her frenemies' faces lose their color. They look closer to death than me.

I pray they don't pass out because they'll land on me.

"Nothing," Tiffy and Hayley say in unison.

"Liars," Penelope pronounces. "And to think I consider you my nearest and dearest!" She rolls her eyes. "That's alright. Once I pull the plug on Peter's reality show, he'll come crawling back." She bares her bleached teeth. "And I'll make his life a living hell."

With my recent forays, I could certainly give her a few pointers.

"We were just saying that Jack will certainly be more popular as a widower than just a DILF," Tiffy admits.

She's found the perfect way to change the topic—and to put a lascivious smile on her BFF's artificially plumped lips. "I'll say!" Penelope murmurs. "And I'll be there to console him."

"So will everyone else," Hayley mutters wryly. "He'll need a stick to fight them off."

"But we'd be the perfect Hilldale power couple!" Penelope insists. "We're both photogenic! It's why we were chosen for *The Hot Housewives of Hilldale* in the first place!"

"I don't think the show mattered to him at the time, so why should it now?" Hayley asks. "And remember: Peter was the only one who came out of it with a follow-up show—without you. Face it, Penelope, your fifteen minutes of fame are over, with or without Jack at your side."

Peter and Penelope's divorce has had tongues wagging for months. Their breakup, after the final episode of the now canceled *Hot Housewives of Hilldale* reality show, culminated in a spinoff production, for him, anyway.

But because celebrities are few and far between in Hilldale, the reality show's producer and showrunner, Addison Montague and Brin Patterson, moved Peter to Beverly Hills.

To Penelope's dismay, Peter parlayed the show into a private bachelor competition. Granted, she has a recurring role as his ever-whining soon-to-be ex-wife, but the real heat is generated by all the starlets and models vying to be the next Mrs. Peter Bing, Realtor to the Stars.

"The producers are going to drop Peter like a hot potato when they see what I've got on him," Penelope predicts.

Tiffy's eyes open wide. "Don't leave us in suspense! What is it?"

"When Cheever admitted he uses Peter's Mac computer to look at his father's porn stash, I told him I'd tell on him—unless he uploaded a spyware program that I control. He did it and now I can access Peter's iCloud account and read his emails and texts," she retorts smugly. "You won't believe all the nasty things he says about his new Beverly Hills celebrity clients—not to mention the producers of his show! And when they're aware of all the sexting he does with his latest slut, from *The Hot Housewives of Malibu*, they'll blow their stacks!"

"But...don't they like that kind of thing?" Tiffy asks innocently.

The thought that she may be right causes Penelope's lips to pucker downward. But before she has a chance to put her underling in her place, Jack walks in—

With Ryan, Emma, Arnie, and Abu.

Needless to say, my neighbors are curious about Jack's entourage. They don't realize it but they've already met two of them. Emma once posed as my Swedish au pair. But at the time, she donned a platinum wig that covered her usual jet-black spiked gamine cut. As my handler, Abu's brush-passes of intel and assignments were made via his ice cream truck, once an afternoon ritual for the children in Hilldale.

He hated the neighborhood's snotty mommy brigade, but he sure misses the pin money.

As they stare dreamily at their fantasy come to life, Jack says brightly, "Ladies, so wonderful to see you! And I'm sure if Donna could speak for herself, she'd tell you how much your visit has meant to her."

For sure, I'd have a few choice words for all their dissing of my body, my relationship, my life in general—

"I've brought out-of-town family with me, who wish to visit in private, so thanks for stopping by." Before they can utter another word, he nudges them out the door, closing it gently behind them.

"Now, let's get to work," mutters Ryan.

My thoughts exactly. But without our little middleman—Nicky —I wonder how I'll be able to convey some of the intel I've collected?

I'm still thinking about that when Arnie begins. "So, here's what's happened over the past twenty-four hours—"

Then everything goes black.

Oh, heck, what is it now, another cyber attack? Why couldn't it have happened when the Bitches of Hilldale were quote-unquote paying their respects?

But it's not an earthly blackout.

Suddenly, I see a ray of moonlight peeking out from a dark cloud, revealing the fact that I'm sitting on a grave in a cemetery.

Oh, joy.

UNLIKE ME—IN MY GOLD GOWN PRE-BULLETED AND BLOODIED, AND sky-high heels—Satan is dressed for the occasion.

Well, let me put it this way: he wears a black suit and tie and is sporting a simple white rosebud boutonniere.

All of hell has turned out as well—or I should say, what is left of its resident sinners. I've yet to find one who hasn't been decapitated, blinded, or otherwise maimed.

Dressed in black, they sob as if they're attending their own funerals.

If only.

The headstone is puny compared to all of the others around it, some of which are three times as high as the average person.

Instead of angels, children, or statues of the dead who lay

beneath them, they are topped by gargoyles, demons, and those who were infamously disreputable.

Some are topped with the Devil himself. Their iconography spans every society's morbid vision of him.

As Satan flicks away an alligator tear, he says, "At last! Donna has arrived!" This only causes his minions to weep all the louder.

"Whose shindig?" I ask.

He holds out a hand to help me up, and then he invites me to turn around.

Carved on the headstone of the grave I landed on is written the following:

**RIP**
**DONNA STONE CRAIG**
**MOTHER, WIFE, ASSASSIN**
**"I intend to live forever, or die trying."**
**—Groucho Marx**

I try not to gasp. Instead, I do my best to stay easy-breezy when declaring, "Aren't you a bit premature?"

"It's cheaper to make such arrangements before the inevitable event," he reminds me.

"It's cheaper to keep her," I counter. "Or so sayeth Johnny Taylor."

"He's not exactly Groucho Marx," Satan points out, "whose statement is quite apt in your regard, don't you think?"

"Frankly, I try not to think about it. And besides, actions speak louder than words." I look around. "Where is my next challenger? Let's get this show on the road. I need to get back."

"This trial may not be as easy as you'd hope." Gleeful with that thought, Satan announces, "I'm sure you'll remember your neighbors, Dave and Midge Kelsey. You left them hanging in your Nordstrom's dressing room."

"You know what they say: three's a crowd," I reply nonchalantly. "Since this trial is a twofer, does that mean this counts as Trials Six and Seven?"

Satan shakes his head. "Sorry, doll, but no. However, should you win, you will get to ask two questions as opposed to one."

I guess I'll have to live with it.

Reading my mind, Satan laughs. "Or die without it. Speaking of which, here are your competitors now!"

The words are barely out of his mouth when I see a shovel heading in my direction. I duck—

And it strikes my headstone so hard that it breaks in half before stabbing one of the mourners, slicing off her head.

As the head rolls past me, she mumbles, "Damn! I'll never get the bloodstains out of this blouse."

Oh, yeah? Well, I've got bigger problems. The way Midge is coming at me with another shovel, I guess I should take off, but it's not so easy. My heels sink in all the way each time they spike the velvety lawn.

I kick them off and run behind a large ornate mausoleum. Its door is open, but I don't dare go in. Otherwise, I'd be a sitting duck. Still, I slam the door shut, to give the opposite impression.

I duck around the side of the mausoleum just in the nick of time.

I wait to hear her footsteps—

And then realize, too late, that she's behind me.

I don't turn around. I don't need to because the moonlight casts enough of a shadow that I can see Midge as she slowly raises the shovel over my head—

But I knock her out with a single punch before she gets a chance to hit me with it.

I then drag her over to an open empty grave and toss her in.

Not a moment too soon. Dave comes at me by way of the mausoleum—

And he's commandeering a giant earthmover.

It rolls over mourners, sarcophaguses, headstones, trees—everything in its way.

When he sees me, this burly guy's gap-toothed grin widens ferociously like a jack-o-lantern's.

I run, but I can't move faster than his new set of wheels. He pins me in the corner of two mausoleums that abut each other at forty-five-degree angles.

Laughing, he jumps out of the vehicle's cabin. He licks his lips as he takes me in. "Well, well, well! If it isn't the prettiest piece of ass in all of Hilldale! Now I get to do the one thing I couldn't do up there: screw the living daylights out of you."

He grabs me by my waist and goose-steps me to the nearest sarcophagus, where he shoves me down against it. 'The worst thing about Hell isn't the fire and brimstone," he insists. "It's the fact that there are no good lays. I mean, look at these bitches! Not one of them is whole!"

"Is that a metaphor?" I ask. "Love it. Spot on, in fact." Needless to say, I'm buying time while he unzips his pants.

I guess he doesn't hear an engine revving up again. Despite being pinned to the top of the sarcophagus, I can still raise my head. I take a quick glance around Dave's girth.

Midge is now behind the wheel of the earthmover. Apparently, she climbed out of the grave, realized Dave wanted to do more than just kill me, and is now a woman scorned.

Not that I blame her.

By the time he's got his pants around his ankles, Midge is just six feet from us. With all my might, I raise both legs and kick off with them, shoving him in the gut—

Right into the earthmover's path.

It runs right over him.

I barely have time to leap off before Midge runs over the sarcophagus as well.

As she chases after me, the earthmover shovels her husband's body along with the rest of the debris in her path. I run as fast as I can through the cemetery, but she's right on my heels.

I'm heading toward a large double-wide grave. The caskets aren't in it yet, but the headstone is already mounted at the head. It reads:

## MIDGE AND DAVE KELSEY

Works for me.

I run faster because I must jump farther to get on the other side of it. Otherwise, I'll fall into the hole before her.

One by one, the faces of my family come to me: Aunt Phyllis, Trisha, Jeff, Mary, and Jack. Should I fail, I'll never see them again. I will never laugh with them, or feel them in my arms.

When it is time for me to leap, it is their voices that urge me to go higher and farther. It is their affirmations of love that send me from one side of the open grave to the other—

Something that the earthmover cannot do. It falls in, taking Midge along with it.

The army of angry souls that were once buried beneath her path of destruction climb out of their now open graves. Their eerie moans create an ear-shattering cacophony of dread, remorse, and anger. They swoop high and low, convulsing into a tsunami that lifts the earth beneath our feet, like a grass rug being shaken by an invisible giant.

The mourners cover their ears and run in fear as a whirling funnel of dirt drops onto Midge and Dave's grave.

Finally, its dusty haze clears. I'm grubby, but I'm still here.

Behind me, someone is clapping.

I turn to see Satan. There's not a speck of dust on him or his suit.

Figures.

"Feel like a sponge bath?" he asks. As if to tempt me, he opens his mouth. His tongue, as wide and long as the Oscars' red carpet, rolls in my direction.

"Thanks, but I'll pass." Brushing the dust off my shoulder, I add, "Now, regarding my two questions…"

VALENTINA PETRECU CRAIG'S NIGHTGOWN IS SHEER AND LACY.

It is also spattered with blood.

She sits on the only gravesite adorned with the statue of a tiny cherub.

I'm sure it is that of her unborn child. She was pregnant with Carl's baby when he killed her for testifying against him at his treason trial.

I was the one who broke the news of her pregnancy to him. Had he known she was carrying it, he would have forgiven her.

Eventually, Jack forgave her for leaving him for Carl. I found forgiveness harder to do because I knew she set Jack up for Carl to kill him.

Now that we are face-to-face again, she asks, "Did Jack let you read my letter?"

I nod. After her death, a priest delivered the farewell letter she'd written to Jack in case of her death.

"Yes. In it, you told him that you had made a pact with the Devil. That he owned your soul and that eventually, he'd come to collect."

She grimaces. "Sadly, a prophetic statement."

"You also wrote that you could never love Jack with the passion with which he'd had for you because you felt passion had to be dark and illicit; that it takes everything and regrets nothing, which was why it was inevitable you were drawn to Carl."

She nods.

"And then you asked for Jack's forgiveness. You 'set him free.'"

Her eyes drop to the ground.

"Only, you didn't, Valentina. He was already free of you."

"I know," she admits. "You made him whole in a way I never could." She wipes a tear from her cheek. "At least something good came out of my taking Carl from you. Can you forgive me for that?"

"There is nothing to forgive," I tell her. "I never had him to begin with."

"Neither did I. He loved one thing above all else: power." Yes, she knew this too.

"Valentina, if Eric has his way, the Quorum will rise again. He has escaped our country's strongest maximum-security prison during a cyber attack. He must have had help from a foreign nation. Which one?"

She stares at me. All of a sudden, she bursts out laughing. Shaking her head, she exclaims, "The wife knows everything."

"Thank you, but it's just a guess on my part…"

I'm stopped when she shakes her head. At that moment, I realize: she's not complimenting me. She's giving me a clue.

But what does it mean?

"Time's up," Satan whispers in my ear.

"But—I haven't had time to ask the second question!"

"Doesn't matter. She's already given you two answers."

"How could she? I never asked it!"

He points in her direction. "Now, wave bye-bye—"

I don't even have time to do that. I'm already back in my comatose body.

"So, here's what's happened over the past twenty-four hours," Arnie is saying.

For once, time stopped for *me*. That's certainly a step in the right direction. I've lost too much time with my loved ones already.

Everyone leans forward, poised to assess the situation, offer opinions, and plan a course of attack.

Everyone includes me.

At least I know who helped Eric. It's…

Okay, not really. But I have two clues that will give me the answer. And since I'm not going anywhere, I have plenty of time to figure it out—

As long as I can stay alive.

---

10

## Loser

---

Performed by the rock band, 3 Doors Down and written by the band's members: Brad Arnold, Matt Roberts, and Todd Harrell.

Released July 2000, it hit #1 on *Billboard*'s "Mainstream Rock Tracks," and stayed there for twenty-one weeks: a record for that chart. It also made it to #2 in the music trade magazine's "Modern Rock Tracks" list, and #55 on *Billboard*'s "Hot 100" list.

The song may have been a winner, but, ironically, not the subject of this song with its sad poignant lyrics: a childhood friend of Arnold's who became addicted to heroin.

*Everyone on earth has felt like a loser at least once in his or her life. All it takes is some callous remark from a parent, some other relative, or even a so-called friend to take away the burgeoning self-esteem of a child, leaving in its place a legacy that lasts a lifetime.*

*Keep in mind these reasons why you are not and never will be a loser:*

1. *You try to accomplish your personal best, regardless of the ability of someone who can do it even better.*

99

2. *When facing an immediate, overwhelming, or life-changing dilemma, your decision wasn't to stand your ground and fight but to turn and flee. In and of itself, the will and the cunning to survive are heroic acts.*

3. *Just because someone calls you, "loser." Remember: your naysayers aren't living your life. They don't know your fears, frustrations, needs, or desires.*

*In other words, no one's opinion counts more than your own.*

"—INCLUDING PIPE BOMBS LEFT IN GOVERNMENT BUILDINGS throughout the country," Arnie is saying. "Little Rock, Albuquerque, Kansas City, San Bruno in California, and just an hour ago, St. Louis."

"Are we talking state or Federal buildings?" Jack asks.

"So far only Federal," Emma replies.

"Population-wise, these are all one-building facilities in relatively small cities," Jack points out. "Why not choose larger targets? Or for that matter, why not choose larger cities that have a plethora of Federal buildings, such as New York or Washington D.C.?"

"Perhaps their sizes, locations, or administrative functions mean that Security wouldn't be as airtight," Abu replies. "Especially when it comes to deterring a cyber-attack, which would shut down the building's electricity and security systems."

"However, if these incidents are supposed to be warnings, they wanted the bombs to be easily found and diffused," Dominic reasons.

"Bingo," Jack murmurs. "Which means they are hiding a different end game..." His voice trails off.

"Arnie, have you found a direct correlation between the cyber attacks on the Federal buildings and the cyber ransoms demanded from the banks, hospitals, and other public utilities?" Ryan asks.

"Yes," Arnie replies. "In fact, the ransomware worm that was released on the nongovernmental facilities was the same."

Ryan nods. "It would explain a lot, since all nuclear facilities must coordinate their security with the NSA as well."

"In other words, the assailants have access to blueprints and security information from the NSA's database," Abu points out. "Are we thinking that this is a foreign agent making a move toward out-and-out cyber warfare?"

"Not necessarily. Domestic terrorists are getting more aggressive as well. My ComInt team and I have been monitoring Alt-Right and Alt-Left chat rooms. So far, we haven't run across any chatter that seems like a lead. Still, you'd be shocked if you saw the amount of government data already leaked all over the dark web! User names, passwords, monitors…for platforms as important as our emergency management systems!"

Jack smirks. "One of POTUS's campaign promises was to strengthen the government's Cybersecurity. But like his predecessors, it's still an afterthought."

"This isn't a gripe session, people," Ryan reminds them. "We're up against a very real and very imminent threat. It may seem random, but there's an endgame here. We just need to figure out what the hell it is—and fast."

Everyone is silent. Jack mutters, "And then there's the question about Eric. Maybe he had nothing to do with it, but used it to his advantage. For all we know, he's sunning himself on some tropical island, enjoying the trillions of dollars stashed away in the Quorum's offshore bank accounts."

I want to shout, *No he isn't! He's in the middle of it all—*

But I can't even get out a moan.

What can I tell them anyway? I've got a bunch of incoherent clues as to what he might be up to and with whom, but none of which indicate where we'll find him.

I guess that's what I should ask in my last trial.

To get the answer, I'll have to win again.

Many lives depend on it—least of all mine.

DEATH TAPS ME ON THE SHOULDER.

I open one eye. "It's about damn time," I mutter.

"You'll see it was worth it," he assures me. "Wait until you see what Satan has in store for you!"

He envelops me in his cape—

And when he flings it off again, we are in a beautiful ballroom: marble floors go on for a mile. Ornate wainscoting is on the lower half of the wall, whereas the top half is covered with gilt oval mirrors or master works by Monet, Matisse, Van Gogh, Degas, Sargent, Klimt, Cezanne, and Renoir, to name just a few.

An orchestra plays on the other side of the room. A Shubert sonata rolls into a Rachmaninoff prelude—both favorites of mine.

Satan would know that.

I see my reflection in one of the mirrors. My hair is upswept and my skin is rosy. My lips are no longer thinned from lack of vitality, but plumped. My lips are now a ruby hue. Even the smallest wrinkle has vanished.

My gown is sheer but covered in fine jewels in a rainbow of colors. Larger stones adorn my neck, wrists and fingers.

Death winks at me. "I'll leave you now to your fate."

"But…you'll be back, right?"

"Sure—one way or another."

"Win or lose?"

He shrugs. "Eventually. I mean, sure, if you lose, you'll have a swan song"—he points upward—"in the Real Life. I'll be there for that. I never miss a performance." He grins. "And if you win… well, you get to save it—and me—for another day. In any event, you've provided Satan a few good laughs, so I owe you for that."

"Oh, yeah? When do I get to collect on it?"

"Soon. Trust me, I'll make it worth your while." He winks. The hourglass comes out again. "Dammit! Late for a pick-up! I'll see you later, Donna."

"*Way* later," I mutter.

His laughter can still be heard long after he's vanished.

I'm not laughing. In fact, I'm scared.

SATAN'S WELCOME ISN'T MADE WITH WORDS, BUT WITH A KISS ON THE back of my neck. When I shiver, he laughs heartily.

I turn to face him.

Satan, sans horns and a tail, is quite handsome.

But he's still Satan.

When a Debussy waltz begins, he holds out his hand to me. "Shall we?"

So, we do.

In his arms, I can do no wrong: I dip deeply, My steps follow his, like a shadow. My intricate footwork would win me international dancing competitions.

"I've searched eons for a partner like you," he declares softly as his lips brush gently against my ear.

"I'll bet you say that to all the girls," I murmur sweetly.

He chuckles. "I don't have to. They throw themselves at me." He shrugs. "I don't know if you've noticed, but the women here aren't exactly marriage material. They're the type who will sell their souls for the silliest things—and have."

"I'm the last person to cast stones," I insist.

"But you do cast them—and with perfect aim, at that," he insists. "Not to mention knives, bullets, grenades, bombs..." He sighs rapturously. "And you cook too! Do you know how unheard of that is in these parts?"

I shrug. "Well, thank you. My mama taught me well." And yes,

I'm relieved I haven't seen her here.

Reading my mind, Satan chuckles. "You're right. She's much too good for the likes of us"—as the music changes to a rumba, he pulls me in close—"but not you. You've got her class, but with your own unique sass. We could have a lot of fun, you and me."

His kiss is a kaleidoscope of orgiastic sensations. Acts of lust flash before my eyes: Each touch leaves me ripe and wanting. Each stroke is a virtuosity of passion. His desire rips through me, depleting me, obsessing me, making me beg for more…

When I open my eyes again, I realize I hate his smile.

The horns are a little creepy too. Try as he might, he can't hide them—and his true nature.

"You'd make the perfect queen," he insists. "*My* queen."

"I'm flattered. Really, I am." Yikes.

"You're just polite." His smile fades. "You're a woman who knows her worth. I like that. In fact, I respect you all the more for it. So go ahead and ask for it. Anything."

"I'm satisfied with the deal we have."

"But the position of Queen of Hell comes with so many fantastic perks! For example, down here, you'll never want for anything."

"Including all vital organs and other body parts?"

"Ah, so you've noticed I use such accouterments as bargaining chips, have you? Very perceptive of you!" He smiles at me like a prideful father with a talented toddler. Suddenly, he pulls a tiny scroll from his inside jacket pocket. "And you can torture each of your enemies as often as you'd like. See? I've already made up a list of them. Of course, feel free to add a few more names. Totally up to you."

I shrug. "I'm not really into pulling wings off flies."

"Metaphorically speaking, I'm trying to keep you from being one of the flies." He frowns and then adds ominously. "You can still lose, you know."

"Yes, I know," I assure him. "But if I win, I get to live. That's more than enough for me."

"Ha! That's what they all say!" He smirks. "As my queen, you'll be freed from the last trial." Like some magic act, a gilded cage holding a white dove appears in his hand. He opens the cage's door and it flies away. "And knowing what awaits you here, you can live life up there to the fullest. You see, I'll just be altering the terms for the Afterlife portion of the Donna Stone Show."

I stiffen in his arms. "You mean the Donna Craig Show, don't you?"

"Slip of the tongue." His grudging admission is not at all sincere.

"I already have a plan for eternity," I retort stiffly. "I'll be at Jack's side."

"Wrong choice," he mutters.

"Thank you, but no thank you," I say in my politest and firmest Mommy-has-made-up-her-mind voice.

"WRONG CHOICE! WRONG CHOICE! WRONG CHOICE!" His words thunder through the ballroom, ripping through the paintings, cracking the mirrors, setting the musician's instruments on fire—

And slamming me to the marble floor. Satan is no longer the charming, debonair man in a bespoke tuxedo. He is a forty-story high blood-red horned demon.

When he picks me up, he shreds my gown with his claws. He holds me close enough to stare me in the eye for one last warning:

"Hell is filled with regrets."

When he drops me, everything goes dark.

I AWAKEN TO THE PUNGENT ODOR OF FRYING SKIN.

Thank goodness, it isn't mine. Still, I leap up onto my feet because the floor around me is hot from the ashes falling from the dark sky above. Every few feet, the ground is pocked with gurgling pits of steaming magma.

The air is heavy with smoke. Flames shoot across the sky; as they fall, anguished screams fill the air.

A flame zips by me, singeing my arm.

My muffled cry brings a laugh from somewhere deep in the steam. A woman's taunts, "This is what it's like. Get used to it."

Tatyana Zakharov.

Once a breathtakingly beautiful woman, this dead and once deadly assassin now wears her pain on the outside. I'm not just talking about the ones earned during spy games, like the broken fingers and the deep scar Jack carved into her face during her stay in Acme's torture chamber, Club Dread; or even the many broken bones she suffered as she and I fell into an open elevator shaft from the nineteenth floor.

I saved myself by grabbing hold of a broken cable. Tatyana wasn't so lucky. The fact that half of her skull is now smashed in is proof of that.

She deserved it. She took Jeff as a captive to be beheaded by terrorists on television.

Tatyana strides my way and she's packing heavy metal. Her flamethrower resembles a bigger badder HK33. "Do you know how long I've waited for this moment?" she crows. "Run, Donna Craig—and don't stop! We both have a lot on the line!"

I shout back, "Tell me, what's in it for you?"

"I get what you turned down—Queen of Hell!" To prove that she's in a take-no-prisoners mode, she fires at me again.

*Why, that fickle Devil!*

I drop onto hot brimstone and roll away, deep into the sultry mist. When I leap to my feet, I shout, "Yo, Satan! Where is my weapon? I'm supposed to have one too, remember?"

Hell quakes from his ear-splitting laughter, causing me to fall to my knees—a blessing in disguise since another of Tatyana's flames soars only two inches from my head.

"Think of what you want and you'll have it—but choose wisely," Satan warns me.

Tatyana appears from the mist. Her surprise at finding me so easily makes her squeal with delight. She raises her flamethrower, cocks it, and aims right at my heart.

This time, though, I won't turn and run.

"I choose Life," I whisper.

It is, after all, the ultimate weapon against Death.

For some reason, at that very moment, I think of one person who made the ultimate sacrifice: Mara Portnoy.

When Jeff was held captive, my bullet took his executioner's life. But Tatyana was determined that, one way or another, the world would witness the terror of a child's execution. Her bullet was meant for Jeff, but Mara, the Acme operative who was to replace me during my self-imposed retirement, jumped in front of my son, trading her life for his.

As if I've conjured a ghost, Mara appears behind Tatyana.

Before Tatyana knows what she's doing, Mara is hugging her—

But not really. At first, Mara's front arm goes high in order to grab one side of Tatyana's face—

But then she lowers her hand to Tatyana's chin. At the same time, her back arm takes hold of what's left of Tatyana's head. With one quick jerk, Mara twists Tatyana's head back as she shoves the heel of her palm up through her captor's chin.

The snap of Tatyana's neck reverberates through Hell.

Her limp body drops to the ground.

"You killed her for me," I murmur.

Mara shakes her head. "No. I killed her for *me*. When you thought of me, I finally had my opportunity for payback." Smiling sadly, she whispers, "Goodbye, Purgatory."

I shake my head. "I don't think you'll be thanking me after you see what it's like here."

Mara laughs. "Who knows? Maybe I'll convince Satan that *I*

should be his queen." She winks. "Don't worry. If he takes me up on my offer, I'll look after you."

"I won't be coming back," I swear fervently—more for myself than for her. "Mara, you shouldn't be here either."

She shrugs. "You're right. In hindsight, Purgatory wasn't so bad." She points upward. "If you get a chance, put in a good word for me."

I nod—

But already she's dissolved into nothingness.

Oh, no! Now I'll never have the answer to my final question: Where will we find Eric?

THE DEVIL APPEARS IN THE EXACT SPOT WHERE MARA WAS STANDING He's holding a clipboard.

"Where's Mara?" I ask warily.

"Initiation," he informs me. "All plebes have to go through it." He sticks out a clipboard. "Just a formality: we like to know your likes and dislikes"—he giggles—"and you can guess which one you end up with."

I don't take it. "Not necessary. I'm out of here. I won. Remember?"

Satan frowns. "I beg to differ. *You* didn't kill Tatyana. Mara did. Ergo, you lost."

I lost?

*No, no, no—*

"Whoa! Wait a minute! I can't help it if she stepped in before I—"

But he's no longer here.

Not good.

I shout into the fog, "Re-do! Okay?"

Nothing.

I need an intermediary. "Death—I know you're here, too—and

you saw what happened! You know I didn't ask Mara to do that! It was all her doing! Please!"

Not a groan, not a whisper, nothing.

Deathly silence.

And then, just like that, I'm back in my hospital room.

I've heard nothing from Death all day. Frankly, I'm worried.

To settle my nerves, I go over all the clues I've gotten thus far:

First off, Varick has confirmed that Eric is, in fact, involved somehow.

For that matter, what did the Gilbert and Sullivan ditty mean? Let's see, how did it go again? Oh yes:

*Three little maids in attendance come*
*To one NOT a maid BUT a bride, Yum-Yum*
*Nobody's safe, for ONE cares for none*
*Three little maids from...*

Not only that, but he got some of the lyrics wrong. It's supposed to be only two little maids in attendance as opposed to three. Also, he said that one of the maids is not a bride like she is in the song. And it's "Nobody's safe for we care for none..." as opposed to the way he sang it: "Nobody's safe for ONE cares for none..."

He's made a muddle of it.

Edwina Doyle's riddle is just as crazy—something about a football, of all things! Did she mean that Eric is planning an attack during a pro football game? Oh, my God–is he going to release a bomb during a pro game?

The third clue—when it happens—is thanks to Robert, who tricked Salem into giving it away: *The clock struck one, and Lee was done.*

For that matter, Catherine mentioned Lee too: Well, what do you expect? He's no Eisenhower...

What has Lee got to do with all of this?

Catherine also said something about "a building filled with ghosts"—to which she also added that, "Carl knows that better than anyone."

Perhaps she means a mausoleum of some sort? And since I never fought Carl in any trial, what does he have to do with any of this?

As to where it happens, Nola's response provided me with another clue—sort of. I say this because for the life (or death) of me I can't make heads or tails of her cockamamie answer: something to do with a setting sun in the west, and a bird with a broken wing…

I'm so confused.

And, finally, there's the clue from Valentina. It makes absolutely no sense whatsoever: *The wife knows everything.*

Was she talking about me? If she meant me, she is so, so wrong.

Maybe that's the problem: *none* of this is real—

Which is why it doesn't make sense to begin with.

Oh, my God—listen to my medical monitors! They're squawking like angry parrots—

And my cardiac meter is zigzagging up and down, up and down—

No—

Just down, down, down while I float up, up, up toward the ceiling.

What is happening to me?

# 11

# She's Not There

Performed by the pop group, the Zombies. Written by band member Rod Argent. Released in September 1964, this was the group's debut single. It spent fifteen weeks on the *Billboard's* "Hot 100" chart, reaching the #2 slot; as well as #2 on the *Cashbox* chart, and #12 on the *UK Singles* chart.

Argent claimed that the inspiration behind the song was his first love: a girl named Patricia, who broke his heart by calling off their wedding just weeks before he wrote it.

*When a woman breaks off a relationship, invariably, her ex will opine, "She blindsided me! I didn't see it coming…"*

*Dude: really?*

*For any guy who can commiserate with this declaration, or who may have an inkling that their own Significant Other is moving in the same direction — that is to say, out the door — here are some telltale signs that very soon she won't be there:*

- *Sign #1: She'd rather be at work than spend time with you.*

- *Sign #2: She'd rather spend time with her family than with you.*
- *Sign #3: Heck, she'd rather spend time with your family than with you.*
- *Sign #4: She'd rather spend time with her girlfriends than with you.*
- *Sign #5: For that matter, she's already looked up your old girlfriends because she wants validation that she should do what they did—get the hell out.*
- *Sign #6: Speaking of life, if every woman you know has come up with an excuse to move on, take it as a very broad hint that you're not living up to their expectations. Time to do a little soul searching. Look at it this way: if you die a lonely old man, you won't have lived up to your expectations, either.*

Frenzied doctors and wide-eyed nurses swarm into my room. Battle stations are quickly assumed. Nancy shouts out my EKG reading, causing one of the doctors, McLanky, to swear. He leaps forward with the defibrillator paddles, placing them on my chest. The other doctor, who sports one big dimple in his chin and is too handsome for his own good, barks the order to zap me while Nancy yells out my readings yet again.

It takes four shots to my chest to raise the semblance of a pulse.

In unison, my medical team breathes a sigh of relief. A couple of the nurses high-five each other. Not Nancy. She looks worried.

And why is Dr. McDimple frowning?

With one hand, he grabs a penlight out of the breast pocket of his lab coat. With the other, he rolls my eyelid open. Shaking his head, he mutters, "This one is definitely LOBNH."

*LOBNH…*

Did he just call me "Lights on but nobody home"? *Why that son of a bitch!*

"The family still believes she'll pull out of it," McLanky insists. "Frankly, I do too."

McDimple frowns. "Wishful thinking on their part—and yours, my friend. The vultures are circling. This one needs to be put out of her pain."

McLanky's tired eyes narrow with anger. Turning to McDimple, he retorts, "What you're suggesting, doctor, may be somewhat premature. As her attending surgeon, I've noted responses on several occasions, including—"

My monitor starts squawking again.

Once again, my medical team scrambles to their positions.

Six shocks later, a pulse is detected—

"Barely there," Nancy declares.

The members of my med team, exhausted, slump against the walls or plop down into the chairs. Jeannette turns to face McLanky. "Doctor, we've tried everything. Maybe it's time."

He purses his lips. Finally he shrugs.

"Poor Donna," Death exclaims in my ear. "Well, hon, you can't say you didn't give it your all."

"I was cheated out of my last trial!" I gasp desperately. "It wasn't my fault–"

I'm interrupted by the knock on the door.

Slowly, it opens:

Jack.

Aunt Phyllis stands beside him. She holds a pie box in her hand. Its sweet cherry aroma is potent enough to widen the nostrils of my medical team. She'll take credit for it with the nurses, but I know Mary baked it. Otherwise, it would have smelled like burnt crust.

My children peek out from behind my husband and my aunt. Mary, Trisha, and Evan hold bouquets of long-stemmed roses. Their yellow petals are tinged a sweet pink. Jeff has my favorite sweater in his hand.

Jack's eyes widen hoping that the gathering of my med team

means good news. But as he scans their faces, the hope in his eyes softens with despair.

Hearing McLanky's sad sigh, Jack's shoulders slump.

"We should talk," my doctor says. "Would you mind following me?"

Aunt Phyllis is no fool. She's lived long enough to know what those words mean. Distraught, she drops the pie box.

As I float out the door after them, I look down at the box. Its top opened in the fall. The pie's lattice top is now broken. Cherry juice oozes beyond the tin, through the broken box and onto the hall floor.

It is the color of blood.

I FOLLOW MY DOCTOR AND MY FAMILY INTO A LARGE CLOSED ROOM AT the end of the hall.

Thank goodness, the room is empty. Its walls are painted a soft moss green. Crisp white molding gives it a homey feel. A couple of settees flank a large coffee table. Comfortable easy chairs face a fireplace, where colorful glass chips, sprinkled over a lit gas grate, send out Tinkerbell flickers across the room. Two more easy chairs are angled toward a window that faces a beautiful walled garden.

No one sits down. Instead, my children and my aunt cluster around Jack. All eyes are on McLanky. While their silence begs him to fill the void, their pursed lips warn him that bad news will batter their hearts yet again.

Despite its serene ambiance, I wonder: how many tears have been shed in this room? Within these walls, how many lives have been shattered by the seven-word sentence now being uttered by my doctor: "There is nothing more we can do…"?

How often is this room remembered as the place in which a patient's loved ones lost hope?

Jack's eyes have glassed up, but his fists have tightened in denial. "Are you trying to tell us that Donna will never wake up?"

Dr. McLanky nods.

"But…but her eyes fluttered when we talked to her!" Mary exclaims.

"She's squeezed my hand—twice!" Jeff exclaims.

"She responded to the ultra-sound," Aunt Phyllis reminds him. "And that was just yesterday—"

"I'm sorry, but brain activity is now negligible. What little there is indicates a persistent vegetative state," the doctor explains.

"In other words, she's no longer Donna. She's just…a body," Evan says, deflated.

I wave my hand in front of his face. No! No! I'm here! Please see me…

"You're wrong," Trisha shakes her head firmly. "Mommy came to me in a dream! She told me that she loves me, and she wants me to never give up on her. She asked me to leave Birthday Bear with her!"

McLanky bends down so that he's eye-to-eye with Trisha. "You walked in just after we'd resuscitated her for the second time in a ten-minute span. Trisha, I wish I could tell you that your mother will wake up, but her organs are shutting down." His eyes then scan the rest of the family for their comprehension of my situation.

Jack's mouth hardens. Seeing this, Dr. McLanky sighs. "I'm sorry, but as of now it's only a matter of time." He places a hand on my husband's shoulder. "When she's taken off life support, it will be a few hours at most. It can be done here"—his pause comes with a wince–"or you can have her transported home if you prefer." He nods to my children. "I'll let you discuss it in private."

My family stays still and silent until he leaves the room.

"We aren't pulling the plug on Mom," Jeff growls.

Trisha nods. "She's in there! She told me she wants to be with us and that it's just a matter of time."

"People say that when they are on their way to heaven too," Mary murmurs.

Jeff is now tall enough to go nose to nose with his sister. "Don't tell me you'd do what he says!"

"No! …Yes—I mean, if she's already gone up here"—Mary points to her head—"and her body is dying, why would we keep her in such pain?"

"She's not in pain!" Trisha insists.

"Really?" Mary counters. "Do you know that for sure?"

Jeff drops his head at the thought that his eldest sister may be right.

"I…no," Trisha admits. "Daddy, does Mommy feel her wound?"

Jack closes his eyes for a moment, as if hoping the right way to answer our youngest child will manifest itself in his mind.

*Jack, please tell her I'm here now with all of you. Tell her I know you'll make the right decision—*

When he opens them again, the serenity I see there puts me at ease.

"Trisha, your mother is here with us now. She knows we'll make the right decision—"

"To…let her go." Jeff's exclamation comes out as a husky whisper.

*What?*

*No! Hell, no!*

Tears stream down Trisha's face.

Mary too is sobbing as she places her arms around her little sister.

I wave my hand in front of them.

And then I thrust it through them—

Nothing.

Jack turns to Aunt Phyllis as if he'll find the courage to stay strong for our children within her frail frame.

I've never seen her look this way. The grief in her face deepens her brow and weighs down on her withered cheeks. She lowers her head before murmuring, "I raised her since she was eleven. I never thought I'd outlive my baby." She shakes from her sobs. "Well, I guess I have."

Jack, please, I shout. I'm still here! Please—

"We'll give our answer to the doctor tomorrow." From the haunted look in his eyes, I now know my fate:

I am doomed.

"Aunt Phyllis, do you mind taking the kids back to the house? I'm sleeping here tonight." I hear his prayer: *One last night with her, God. Please.*

"A shame," Death snorts gleefully. "Don't you wish you could make it worth his while?"

I whip around. He is no longer an angel, but a hovering skull.

I put my hands through his eyeholes and fling him toward the fireplace wall.

When the skull hits the back of the fireplace, it shatters into a million tiny pieces.

A shower of glittering sparks roar beyond the hearth before dissolving into smoke.

No one sees it. They're already out the door.

"The Afterlife isn't so bad."

My mother's voice shocks my soul into lifting the veil of dread that I now hover beneath.

She is standing beside me, gracing me with the gentle smile that always had the effect of the sun's rays on a lake after a tumultuous storm—

That the worst is over.

That life goes on.

But mine will not. Like hers, it is over.

She is beautiful. Her makeup is flawless, as is her up-do: a

French twist. Her brows, arched over her warm brown eyes, are the perfect complement to her cupid-bow lips. She wears one of her many little black dresses. As always, she's accessorized it with three tight strings of pearls. The only thing missing is the locket that she always wore.

I now wear it.

Yes, there it is: on the shell of the body that was once mine.

As I stare down at it, I whisper to her: "I've missed you."

"I know." Mother lays her hand over mine. It is as soft as silk. "But I've always been there, right beside you."

"I wish told me about…your cancer." I'd always wanted to say that to her.

Mother's smile goes flat, but the love in her eyes only burns brighter. "I didn't want to spend my last months watching you sad and angry over something neither of us could stop. I needed to remember you filled with happiness and hope."

Lightly, she places her hands on both sides of my face, tickling precious memories of us. She must be reliving them too because her lips lift again in our shared joy:

She gives in to my plea to push me high enough on my backyard swing so that my foot can touch the tree branch just out of reach, all the while admonishing me to "hold on tight, my little daredevil!" But she laughs just as heartily in fearless glee when my foot taps it;

She dresses the cut in my finger—an accident from the very first time I pared apples for her pies. "There will be many more of these," she warned me. "This is part of the spice that makes baking all the sweeter."

As we lie outside on a sheet on a warm summer night, as she points out the constellations until I too can see them. "If you learn them, you can always find your way home," she explains.

I am no longer sad, just honest when I tell her, "You were my home—and Dad's."

She knows what I want to ask next. Instead, through her eyes, I see him: He sits in a fog.

"He isn't with you." It hurts to realize his eternal limbo.

"His heart was too heavy. Our lives are too precious to waste," she explains sadly. "I'm proud of all you've done with yours."

I TURN TO HUG HER BUT I'M TOO LATE. SHE IS ALREADY FADING AWAY.

Confused, I ask, "But…didn't you come to take me with you?"

"Soon," she whispers. "Dear Donna, don't worry. When it happens, it's over in the blink of an eye…"

She's gone.

Until then, I'm alone.

With whatever is left of me.

# Sacrifice

RECORDED BY ELTON JOHN, A SONG HE WROTE WITH BERNIE TAUPIN. Released October 1989, the song spent fourteen weeks on the greatest hits chart, reaching #3 on U.S. *Billboard* "Hot Adult Contemporary Tracks" chart. In 1990, it also reached #3 on *UK Singles* charts.

*There are three big differences between a compromise and a sacrifice:*

- *Difference #1: In a compromise, you may not have won all the marbles, but you'll walk away with some of them. In a sacrifice, you lose something you want dearly—and it's probably worth much more than a few glass marbles.*
- *Difference #2: In a compromise, you save face. When you sacrifice, you've lost your shirt.*
- *Difference #3: You compromise because you can afford to lose something. In a sacrifice, you've just lost everything.*

*Should you find yourself outnumbered in a bar fight, don't even think about compromise. Otherwise, you sacrifice everything.*

JACK CAN'T HEAR MY SCREAMS, EVEN WHEN I STAND DIRECTLY IN front of him. I try kissing him, but he swats away my lips as if they are moths. I even try slapping him. Its effect is negligible: he rubs his cheek as if remembering a kiss.

If only.

My emotions well up inside my soul: denial, frustration, anger, fear—and become a funnel of energy that whips around the room. In his subconscious state, Jack may not be able to feel it, but it is causing chaos with some inanimate objects. The window's blinds ripple. His water glass shakes so much that the water within it washes back and forth as if hit by a mini tsunami. The blanket on his prone body falls to the floor.

And yet, nothing from my sleeping prince.

Exhausted, I let my feelings of remorse envelop me.

All movement stops.

And just in time. The doorknob creaks as it turns ever so slowly. The door opens just enough to allow a sliver of light from the hallway beyond. It falls on my comatose form, allowing my new guest to gaze at my still and bloodless form. The ray grows larger, revealing the machines that now ping and beep listlessly like robots whose batteries are dying.

Soon, the door opens wide enough to let in my visitor: the nurse, Nancy. Her right hand is in the pocket of the lab coat she wears over her scrubs. Her smile is harder than usual.

Her eyes scan the room. They pause when she sees Jack. Her grimace drops into an angry frown.

Still, she enters the room, closing the door behind her.

By the time she turns around, she's pulled something from her pocket: a vial and a needled syringe.

She stabs the vial with the needle and watches as it fills the syringe.

Satisfied that there is enough in it, she makes her way—

To Jack.

Dread darkens my soul. I run to stop her—

Only to face Carl.

I stop short. Stuttering, I ask, "Don't tell me I'm in Hell!"

"Well, hello to you too." Carl grins. "You'd think you'd be a little more pleasant, considering all we meant to each other. Honestly, I guess I should say 'done to each other.'"

"Hardly," I snort. "Out of my way! She's after Jack!"

"Not to worry. We have a few seconds to catch up." He steps sideways to make his point.

For once, he's not lying. Nancy is now a living statue. Her left leg is suspended in mid-dash. The syringe is grasped in her raised right palm. Her smile is cruel with determination.

"Did you do that?" I ask cautiously.

"Sadly, I can't take credit. The Angel of Death gets the brownie point."

"Why did he…Carl, why are you here?"

His smile wavers. "When the all-points-bulletin went out for those who wanted to put you in your place—that is, in the Afterlife with the rest of us—I thought I'd see if I could make the cut."

"So, you're here to take me out?"

"Depends." He moves behind Jack. "Wifey, let's be honest. What's he worth to you?"

"Ex-Wifey," I remind him, "and he's worth everything to me."

"Even your life?" Carl's voice tightens as he adds, "Now, be completely honest with me."

Can I be anything else? My every thought is exposed.

Not that it matters. There is only one answer:

If it came to my life or Jack's, yes I'd sacrifice myself.

Since the bullet put me in a coma, I've had plenty of time to make my peace with my ultimate fate. I've accepted that I will never be able to touch my children; to kiss away their tears; to reward them with my smile.

I won't be there to cheer on my friends and celebrate their accomplishments. I won't be at Aunt Phyllis's bedside when it is her time to go. Hopefully, though, we will find each other in the Great Beyond.

And I won't be here to laugh with Jack; to feel him inside me; to grow old with him.

But he will be here to comfort those who mourn me. He will share his memories of me with them. He will love them as much as I did.

So, yes, because I'll live on in him, I can make the ultimate sacrifice.

Carl knows this to be the truth. It's why his mournful sigh is strong enough to shift the window curtain.

"I was a fool," he murmurs.

"For leaving me?" I wonder.

"Okay, yeah, maybe that too." He shrugs. "But, more importantly, I made a bet with Death. If he's right, Jack's the goner."

"And if you're right?"

"You live." He nods toward the human tableau below us. "But either way, Death always wins, right?"

I nod. "You were a fool to bet against me, Carl."

He chuckles. "Who said I did? I know you too well to ever doubt what's in your heart, Donna Stone."

The sound of my old name—*his* name—no longer shames me because in the end—*his* end, now—I realize that he has just saved me.

"I tried to be the best husband to you. You have to believe me," he pleads.

"I do now." How could I not? Like mine, his soul is fully exposed.

I'm almost afraid to ask, but I must: "You didn't come here to fight me but to help. I suppose…"

"That my request to see you once more came at a very steep price?" He nods.

"What does Death want from you in return?"

"You had to ask, right?" The edge in Carl's voice cuts me like a knife. "Despite all my bad deeds, my one redeeming quality kept me in Limbo."

"Hell's first circle," I murmur.

"You got it." He shrugs.

"What stopped you from going all the way to the basement?"

"My love for you and the children." The levity is gone from his voice. "It was my trump card—until now. So it's the 9th Circle for me, I'm afraid."

"Treachery," I murmur.

"Appropriate, wouldn't you say?"

To be trapped under a frozen bed of ice? My heart swells at the thought of the pain he'll find there.

While his earthly body floated through a watery grave, what thoughts went through his mind at his moment of death? I wonder.

Again, unbidden, he answers. "The letter I left for you—in your recipe book. Did you find it?"

"What? A letter? No…" A veil of sadness drapes over me, only to be swept away on a forgiving breeze.

"A shame. It explained why I went deep cover. And how I would never have deserted you"—his whisper rings in my ear —"and how I loved you, always."

Tenderly, I reach out for him. I am resigned that I will feel nothing.

I am wrong. For a moment, he *is* real.

My palm lands gently but solidly on the angular plane of his face. He shifts so that his lips can brush against my hand—

But just for a moment.

In that one touch, Carl's emotions smack me like a wave. They are a tumult of grief, regret—

And yes, love.

He reads my mind: *Too much, too late.*

"Donna, one more very important thing—and please don't kill the messenger." He laughs. "Not that you could."

Yet one more trial? Ouch! I brace myself and then nod.

Still, he's wary enough about my response to take a step back. "When you get back, you, uh…well, you must kill Jack."

I shake with anger. "What is this, some kind of game? Really, Carl? You just redeemed yourself!" If he hadn't already lost his jawbone, I would have pulled it out with my own two hands.

Nancy's sneaker gives a faint squeak as it hits the floor.

Only I can hear Carl's regretful sigh. "It's the only way to stop Eric. When the time comes, you'll feel it in your gut. Trust me, Donna. Please!"

His soul shimmers for a just moment before fading into the darkness.

If only I could say the same for Nancy.

In no time, she is at Jack's side. Her raised arm begins its downward trajectory toward his left bicep.

With all my might, I shove her aside.

She falters and then freezes: not because she felt me, but because the machines hooked up to me are chirping so loudly—

Enough to wake Jack.

Because Nancy is staring over my still comatose body, she doesn't notice that Jack's eyes are now open.

When he realizes what she's doing, he tackles her into a wall. She is stunned enough to drop the syringe, but she's not knocked out. Her kick catches him in the chest, sending him reeling back toward my bed.

He barely touches it before Unearthly Me shoves him back toward her.

She has crouched down to pick up the syringe but his kick gets her in the ribs, sending her into the wall again, and knocking her out.

By now, my bed is surrounded by three other RNs and the doctor on call: McDimple. They came in to attend to me only to find Jack standing over their coworker.

"I woke before she could stab me with whatever is in that syringe," he explains. "But I don't think she knew I was here, so I guess it was for Donna."

While two of the nurses check my vital signs, McDimple warily makes his way around Jack to Nancy. "She's breathing, but unconscious," he tells the third nurse. He then picks up the vial in one hand and the syringe in the other. He stares down at the vial, reading its label. "It's aconite." His eyes shift to the syringe. "And there is enough in here to take down a horse." McDimple nods to the third nurse. "Call Security."

In an instant Jack is at my side. He's noticed that the monitors' chirps and clicks are now steady, but to my ear they seem to get increasingly softer until they fade away altogether.

For that matter, I'm fading away too.

As I am sucked into a dark tunnel, the med team's voices become even louder. I do my best to block out the sound so that I'll remember all that I've learned since making my pact with the Reaper:

That Eric escaped with the help of—wait, give me a moment! It'll come to me. It has something to do with...

Gilbert and Sullivan? A football? A dove? None of that makes sense!

And that his destination is...is...somewhere near water? And he'll go by boat?

And that Eric's goal is to...to...

What is it again he's going to do?

And then there's that cryptic plea from Carl, telling me that the only way to stop Eric is to...to...

Do something bad...to Jack.

I can't...

But...I must.

My medical team's excited chatter reverberates all around me. Shut up, I want to scream. I need to remember so much…

But then I hear the one calm voice that beckons me forward. Jack's gentle but insistent declarations—that I'm alive, that I'm okay, that he loves me—are the breadcrumbs that guide me out of the darkness and back to the world I left.

*I'm back, Jack.*

*Thank you.*

------

## 13

# Home

------



Written and performed by Cheryl Crow. The song became Crow's ninth top-40 hit in both Canada (topping out at #40) and the United Kingdom (hitting #25). It was not initially released in the United States.

She recorded the music video at a village car-race festival—a perfect example why it pays to go to any event where they serve deep-fried everything on a stick!

*The definition of "home" depends on whom you ask.*

*To the lonely, an empty home is the consolation prize awaiting them at the end of a day in search of companionship.*

*To a young child, home is the lap of his mother and the reassuring voice of his father.*

*To a loving couple, home is the bed they share while in each other's arms.*

*To an unhappy couple, misunderstanding meets them at the door and frustration silences them. They sleep with anger as opposed to each other.*

*The perfect home isn't in any particular neighborhood or filled with designer furnishings. Nor does it boast a specific number of rooms.*

*It is not a place; it is a state of mind. Trite but true: home is where the heart is.*

My children won't stop petting me as if I'm some exotic bird.

Jack is the same way. Does he notice how I find a reason to let go of his hand within a few minutes? Or that I turn away from his adoring look?

I can't help it. Since I've awakened, whenever I look at him now, I hear Carl's voice in my head, urging me to do…

Something.

To Jack.

And it's not good.

I wish I could remember what…

In any event, I feel ashamed because I actually believe I must do it in order to accomplish our mission.

Jeff waits until we're home and I've settled on the couch before shyly asking, "So, what was it like to be in a coma?"

Hearing him, the other children freeze. Despite their awe at his boldness in broaching this curious topic, they can't help but hover, like stubborn snowflakes on a frigid day, within reach.

I clear my throat if only to give myself some time to think through a way to tell them that I've literally been to Hell and back.

Of course, I can't. And so I don't. Instead, I tell them what I think they want to hear. "I was never in pain. And although I couldn't move or speak, sometimes I could hear you."

"Do you mean like a ghost?" Mary asks.

"I guess it was like that. There were times that it felt as if I left my body. I'd float over myself…and others."

Trisha nods emphatically. "You came to me, Mommy! Do you

remember? You told me to bring you Birthday Bear!" She still has it with her. She lifts it to show me.

I can't lie to her, so I nod. But when I do so, I notice that Jack frowns.

Whether he likes it or not, I want to assure her that it wasn't just a dream. "I told you that I loved you, that I'd always be with you, and I begged you to never give up on me."

Trisha gasps along with the others.

For the longest time, no one says anything. I gaze at each of their faces. When my eyes meet Mary's, I see them glisten with her tears. "Then you heard me too."

I put out my hand to her. "Please, Mary, don't feel guilty. You spoke out of compassion. You thought I'd already left my body."

She smothers me in a hug.

"And when Aunt Phyllis cried and called me her baby—"

My aunt may be snorting, but she tears up nonetheless. "I probably struck you as a big bowl of mush!"

"No, I thought it was the sweetest thing you'd ever done. And you've done *a lot.* Mother thought you were a bit mushy, though. She let me know she still watches over us—"

"My sister, Mary…she sees us?" The blood leaves Aunt Phyllis's face and she faints.

Thank goodness Evan is there to catch her.

"By the way, Evan, your mother truly appreciates your prayers on her behalf."

Evan's mouth flies open. When his arms falter, Jack lunges toward Aunt Phyllis, catching her before she hits the floor.

Trisha grabs the ever-present water bottle from her great aunt's purse and squeezes some of it onto her face. Phyllis sputters as she comes out of her shock.

I notice that Jeff's cheeks have turned a deep red. "Oh—heck!" he murmurs. "Then, when Cheever—"

"Yes," I inform him crisply. "And the next time I see that little pervert, I'm going to—"

Jack growls, "Donna, can we speak—alone?"

Before I can answer, he stalks upstairs.

I hesitate because I don't know what got into him.

I turn to the children. They stare as if they see a ghost.

Oh, heck. Maybe I've said too much, too soon?

My guess is that, at the very least, Jack thinks so.

There is only one way to know for sure. I follow him upstairs.

WHEN I ENTER THE MASTER BEDROOM, HE FIRMLY CLOSES THE DOOR behind me. "Donna, just what the heck were you doing down there?" he asks.

"I...I thought I was sharing this incredible experience with you, the kids, my aunt—"

"First of all, being on the brink of death isn't an 'incredible experience'! It's torture for those who love you and thought they'd lost you forever!" Frankly, I've never seen Jack like this. He's pacing the floor as if his feet are on fire. "And another thing: letting the kids know you could hear everything they were saying was scaring the bejeezus out of them!"

"It didn't seem that way to me," I sniff. "In fact, I think they were fascinated."

Jack freezes to glare at me. "'Fascinated?' Is that what you call it? Phyllis fainted out there! What if you'd given her a heart attack or something?"

"I get it, Jack. It's shocking to hear that someone who you thought was dying—or dead—heard things that you thought they'd never hear." I look him straight in the eye: "But, Jack, I did. I heard it all. And I believe I've been saved for a purpose—"

"I do too." Tenderly, he touches my cheek with his palm, as if he can't believe I am truly there at his side.

To prove I'm very real, I turn my lips so that I can kiss his hand.

Soon, his lips are on mine. His hand roams under the surgical scrub top graciously lent to me by the hospital to replace my bullet-torn, blood-soaked evening gown I wore to the hospital. His palm spans the small of my back as he eases me down onto the bed.

When he drops down beside me, I put my hand over the zipper of his jeans. I'm not at all surprised that he's already rock hard.

He knows an invitation when he feels one. He lifts my arms toward the headboard so that he can pull my top over my head and—

*Nothing.*

"Hello?" I ask. I can't see through the top so I have no idea why he stopped. When he doesn't answer me, I wriggle out of it myself.

He's staring at the wound in my abdomen.

When I look down, I see why. My jagged stitches look as if they are barely holding my purple mottled skin together. I guess if Acme doesn't take me back, I can always try out for the role of an extra in a horror movie.

When he finally looks up, his eyes are filled with despair. "If only I'd shown up a few minutes sooner—" he says angrily.

"You didn't. But you came in time to save my life," I remind him.

"I'll kill the son of a bitch who ordered your hit," he swears.

"I know you will." Hearing the steely tenor of my conviction, he smiles again. "This is an odd thought but I think I should throw it out there. Could it be related to our new mission?"

His grin fades. "Donna, hon, it's not your mission anymore. You're sitting this one out. You just got out of a four-day coma —remember?"

"But, I'm here, and I'm alive," I insist. "Not only that, I've been fully briefed on it."

His right brow inches up. "By whom?"

"By you—and Ryan, Emma, Abu and Arnie." I shove his pillow between us. "I heard everything—remember?"

"You may have heard some things, but there's a lot you missed."

"Oh, yeah? You mean, like Eric breaking out of Magic Mountain Maximum Security Incarceration Facility in Utah?"

Jack stares at me. "You heard that too?"

I nod. "It took place during this most recent outage. Remember? You and the others were in my hospital room while it went dark. The other outages were tests, ruses, and diversions to cover Eric's tracks for when he made his great escape. Eric broke out right then and there. In fact"—I take a deep breath in the hope that this adds velocity to Jack's leap of faith—"I asked little Nicky to say Eric's name so that you'd know he'd planned it."

"Nicky...was just testing out sounds," Jack insists. "Or maybe he heard the name while we were talking—"

I shake my head adamantly. "You're wrong. He said it because of me. Don't you get it? I was warning you!" I sigh. "But I was too late!"

Jack laughs nervously. "Tell me then. How did you know?"

The vision of Varick dressed as a kabuki comes to me. Hesitantly, I admit, "Eric's old chum, Varick, told me."

Jack shakes his head. "Now I know you're delusional. I killed Varick!"

"I know you did. I received his head in a pretty gift box, thanks to Eric." I shiver at the memory.

"Why would Varick of all people have told you that Eric was going to break out?" Jack demands.

"Because I asked him," I huff.

"Where? Was he in your hospital room too?"

"No! He was in...in Hell."

"Ha! Well, that doesn't surprise me in the least." Jack leans against the headboard, concerned "How did *you* end up in Hell, anyway?"

"I...made a pact."

Jack's eyes narrow. "With the Devil?"

"No. Well, yes—sort of. Really, it was with the Grim Reaper."

"I see." He smothers a grin.

"No, you don't. You're smirking," I mutter. "It's very unbecoming."

"Pardon me," he says, but the smirk is still there on those lips I adore. "Donna, you have to admit it sounds pretty farfetched—"

"Oh, my God—Varick gave me another clue! Really, he sang it —something from Gilbert and Sullivan! What was it again? 'Pirates of Penzance? No, no… 'The Yeomen of the Guards'? … Agh! No, not that one~"

The melody flits about in my memory, but the words escape me.

For some reason, Jack apparently finds my frustration hilarious. He chortles, "That coma of yours was one hell of a dream factory!"

"I'm telling you it wasn't a dream! It was all very real!" Furiously, I shake my finger at him. "You're trying much too hard not to believe me."

"And you're trying much too hard to convince me that you weren't delusional while you were in your coma," he insists, still laughing.

At the moment, his lack of belief hurts more than my wound. When he leans in for a hug, I shove him away. "I'm tired. It's already been a very long day."

He frowns, but nods. "Sure. Totally understandable, hon." He sits up in order to take off his jacket and shirt.

When he stands and unbuckles his belt, I turn around, embarrassed. It's been a while since we've seen each other naked. Considering his reaction to my wound—and mine, to his jokes about my Afterlife adventures—intimacy may be a long time coming.

I'll reconsider if Ryan lets me back on the mission. But until then, his love life just went AWOL.

He gets the message when he sees what I pluck out of my

lingerie drawer: a flannel granny gown adorned with all the Smurfs. It was my Mother's Day gift from Trisha.

I take it into the bathroom with me and shut the door. After stripping out of my scrubs, I take a long hard look at my dark, ugly Frankenstein wound. I hurt like heck, and I look like hell.

Still, I know, I'm very lucky to be alive.

I awaken to Carl's whisper:

*Donna, one more essential thing…you must… Jack.*

Jack's arm flings off my waist when I sit straight up in bed. Apparently, we've been spooning.

What did Carl mean about Jack?

My heart is pounding so loudly that it takes me a while to figure out that Jack's cell phone is buzzing too. I reach over him to his bedside table. The screen reads OFFICE.

Hearing it, he mumbles in his sleep. I hesitate, but then I shake him awake.

He groans, but at last, he opens one eye.

I put the cell phone in front of him. He sighs but takes it and reads the text. "It's from the office." He kisses my forehead and then leaps out of bed. "I've got to go. All hell's broken out…" He turns red. "Sorry! It wasn't a joke at your expense, I swear."

"None taken." I hop out of bed. "I'll get dressed and go with you."

Jack pushes me back down onto the bed. "Oh, no, you don't. You're still weak as a kitten."

I smack his hand away. "Funny! You were treating me as if I were a wildcat when we entered the bedroom."

"More like a cougar." He winks at me. "And I'm ashamed that I almost took advantage of a thirty-something married woman in a highly suggestive state of mind."

Really? Is he going to bring up my so-called delusions again? When I throw his pillow at him, he ducks out of the way.

No need, because it falls several feet short of him. My arms are still too weak.

Watching me wince from the pain, Jack says softly, "Listen Donna, tomorrow you start physical therapy. The sooner you do, the quicker you're back on the team. Seriously, hon, the best thing you can do for yourself—and all of us, for that matter—is to get some rest."

He tosses the pillow back at me.

I'm afraid to reach for it. Instead, I let it hit me in the chest and I hold it there. "Right. Good." I shrug.

"And…well, don't be surprised if Ryan insists on a psychiatric evaluation."

I frown. "Why would he? Are you going to tell him that I'm delusional?"

"No, of course not. Look, even if your surgeon hadn't recommended it, Acme protocol would insist on it. You've suffered a major trauma, remember?"

I retort, "You certainly won't let me forget it."

When he reaches the door, he turns around. This time, though, he's not smiling. "A word of caution: spouting off crazy stuff—you know, like making a pact with the Grim Reaper and seeing Varick sing light opera—won't get you back on the mission team anytime soon."

In other words, I should keep my mouth shut.

But I can't. And I won't. Not with so much at stake.

Now, if only I could remember what I think I know.

# 14

# Life Goes On

Performed by Fergie. Written by Fergie, along with Tristan Prettyman, Keith Harris, George Pajon, Jr., and Tobias Gad.

The song was released on November 11, 2016, on the songstress's Double Dutchess album, hitting #39 on *Billboard*'s "Top 40" list.

*Are you feeling as if life is passing you by? Here are some telltale signs that it is!*

*Sign #1: You can't name any current celebrities or Top 10 songs.*

*Solution: Pick up a copy of* Vanity Fair *and read every article in it. Also, turn on a Top 40 radio station and listen to it for a full day.*

*Sign #2: Your memories of the past are crystal clear, but the thought of you taking a chance on a new job, new home, or a journey to a place never visited leaves you trepidatious.*

*Solution: Plan a trip where they don't speak your language. Take a friend and a camera. After that, any other changes you make will seem easier.*

*Sign #3: It takes you longer to carry out an execution. And sometimes you miss. Solution: Get out of the game—before you're hit back.*

Life is beautiful.

I look up at a baby blue sky from the double hammock hanging between the twin Heritage oaks in our backyard. Now and then a lazy cloud drifts overhead, but not for long. The Earth sighs and reluctantly it moves on.

When hit by the sun's golden rays, the oaks' verdant leaves give the impression of fluttering. I know it is merely an illusion, but through half-closed eyes, I can believe it's actually happening.

Illusions are like that.

Behind my whitewashed picket fence, I hear the conversations of those walking past our house. A child's plaintive plea gives way to a squeal of delight when a father gives in to his offspring's request for ice cream. 'Tween girls giggle at the adorable antics of the puppy that runs at their side. While relaying her dismay over their mutual friends' peccadillos, a woman's voice modulates from shock in a scherzo tempo to a requiem of concern in a minor key. Her companion's anger comes out in a trill of the anecdotes that foreshadowed what they both now know.

My senses seem keener now.

I may be fooling myself. At the time, my journey to Hell and back seemed so real. But in the space of a few days, it now seems like a dream.

Out of the corner of my eye, I see someone. Dreading that my mind is playing tricks on me, I turn my head so quickly that I almost fall out of the hammock.

It's a very real Jeff. He wears his Hilldale High Junior Varsity basketball uniform. Jeff twirls a basketball on the tip of his index finger without looking at it. "Mom, we better hurry or I'll be late for my game!"

He's very proud of making the team—as he should be, considering the number of kids who turned out for tryouts.

*Yes!* Watching Jeff hit the hoops is exactly what the doctor never ordered, but what I need so dearly.

"Let's do it!" I rise in order to follow him into the garage.

Trisha and Aunt Phyllis are already standing next to my SUV. My aunt is huffing and puffing over the weight of the cooler in her arms. A pair of pompoms and a bullhorn balance precariously on top of it.

Seeing her distress, Jeff grabs one of the handles to help her put it into the vehicle. Trisha grabs hold of the pompoms and the bullhorn before they topple onto the driveway.

My eyes widen when I realize that Aunt Phyllis is also wearing an identical jersey to Jeff's, but the number on it is 99. Her spindly legs peek out from under it.

"What exactly are you wearing?" I ask.

"It's supposed to be yours, but since you were…er, indisposed, I took on the duties of team manager in your place."

"I…I don't remember signing up for that," I murmur. Did I? If so, did my injuries affect my memory?

Jeff sighs loudly. "You didn't. Aunt Phyllis signed you up for it *in absentia.*"

"And it's a good thing I did, young sir! When it comes to keeping you and your teammates hydrated, those so-called mothers of your teammates refused to help," Aunt Phyllis sniffs. "Heaven help them if they broke even one manicured nail! They'd much rather be checking out the DILFcake from the stands."

Trisha licks her lips. "What does DILFcake taste like?"

Jeff snickers at her naivety.

Before Phyllis can answer her, I ask Trisha, "Honey, where did you get those pompoms?"

"They belong to Aunt Phyllis. But she promised me I could shake them when she's on the bullhorn."

Jeff slaps his forehead at the vision presented by his younger sister.

"Now that I'm here, I guess I should take over," I mutter uncertainly.

"No, no, no!" Aunt Phyllis insists. "You're still recuperating, remember? Why, it may take you all season to get better." Her eyes plead with me to play along.

Sure, why not? Very soon, my schedule won't be so flexible anyway. Ryan is setting up my physical therapy sessions. And as Jack so pointedly declared—I'll also have to pass a shrink test before Ryan takes me back, but so what? Easy peasy!

Still, if Aunt Phyllis is going to sub in for me, she's got to look at least presentable. "Shouldn't you wear a pair of pants with that jersey?" I drop my eyes pointedly to her bare legs.

"Can I help it if they're short-shorts?" She raises the jersey, revealing matching trunks that she has raised above her stomach.

I give up. "Okay, let's get this show on the road," I sigh.

Now that Jeff's in high school, there are some battles he has to fight for himself.

THE PARKING LOT IS ALREADY FILLED WHEN WE PULL UP TO HILLDALE High School's gymnasium. The bus for the opposing team, the Mira Costa Mustangs, is right behind us.

While Aunt Phyllis and Jeff hustle to join his teammates, Trisha and I climb the bleacher steps. Penelope Bing, who's there with Tiffy and Hayley, does a double take. Her nudge to Tiffy elicits a gasp from her BFF. When she sees where Penelope is pointing—at me—she squeaks in surprise.

As Hayley follows their eyes, she declares "Mother of God!" It's not this blasphemy that causes her to make the sign of the cross. It's seeing me alive.

Frankly, I'm glad we're not in church. Otherwise, she might feel the need to drown me in Holy water.

I wave at them, but I'll be darned if I sit anywhere near them. I'm sure she's dying to hear the details of my miraculous recovery.

Ain't happening.

There's no better reason for me to park myself right in front of her soon-to-be ex-husband and his current arm charm in the hope that she'll be too intimidated to walk over.

I'm sure it grates on Penelope to have him back on her turf with his current squeeze, a winsome beauty who, from the looks of her, is at least a decade younger than his wife and barely a decade older than their brat, Cheever.

Well, what do you know? Penelope and her momtourage are on their way over anyway. Could it have something to do with the ever-present cameraman who's always within a few yards of Peter? Or are they curious as to why I'm up and about, cavorting with the living?

My guess is the latter, despite Penelope's blunt exclamation, *"You survived?"*

I grace her with a smile. "Why, hello to you too!"

Tiffy pouts, "But…we were told you were at death's door!"

"By whom?" I ask.

"That nurse," Hayley replies. "What was her name again? Oh, yeah—Nancy."

I click my tongue. "Ironically, it's Nancy who's no longer with us."

"She died?" Tiffy's eyes open wide.

Penelope eyes me suspiciously. "You didn't have anything to do with that—did you?"

I shake my head. "In jail. Attempted murder. Mine."

"Too bad she got caught," Hayley mutters. Glancing at Penelope, she shrugs her disappointment.

As if reading her mind, Penelope snickers. Then, turning to me, she innocently explains, "What Hayley means is that she seemed so nice."

"By the way, even if Nancy had succeeded, you'd have been the last person Jack would ever date," I inform her.

Penelope's jaw drops practically to her surgically enhanced chest. She recovers quickly enough to growl, "Which one of these loudmouths told you that?"

"Neither," I assure her. "I heard you say it myself."

"Impossible!" Penelope retorts smugly. "You were dead as a doornail—well, almost."

"In other words, you deny that you called Jack 'the hottest DILF in Hilldale?'"

Tugging on my T-shirt, Trisha exclaims, "Mommy, does that mean Daddy knows how to bake a cake too?"

"Trisha, why don't you help Aunt Phyllis hand out the Gatorade?" I suggest sweetly.

Trisha winks. "And if there's any left over, we can have it with Daddy's cake!" She skedaddles in the direction of my aunt.

I'm about to follow her when Penelope grabs ahold of my arm. "Hey, not so fast," she growls suspiciously. "What else did you hear?"

I grab her wrist and fling it away. "If you're asking if I heard you telling your besties here about the spyware you coerced Cheever into planting on Peter's computer and iPhone when he was at his father's house, then, yeah, that also came in loud and clear."

Just as loud as I am speaking now, in fact—which is why Peter quits his canoodling with Arm Charm to glare at Penelope. "You had our son put spyware on my stuff?"

Tiffy and Hayley exchange guilty glances.

On the other hand, Penelope's eyes are on the television camera. The most important thing she learned during her time on the reality show: when the camera's little red light flashes, it's show time. "You betcha," she declares. "And my lawyer is going to make sure your clients and the producers know what you think of them."

The Bings' bickering is now so loud that neither notices that warm-ups are over and the game is about to begin.

The Mustangs' team captain slaps the ball in the direction of his forward, who dribbles the ball down the court at a furious pace. The crowd leaps up when Jeff intercepts the boy's pass to his teammate and moves back in our direction—

Only to be tripped by Cheever.

Jeff slides across the slippery gym until he slams head first into the nearest wall.

On the other hand, Cheever grabs the ball before it goes out of bounds. He smirks as he heads off with it. He shoots a basket from center court and revels in the crowd's spontaneous cheer.

I run to my son.

His coach, Mr. Morris, is also running toward Jeff from the other side of the court, all the while motioning the referee for a timeout.

I reach Jeff first. Falling on my knees, I look into his eyes. He's having a hard time focusing. Frantically, I ask, "Jeff! Can you hear me?"

"Yes," he murmurs sluggishly, but at the same time, he closes his eyes.

Memories flood me:

Of my shock at being shot;

Of my soul leaving my body;

Of my despair at the thought of leaving my family—of missing out on their joys and triumphs in the coming years.

Is that what Jeff is now thinking?

I won't let him go—ever.

I shout frantically, "Jeff, please! Stay with me!"

By now, Coach Morris is beside us. He helps me prop up my son, murmuring, "Jeff—son, how you are feeling?"

Jeff takes a deep breath before nodding lethargically. "I'm just a bit…dazed. Mom, I'm okay."

His teammates have gathered around us, including Cheever, who rolls his eyes at the drama surrounding his act of selfishness.

Glaring at him, I exclaim, "My son may have a concussion! Where's a doctor?" I look around at the stunned crowd in the stands. "Is there a doctor here? *Anyone*?"

Aunt Phyllis taps my shoulder. "Lila Hanover, the school nurse, is here." She nudges the woman toward Jeff.

Ms. Hanover takes a penlight out of her pocket. After shining light into Jeff's right eye and then his left one, she murmurs, "His eyes are following it." Smiling encouragingly at my son, she asks, "Tell me, Jeff, do you have a headache?"

He shakes his head. "Nah."

"Where were you hit?"

Jeff touches the side of his head that met the wall.

"Do you mind if I touch it?" Nurse Hanover asks.

Cheever snickers, "That's what she said."

I grasp my hands tightly—not around Cheever's neck, although I seriously believe I could beat a murder rap if the jury were made up specifically of the multitude of other Hilldale parents who shudder when the Bings are in sight.

Jeff frowns at Cheever. Ignoring him, he mutters, "Go ahead."

Tenderly, she places her fingers on the spot. "Any pain?"

Jeff shakes his head of dark curly hair. "I knew there was an advantage to letting my hair grow out." He rises slowly.

"Any dizziness or nausea?" Nurse Hanover asks.

"Nope, none," Jeff assures her.

"Helmets!" I insist. "I'll never understand why they aren't used in basketball—"

"Mom—it's okay!" It's shame, not a concussion, that reddens Jeff's cheeks. "I was just stunned is all."

"Sure, okay," I mutter uncertainly.

Leaning over us, Cheever jeers, "You've got two left feet, Stone."

"My last name is Craig," Jeff retorts.

Cheever snorts. "Are you sure? You were out cold for a while there. And the way your mom goes through men, she may have already found another daddy for you by now."

Angered by Cheever's chiding, Jeff staggers to his feet. "Are you calling my mom a—"

Coach Morris jumps in between them. "Take it out on the Mustangs boys—not on each other."

Ignoring Cheever's smirk, Jeff nods reluctantly. "I'll just sit out the first half. Right coach?"

Coach Morris's eyes shift in my direction. My silent plea comes with a firm shake of my head. Reading me loud and clear, Morris shrugs noncommittally. "Let's play it by ear."

Jeff frowns. Nope, that wasn't the answer he was looking for. Still, he shuffles off to the bench with the rest of his teammates.

Before Cheever heads toward the bench, I tap his arm. "Cheever, darling, may I have a word with you?"

He's isn't used to seeing me smile so sweetly. Stymied, he nods.

No one seems to notice when he follows me down the hall toward the locker rooms.

We only make it as far as a utility closet—conveniently out of range from any security cameras. Before Cheever knows what's happened, I shove him inside, closing the door behind us.

While he's off balance, I yank his jersey over his head. As he flails around, I grab a jump rope and an athletic sock off a shelf. He doesn't realize I've lassoed his wrists to his ankles until it's too late. When he does, he opens his big mouth to shout—

But he can't because I cram the sock into it.

Cheever stumbles when I shove him down onto a large mesh

bag filled with soccer balls. He inchworms his way to the wall, but he can't escape me. I bend down over him and hiss, "I didn't like what you did to my son. And while we're having this little heart-to-heart, let me make this perfectly clear: I didn't like what you *almost* did to me either."

"Whah dhoo you meewn?" His words are muffled, but I can make them out.

"In the hospital, you little pervert! Before Jeff stopped you from making the biggest mistake of your life."

Cheever's eyes widen. "He…tohl you?"

"He didn't have to. I saw it with my own eyes."

This realization startles him enough that he shakes uncontrollably.

Before we both drown in his sweat and piss, I growl, "Now, let me make this very clear to you, Cheever Bing. Unless a gentleman is invited to do so, he should never touch a woman inappropriately. Should you try—and I hear about it because all bullies have to brag about their bad behavior—*you will never walk upright again.*"

To drive home my point, I kick the bag out from under him. He falls to the floor, but the way I've got him tied up, he can't get up again.

Too bad.

I close the door behind me.

I ENTER THE GYM TO THE CLANG OF THE BUZZER ANNOUNCING THE END of the first half.

Jeff isn't one of the players chosen to hit the boards. Scowling, he slumps low in his chair.

Trisha waves me over to the home team bleachers on the opposite end of the stands from the still bickering Bings. They're mugging so hard for the cameraman that they haven't even noticed that their son has vanished into thin air.

Not Aunt Phyllis. During the last quarter, she sidles over to me. "*Pssst*! Where'd you drop the body?"

I shrug. "I have no idea what you're talking about."

"You know—the Bing brat! Creepy Cheever! The Hilldale Hellion!" Eyebrows arched, she leans in. "Where did you plant that bad seed?"

Batting my eyes innocently, I murmur, "Can you be more specific?"

Aunt Phyllis throws up her hands. "The kid who's been a thorn in our family's side since you moved into this hellhole of a planned community."

"Ah, yes—Cheever *Bing*." Sighing, I roll my eyes. "I thought it best that we talk in private. I counseled him on ways to ignore any untoward urges to play class clown."

"You mean class bully," Phyllis mutters.

"In any event, it worked."

"Really?" Aunt Phyllis's tone drips with suspicion.

"Yes. To my delight, he agreed with me that his naturally aggressive nature was hindering the team's collective vow of good sportsmanship."

"Ha!" Aunt Phyllis scrutinizes me suspiciously. "So then, where is the little jerk?"

I look around. After taking note he's nowhere to be found, I say, "Meditating, perhaps?"

Before she can retort, the scoreboard buzzer rings, announcing the end of the game.

Jeff joins his team in shaking the hands of the victorious Mustangs. With the Wildcat's top two players sidelined, the win was inevitable.

My son's silence on the drive home is deafening.

I wonder how Jeff will react when I start a school petition for helmet use in all sports?

WE PULL INTO THE GARAGE. JACK'S CAR IS THERE.

Evan's, however, isn't in the driveway. Perhaps he's taken Mary grocery shopping. Although I'm home from the hospital, my sweet Mary has insisted on making dinner every night, as she did during those days when I hovered between life and death.

Evan has been helping her. However, his sabbatical from college ends after this weekend. Cooking together is just one more way they can make the most of their time together before he leaves tomorrow for Berkeley.

Jeff storms into the house, leaving the front door open. The sound of his bedroom door slamming reverberates throughout our home.

Trisha, Aunt Phyllis, and I hustle out of the car just as Jack appears at the front door. "What was that all about?" he asks.

"His team lost," I mutter.

"Because Donna thought it best that he not play." By Aunt Phyllis's tone, I can tell she questions my decision.

I stick out my tongue at her.

"And then Cheever disappeared!" Trisha adds dramatically.

Jack's stare shifts from me to Aunt Phyllis to Trisha and back again. "Ladies, something seems to have gotten lost in translation."

I'm about to make my case when Evan's car screeches into the driveway before lurching to a sudden stop.

Mary is behind the wheel.

Evan is riding shotgun. I don't blame him for wincing.

But Mary grimaces too when she sees the shocked look on my face.

I storm inside.

The others follow, carrying the groceries.

Considering how I feel right now, the kitchen and its many

knives may not be perfect place for this discussion, but it will have to do.

❧

EVERYONE WAITS FOR ME TO SPEAK. MY ATTEMPT AT CIVILITY IS IN MY words if not my icy tone. "Why was Mary driving?"

"Mom, please—don't be so upset! It's not the first time I've driven Evan's car."

I glare at Evan. "Is that true?"

Reluctantly, he nods. "She passed the test for her learner's permit the day you were"—he pauses—"you know, when you ended up in the hospital. We were going to surprise you."

Ah, great. One more thing I missed while unavoidably detained by the Grim Reaper. "Mary, let me guess. One of the questions on the test you missed was that you must drive with a licensed driver who's at least twenty-five. Am I right?"

Mary's face loses all color. "No. I aced the test, including that question. Still, we felt that your situation was an emergency. With you incapacitated and Dad's work schedule..." Her voice trails off.

Evan jumps in: "What Mary is trying to say is that having another safe driver in the family might soon be a necessity."

"Had your mother...well, let's just say I'd always be around to pick up the slack," Aunt Phyllis reminds them.

"But they said, 'safe,'" Trisha reminds her.

Jack's grin reflects what the rest of them are thinking.

Why am I the only one who doesn't find any of this funny?

Angrily, I face Jack. "Did you know about this?"

"No," he admits. "Nevertheless, as Mary just pointed out, things have been a little hectic while you were away."

I shake with disgust. "You make it sound as if I were on holiday."

"Not at all," Jack says in an irritatingly calm murmur. "Honey, no doubt it was hard to lose those days. But this past week aged all of us—let me say that differently. It *matured* us greatly." He puts his hand on my shoulder.

I fling it off. "I don't think I'm overreacting, Jack! What if Mary had been in an accident? What if, God forbid, she and Evan had been injured? Or worse yet, killed?"

"But they weren't," he reminds me. "And they're smart, trustworthy young adults."

"What about me? Aren't I a trustworthy young adult too?"

We turn in the direction of Jeff's voice.

"Of course you are," Jack assures him.

"Mom, do you think so too?"

I nod, but I can guess where this line of conversation is going. "Yes, I think you know that."

"So, when I told you I felt good enough to play ball, why did you ask Coach Morris to bench me instead? You did that—right?"

I shrug. "Not in so many words, but, yes, I suppose that, like me, he realized your health was the utmost priority—"

"I could have played the second half! And maybe I could have turned the game around!" Noting the grimace on my face, he throws up his hands in frustration. "And for Cheever to bail on us too…" He frowns. "When you talked to him, what exactly did you say?"

If Aunt Phyllis thinks that her fake coughing jag will cut the tension between my son and me, she's wrong. Only Trisha is truly worried about her. After slapping my aunt on the back several times, she reaches into the cooler for a Gatorade bottle. "Here, sip some of this," she suggests.

"The way this is going, I may need something stronger," Phyllis mutters.

I reach into a cabinet and pull out the bottle of cooking sherry. Handing it to her, I declare, "Go for it."

My aunt's eyes grow to the size of cornflowers, but she doesn't dare uncork the bottle. She'd much rather have my wrath aimed at my children and my husband.

She's getting her wish. As I circle them, I growl, "I may have awakened from a coma only two days ago, but I never stopped being a mother. *Your* mother." I let the words sink in. "And as such, I'm laying down some ground rules for the health and safety of this family so that your own experiences with death aren't caused by lousy odds, bad judgment, or stupidity on your part. Rule Number One: If you're to play a sport, you do so with a helmet and padding to all joints."

"But…there are no helmets in basketball!" Jeff declares

I turn my no-nonsense gaze on him. "There are now—for *you* anyway."

"No way!" Disgusted, he shakes his head. "I won't be the only person on the court wearing a helmet. I'd look like a jerk!"

"Okay, got it. So you won't play at all." Before he has a chance to protest, I add, "And that goes for baseball as well."

Jeff fumes for a moment before muttering, "Welcome home!" as he stalks off.

I turn to Mary next. "You blew it. You should have waited for either your father or me to accompany you. Instead, you took a chance on something that could have cost you dearly—*your life*. This lesson comes with a consequence." My pause is not for dramatics, but because I must think of something that will make her think twice next time. "You're not to drive again until your eighteenth birthday."

Mary tears up. "Mom…seriously? Are you kidding me?"

"No. This is for real."

"It's—not fair! I wish…I wish you had died!" Mortified at her words, she flees the room, sobbing.

Trisha's lower lip trembles. "Does this mean I can't play soccer?"

I kneel in front of her. "Of course you can, sweetie—*with a helmet.*"

Trisha bursts into tears and runs up the stairs after her sister.

Evan stares after them. When he turns toward me, he's more

sad than angry. "Donna, we know you love us. We love you too. But we can't quit living our lives because you're now too afraid to live yours."

He treads off to his room over the garage.

Aunt Phyllis murmurs, "I'll leave you two lovebirds alone."

The look in Jack's eyes is anything but love—more like pity.

"Evan is wrong," I insist. "The last thing I am is afraid to live my life."

"Frankly, it wouldn't be a bad thing if you took it easy," Jack counters.

"And yet, at the same time, you feel I'm being too protective with them?"

He says nothing.

"Admit it!" I dare him.

He nods. "Okay, yes. I think you're projecting your fears onto them."

"Who asked you to play shrink?"

"I wouldn't dare take on that role for you," he counters. "You're too likely to shoot the messenger. Speaking of which, Acme lined one up for you, along with a physical therapist. You're to start Monday with him for daily sessions, and you'll see the psychiatrist on Wednesday." He hands me two business cards. "By the way, Coach Morris called."

Seeing me wince, Jack frowns. Nonchalantly, I ask, "What did he want?"

"He said he found Cheever bound and gagged in an equipment storage room. He wondered if you knew anything about it?"

"Hmmm…" I widen my eyes in mock innocence. "I wonder why he'd think that?"

"Other than it was Cheever who shoved Jeff into the wall, and that you were the last one seen with him? Gee, you've got me."

"What does Cheever say about it?"

"He claims he never saw his assailant." Jack can't help but smile. "You must have scared the piss out of that brat."

"Oh? Did he leave a puddle?"

"Luckily, no." Jack's grin fades. "At this point in your recovery, erratic behavior in public can, and will, find its way back to Ryan."

"By whom, Jack? You?"

"A complaint filed at the school by anyone—say, the Bings—will be picked up by Acme's Clearance Division. You and I both know that." He reaches for a lock of my hair. Tucking it behind my ear, he murmurs, "I'm not the enemy, Donna."

"Prove it," I reply. "Stop working so hard to keep me off this mission."

"If I'm 'working hard' at anything, it's to keep you from"—he struggles to find the right words that don't express his fears —"from getting hurt again."

I reach for his hand. "Please, Jack! I'm here. I'm alive. And I want to get on with my life! Don't stand in my way."

"I don't see it that way. In fact, I may be saving you from yourself."

When he puts his arms around me, I flinch at his touch.

He reads that to mean he's somehow hurt me.

He has, and yes, the bruise is internal: my heart.

I head for our bedroom.

By the time I drift off to sleep, he's holed up in the guest room.

# 15

# To Lose My Life or Lose My Love

THE SONG WAS ON THE DEBUT ALBUM OF THE BRITISH INDIE ROCK band, White Lies. When released in January 2009, the album immediately hit #1 on the *UK Albums* chart, and it was the first album that year to debut at #1 worldwide. It also held Top 40 slots in six European countries.

The single itself also hit #146 on the *Billboard* "200" chart; and #4 on the *Billboard* "Top Heatseekers" chart.

*The loss of a life? Deadly. The loss of a love? Devastating, but there is a chance at recovery—if you remember these three Don'ts:*

1. *Don't let it obsess you. After hearing your woe-is-me blather for the umpteenth time, your friends will be the first to tell you: It wasn't something you did. In truth, it had to do with the many somethings you are. Or, for that matter, your ex's many somethings have a lot to do with it as well. Sometimes, too many somethings can add up to a whole lot of nothing.*

2. *Don't act as if it's the end of the world. Shakespeare said it best: "Better to have loved and lost than to have never loved at all." Babe Ruth's famous saying is the perfect metaphor: "I had the most home runs because I had the most times up to bat." In other words: get out there again.*

3. *Don't think you'll ever fall in love again? Great news! It's like riding a bicycle. Once you know how it's just as easy to do a second time…and a third…and a fourth…*

"YOU ARE ONE LUCKY LADY!" THE AWE WITH WHICH JONAH KYLE, MY physical therapist, says this makes me wince even more than my latest rotation of arm-strengthening exercises. "You've only been home a week and look at you! I have clients who take months—sometimes years—to get their motor strength back to even that."

Even that.

Apropos, since I'm moving as slow as frozen motor oil. Whether curling, jogging, reaching, or even walking, my gut hurts with each pull on my abdomen.

But if Jonah gives me a lousy prognosis, there will be no way to convince Ryan that I should be on the mission to find Eric.

Not that I'll let Jonah know this. I smile up at him. "Just call me Wonder Woman."

"Trust me, I do." His grin is tepid at best.

"You don't sound too convinced," I retort.

"Frankly, I think you're pushing yourself too hard." He squints at me as if preparing to catch me should I falter from the pain that he thinks I'm feeling.

I am hurting—but I'll never admit it.

Finally, he shrugs. "Donna, we've both seen your x-rays. Luckily, the bullet dodged your organs. You were stitched up by the best, and that's a big plus. Still, it's going to take a while until you're fully healed. All the more reason to go slow and steady."

I nod meekly.

And then I do twelve more rotations on each arm at an even faster pace.

Jonah sighs.

Too bad. I'm here on a mission. Nothing will keep me from it.

Certainly not my mortality. I've already proven that once.

ACME'S RESIDENT PHYSICIAN, DR. FRIEDMAN, SLOWLY UNWRAPS THE bandage on my wound. I'm lying down on his patient table so I can't see it, but I can gauge the emotions I see in his face.

At first, his eyes open wide before narrowing again in concern. He grimaces as he takes a closer look. With gentle fingers, he presses down.

This time, it's me who reacts: I stiffen, but I hold back a yelp.

"Ah," he murmurs.

"What does 'ah,' mean?" I ask warily.

He shrugs. "It's shorthand for 'it's going to take some time to heal.'"

I ease myself up on my elbows. "We have an active mission right now—"

"Yes, I know." Friedman frowns. "And I know how badly you want to be a part of it. Listen, Donna: in one regard, you were lucky. That bullet could have done some serious life-changing damage. With what I'm seeing here, it may take a month, maybe two, until you're completely healed and ready to go back into the field"—he hesitates, then adds—"depending on your psychological assessment, of course."

Seeing my crestfallen face, he sighs. "By that I mean sometimes a near-death experience will set off PTSD. Just take it easy for the next few weeks. Allow yourself to heal, both physically and emotionally. Your life depends on it." Chuckling weakly, he adds, "Hey, consider the alternative."

Been there, done that.

I wait until he walks out of the room before groaning.

Yes, out of frustration. And yes, from the pain.

"Do you want to talk about your visions?" My Acme-appointed psychiatrist, Dr. Alfred Bellows, scans the dossier in his hands.

I've been admiring his wall art: beautifully framed Rorschach blottings. At some point, will I be asked to give an opinion of what I see in them?

So far, all he's asked is if I prefer to sit in an easy chair or on the couch. I ease down onto the couch so that I can lie down. My gut is sore and throbbing from my workout. No pain, no mission. I'll live —I hope.

Not that I need Dr. Bellows to feel it on my behalf. "Yes, let's talk about them," I say, perhaps a bit too cheerily.

The good doctor nods, but then adds hesitantly, "Because of your security clearance, you know that everything you say here must be reported to your Acme superior, Ryan Clancy."

"Yes, I know."

"Good." He writes something in my file. "Well then, let's start with how and when the visions began."

So I tell him:

About leaving my body the moment the bullet entered me;

And about seeing Jack's frantic and caring reaction when he discovered my comatose body;

How I appreciated Jack's tenderness and concern as he sped to the hospital, all the while trying to keep me from bleeding out;

How my soul watched while suspended over the surgical team–

And then the Grim Reaper showed up.

Hearing this last bit of news, Dr. Bellows stops scribbling. He looks over his glasses to scrutinize me. "Um…so, what does he look like?"

"To be honest, he changed his look several times over the course of our visits. Sometimes he was the wraith in the hooded robe and holding a scythe. At others, he was a dark angel with wings as wide this room, large gnarled fingers, red eyes…" I shudder at the memory. "Once, he was just a floating skull. Charon on the River Styx, Thanatos, Ankou, Banshee…" I shrug.

Dr. Bellows nods solemnly. "You know your death mythology."

I can't tell if he's being sarcastic. "So, you do believe me?"

He pauses but then shrugs. "You seem convinced. That's all that counts."

"It counts? How so? Does it count as far as committing me to some loony bin?"

"We don't call them loony bins anymore. They go by sanitarium, or spa—"

"Let's not parse words, Doc." I sit up on the sofa. "Do you think I'm nuts?"

He shakes his head. "I think there's a reason for everything we see and hear. If you're asking me if what you perceived was fact as opposed to a delusion, I'll have to hear a little more." He nudges his glasses higher on the bridge of his nose. "I assume he talked to you?"

"Yes. He told me I was dying. I believed him because of what I heard between my surgeon and the trauma team."

Even as he takes notes he asks, "So, you could hear the doctor?"

I laugh mirthlessly. "Among others. I heard everyone who came to visit: my husband, my family, my mission team, my neighbors, the President and the First Lady—"

"Wow. You do have friends in high places."

"Yeah, lucky me." Not that I want to get into my very complicated relationships with Lee and Babette. Better to save that for another visit.

"What did he say to you?"

"Who, POTUS?"

*You mean, like, that he loved me, and if I woke up, he wanted to marry me? Sorry, my lips are sealed, Doc—and not just because you'd chalk it up as a sex fantasy.*

"I meant the Grim Reaper," Dr. Bellows explains. "You said there were several visits."

"Yes, well, I was crashing, so I offered him…a deal."

Dr. Bellows's pen freezes. "What kind of deal?"

I take a deep breath before answering. "To be honest with you, I told him I…well, that I'd help him with his harder cases if he needed it."

Dr. Bellows nods slowly. "I see."

"You know, since it's my line of work anyway, I thought it might have been a no-brainer." I shrug. "But I made it very clear to him that I wanted to handle only the worst cases. Now, in hindsight, the whole concept may have been a bit presumptuous on my part."

"Yes, well, he's been a solo act for years, so…" The good doctor's voice trails off. Finally: "But since you're here, I suppose he agreed to an alternate proposal?"

"You could call it that. He pitched Satan on a few death matches—seven, to be exact. I guess a more apt term would be 'un-death matches—at least, in my case." I giggle weakly. Frankly, I shouldn't take credit for this little joke since it was Death's bon mot.

"'Undeath matches'…I get it." A shadow of a smile rises on his lips. In fact, he writes that down.

Yikes. Is that a good thing?

"Now that I'm far removed from it, un-death matches made sense on a couple of levels," I assure him. "As Satan explained it, if I won, it shattered any sinner's hope of ever getting out of Hell for, you know, the Good Place. And if I lost, I would have to pay the ultimate price."

"Did the thought of losing scare you?" he asks.

"Yes, very much so! But I figured that I'd already killed my adversaries once, so maybe—to paraphrase *The Hunger Games*—the odds were in my favor."

Suddenly, Bellows is scrawling furiously. Dammit! Why did I quote Effie Trinket? Maybe he thinks I didn't take my dire situation as seriously as I should have.

To prove that theory wrong, I quickly add, "The fights were surreal! There were millions of sinners there, watching, cheering, or jeering—by the way, sinners is what he called them, not me."

"He, meaning the Reaper?" Dr. Bellows asks.

"Um…no. Satan." I rise. Just a theory here, but I don't think now is the time to mention that the Devil wanted to make me Queen of Hades, so I add fervently, "I just want to make this clear: I did everything I could to come back here."

Bellows nods sympathetically. "I'm sure you did, Donna."

I wish he'd quit taking notes. It makes me feel like a freak.

"Is there anything else you'd like to tell me?" he asks.

"Yes! You see, whenever I won a fight, I was rewarded with a visit from a deceased friend or colleague."

"I'm sure these were, er…heartfelt reunions," he murmurs.

"Yes. I was truly touched that these souls came to pay their respects." Hoping I'm not making this sound like a high school reunion, I lean forward and add, "More importantly, they gave me intel on my team's latest mission—some of which I was able to feed back to Ryan and my team."

His pen pauses in mid-air. "You mean, while you were still in the coma?"

I nod.

"How…how did you do it?"

"Apparently, some of us are more susceptible to psychic phenomena than others—especially children. One of my team members brought her toddler, Nicky. He's just now saying words. I came to him and taught him to speak the name of the person who is now our prime suspect."

"I see," Bellows murmurs. However, he doesn't write it down. "Was your intel confirmed by, er, the living?"

"Yes, that very day, in fact. Almost simultaneously. You see, while the team visited, Mr. Clancy got a call informing him that the suspect escaped his cell that very morning."

Once more, Doctor Bellows puts pen to pad. From the amount of time he's taking, perhaps he feels he's got the makings of an interesting white paper on a coma patients' ability to commune with those in the Afterlife. How exciting! Maybe it will appear in *The American Journal of Psychiatry*, or *Lancet*, or *The American Journal of Medicine*, or *International Journal of Medical Sciences*—

How very *Three Faces of Eve*! I'll be his Sybil! When he confirms he's actually doing this, I'll suggest that the title could perhaps be *The Seven Trials of Donna*.

I'm so excited at my shot at immortality in the annals of medical research that I have to ask: "What do you make of all this, Doc?"

Bellows puts down his pen with a sigh. "Right now, I'm leaning toward delusions from Post Traumatic Stress Disorder."

*What the...*

No! Just—*no*. "But...how do you explain the validated intel?" I ask indignantly.

"You were in the coma for several days. Tell me, Donna: on which day did you give the toddler the suspect's name?"

"I...I can't remember," I retort. "It wasn't as if I was wearing a watch or anything. When you're in a coma, time stands still, or races ahead like fast-motion photography."

"Perhaps you could have heard your team mention the suspect's name on one day. Then, in your unconscious state dream, you might have *thought* you'd given it to the toddler the next day. Or, perhaps he just heard it while there in the hospital room, like you."

"In other words, you think I'm delusional." Which means I won't be getting anywhere near the mission.

Bellows coughs apologetically. "You have to consider that the images that appeared to you—the Reaper, Satan—represent your deepest darkest fears: death and the Afterlife that we can only guess at. For some, the thought of dying is filled with sadness, anger, and loss of self." He leans forward on his desk. "As for the fantasy of re-connecting with loved ones who'd died, I'd say it represents your hope that they'll be there to greet you when it is your turn to, as they say, 'cross over.'"

"Interesting," I mutter. *Not.* "Are you also doubting that I may have heard those around me while in the coma? Or that I might have connected with Nicky?"

"Not at all. Such psychic phenomena occurring to coma patients has already been reported, so yes, it's always possible." He tents his fingers on his desk. "As for those 'un-death matches,' perhaps they were the manifestation of guilt on your part for the lives you took—"

"I have no regrets," I interrupt. "Neither the first time I killed them, nor during the un-death matches." I too tent my fingers at my waist. It's the only way to keep from grabbing his pen and stabbing him in the neck with it, which wouldn't get me what I want: back with my team.

Bellows nods as his pen scratches his pad. "Even those who may have been collateral damage?"

"What do you mean by that?" I ask warily.

"Most people have some code of ethics or morals. Granted, some in your profession can fit theirs on the back of a business card, but there are some lines that are taboo to cross. And when exterminations go awry, there can be…regrets." He pauses again. Then, he hesitantly adds, "No one is perfect. I'm sure you've had some too."

Instead, I murmur, "But of course, Doctor. Makes perfect sense."

A pleased smile accompanies his less-than-modest shrug. "One last question, Donna: are you still having these delusions?"

*Yes, Doc. I hear voices in my head. I see dead people. My ex visited just this morning...*

"Who...me?" I shake my head. "Nah. All gone now, thank goodness!"

He sighs disappointedly. "Quite an interesting case. Do let me know if they come back...you know, as visions or nightmares. Anything."

*Like Hell.* "Will do! Good-bye Doctor."

I'm trying to keep my voice positive, but he's an intuitive shrink. When I slam his door, a few Rorschachs fall to the floor. Gee, I hope he doesn't pick up on my disappointment.

I HAVE NO NEED TO GO DIRECTLY HOME, SO I WON'T. THERE'S NO ONE and nothing waiting there for me.

At first, I meander aimlessly, driving north on State Route 1 until it turns into the Pacific Coast Highway.

Finally, I pull off the road far north of Malibu.

I get out in order to walk on the beach.

The coarse brown sand fills my shoes, so I kick them off and just keep walking until I reach the surf. In no time, I've strolled out far enough that the tepid waves are lapping at my thighs.

I leap in.

My breaststrokes take me far out into the dark turquoise ocean. I barely feel the frigid water. I'm already numb from despair.

My dead man's float allows me to me look up at gauzy clouds, pulled into thin wisps by ocean gusts. Is it a scrim hiding the Heaven of our dreams?

In any event, I am not worthy of it.

So then, why am I here?

I don't mean out here in the Pacific, or even Malibu. I mean here—as in *alive.*

We tell ourselves that life is precious. What we don't want to accept is that it goes on without us; that after loss, grief may follow, but acceptance is inevitable.

Memories fade. People forget. What's left to be said about you can easily be carved onto a headstone: your name, a couple of dates, and some innocuous homily.

What is it all for?

And in my case, was coming back worth it?

In the eyes of my husband, I'm an invalid whose sanity—a frail skein of tangled thoughts, emotions, and deductions—is now hanging by a thread. I overreact to threats against the safety of my precious children while ignoring my own brush with death.

No doubt, he'd second every conclusion reached by Bellows: that I'm delusional. That my lack of concern for my safety is rooted in guilt for those lives taken—both directly and indirectly.

Perhaps he's right. I count on my fingers those affected by my words and deeds if not my assassin skills: the witnesses who were at the wrong place at the wrong time, or the women who I vetted as my replacement when I considered retirement.

Even Mara Portnoy was such a casualty.

And now that my obsession with my job has moved beyond its original motivation—avenging a loved one's death—is the good doctor right in assuming that it's fueled by a different obsession: the thrill of the kill?

If so, then I am a monster.

The sea is filled with them.

It took Carl. It could easily take me too.

Because my ears are underwater, I didn't hear the arrival of the surfer who now stares down at me. Despite his smile, I hear the concern in his voice when he asks, "Hey, doll, need a lift?"

I know better than to take too long to answer. I nod. "Sure, why not?"

I hop in front of him on his surfboard and we paddle back to shore.

He doesn't ask how or why I'm out here. Something tells me I'm not the first person he's found out swimming in a tidal pool of despair.

They say salt water heals wounds. I hope it can heal hearts too.

# 16

# Live Like You Were Dying

PERFORMED BY COUNTRY SINGER TIM MCGRAW. WRITTEN BY THE songwriting team of Tim Nichols and Craig Wiseman. It was the lead single from his eighth album of the same name released in 2004. The writers' lyrics were inspired by those they knew who suffered serious illnesses and changed in order to live life to its fullest.

The lead single from the album, the song became an enormous success in the U.S. It spent seven weeks atop the *Billboard* country music charts, and was touted as the biggest country song of the year. It won "Single of the Year" and "Song of the Year" at both the 2004 Country Music Association Awards and at the 2004 Academy of Country Music Awards. It was also awarded the 2004 Grammy Award for Best Country Song.

~

*In the immortal words of George Burns: "You can't help getting older, but you don't have to get old."*

*In other words, live like you're dying. As if every day may be your last.*

*To make that ideal a reality, make this a part of your daily routine:*

- *Change #1: Don't be afraid of what others say or think about you. If you're true to yourself, the only opinion that matters is your own.*
- *Change #2: If something in your life doesn't work, change it. If you aren't happy, no one else will be either.*
- *Change #3: Not every day will be a great one. When a great one occurs, celebrate it in the moment.*
- *Change #4: If something doesn't work in your life, quit doing it. If someone doesn't work in your life, walk away from him or her. If someone is threatening your life, stand tall—and make sure they fall hard.*

"You're still in bed on such a beautiful day like today?" Aunt Phyllis pulls my comforter away, exposing my Smurfs granny gown for the world to see.

I guess I'm exaggerating since we're the only ones in my bedroom—quite evident to my aunt, who winces as she mutters, "It's already ten o'clock! And you wonder why Jack jogs every morning at the crack of dawn when he should be under the covers with you, doing the dirty—"

"Jogging is a new obsession," I retort.

Aunt Phyllis's admonishment comes with a frown. "You've slept for two days straight," she counters. "It's time you quit hiding out!"

"Me—hiding? That's rich!" I retort. "From whom? From what?"

"From your family. From your husband." She moves in to make her point: "From your life."

I frown. "That's not fair! I've gone through a traumatic experience—"

Aunt Phyllis shakes her head. "So, you've decided to give up?"

"You don't know the half of it," I mutter.

"My dear niece, I may be blind, partially deaf, and yes, a bit brain-addled—but I'm not stupid." Aunt Phyllis's right brow arches. "You're scared. We all get it. But we can't change that in you. We can't be you for you. In other words, only *you* can fix this." She takes my hand. "Start by staring it in the face. Whatever haunts you—*it will blink first*. And when it does, you'll finally recover that unique courage that sets you apart from everyone I know."

I nod because I know she's right. Before I can do so myself, Aunt Phyllis wipes away the tear rolling down my cheek. "I know you're going to tell me that I'm sticking my nose where it shouldn't be, but you'd be wrong. The happiness of this family is just as important to me as it is to you—all the more reason you should kiss and make up with Jack. He never left your side, missy! Not for a moment. Not even when the doctor told us you were a goner. Now, why are you doing everything you can to push him away?"

"That's between Jack and me," I declare. "Please respect my wishes to handle my husband as I see fit."

"The way you're 'handling' him, he may not have that distinction for much longer." She stalks out of the room, slamming the door behind her.

And not a moment too soon. My cell phone rings. Caller ID says it's Ryan.

*YES! YES! He really, really loves me!*

I answer immediately. "Yes, my king, my liege?"

"You flatter me," Ryan's response is not only uncertain, it's cold. "Despite that, we need to talk."

"Sure." I mean, it's that or watching my toenails grow. "Should I wait and come in with Jack?"

Ryan coughs. "Not necessary. I'll just expect you sometime today."

"Duly noted. I'll be there at one-thirty," I reply nonchalantly. It's better to know Ryan's opinion on my status as soon as possible.

"That will work perfectly. I've got an out-of-office meeting scheduled for three. I'll need time in between to prep for it. Come in through the back entrance."

Ryan has a secret door into his office. It's his way of saying he'd like to keep our conversation on the down-low. I'll be in and out before anyone at Acme realizes I'm there—including Jack.

I've got no problem with that. No matter how Jack feels about my quote-unquote delicate situation, Ryan's take on my experiences may be different. And if he feels I'm good to go, then Jack's opinion won't matter.

But if Ryan feels I'm no longer a viable Acme asset, there will be other days spent in bed.

Perhaps months.

As I expected, by the time I enter Ryan's office, he's lowered the scrim that shields his office, making us invisible from the rest of Acme.

Ryan uses the file in his hand to point to the chair in front of his desk. "Sit down."

I ease myself into it, but keep my mouth shut until he's ready to talk.

"We have a lead on your attempted assassin," he says.

Ah, this should be interesting. "He was a former Russian operative. He's been rogue for a few years, so we're going on the assumption that it was a hit for hire."

"Which doesn't bring us any closer to who hired him," I mutter.

"Neither did our interrogation of Nancy Carr. While at Club Dread, she admitted that if you weren't close enough to expiration on your own, she'd been paid to help you 'cross over.' Unfortunately for us, she managed to take a poison pill before she'd divulged her client's name."

"I guess she wasn't just playing Angel of Death." I flinch. Considering my encounter with the real deal, you'd think I'd know better than to use that term of endearment. "Do we know her real name?"

"MI6 pulled up a partial match on her little pinky: an IRA operative who disappeared a couple of decades ago. They started them so young back then." Ryan shakes his head. "Our guess is that she immigrated to the States to get a fresh start, got her nurse's degree, and lived a clean life—until your enemy either blackmailed her, or tempted her with enough cash to make assuring your imminent demise worth her while."

"A Russian assassin and a former Irish terrorist?" I shake my head. "I guess I'm hated all over the world."

His way of changing the subject starts with a gentle smile. "How's the physical therapy going?"

I flex a muscle. "Jonah says I'm almost back to optimum strength." Whatever else he's saying has got to be in that file, so I guess I better not exaggerate too much.

He walks over to my side of the desk. Leaning against it, he asks, "And your wound? Still tender?"

No. It hurts like hell. Not that I'll admit it.

Instead, I lift up my shirt to show him. I wrapped it nice and tight so that the bruise is fully covered. With the fingers on one hand I pretend to press down on it. "Nah, not that much. See?"

He nods appreciatively.

"Want to feel it? Go ahead, don't be shy." I'm teasing, but I pray he doesn't take me up on it.

His eyes scan my face as if he'll find some deep truth there. Finally, he replies, "Thanks, but no. I don't want it getting back to Jack that I manhandled his wife in my office."

Noting my shrug, he asks, "How are things between the two of you?"

"He's been…very protective."

Ryan nods. "That's to be expected. He thought he lost you once. Should it ever happen, he'd be…inconsolable, to put it mildly."

I nod.

"The emotional wellbeing of my operatives is always my top priority—not just because it could jeopardize their missions, but because they are my family." Ryan's eyes never waver from mine. "You told Bellows something about visions you had, starring the Grim Reaper?"

"Yes." Oh, darn! Here it comes—

He frowns. "And with Satan."

"Yes."

"Do you mind telling me about them too?" Ryan's eyes search mine as he waits silently for my answer.

Should I parse my words to fit what I think he wants to hear in order to ensure that I sound sane enough to stay on the team?

No. If that is indeed Bellows' report in his hand, he already knows.

Besides, Jack might have already expressed his concerns about what he calls dreams despite telling me that he wouldn't.

If so, I'll certainly be upset about it.

I trust my gut that Ryan wants to know the truth. And yes, he'll make the decision that is right for the team.

But I also feel he'll know what is best for me too.

So I tell him:

About my pact with the Reaper: seven hellish rematches with those I'd previously assassinated;

About the six trials that went right, and the last one that was stolen from me;

About the clues I was given, and how I was able to pass Eric's name to them by way of Nicky while they discussed the mission in my hospital room. His face, devoid of emotion throughout the baring of my soul, now opens up with a wide grin.

"You think I imagined the whole incident, don't you?" I mutter crossly.

"The tyke was adamant," he admits. His smile fades. "And I saw the blocks he'd laid out on the chair—not to mention the tear on your cheek."

Hearing this fills me with relief. "So…you do believe me!"

"I believe you, Donna. I also believe there's an Afterlife and that sometimes those that went before us reach out to protect us." He pauses. When he speaks again, it's a soft whisper: "Natalie—my wife—comes to me in my dreams."

So, yes, he truly understands. I am validated.

"These other clues you received—can you remember them?"

I look down at my hands. "Sort of, but not really—just bits and pieces that don't make sense. Not that they did when they were given to me, either! None were straight answers. More like riddles that I'd have to solve…"

Ryan looks so sad. Maybe it's because I sound so pathetic.

He sighs. "Believe it or not, your coma was a gift. But do us both a favor: For now, keep your experiences to yourself. And Donna, if anything—no matter how incoherent—comes to you, please write it down and pass it to me. I'll have Emma's team run them through computer analysis and follow up on them—"

"I'll coordinate with Emma myself," I retort hotly. "Unless what you're telling me is that I'm off the team."

"Not at all. Just not out in the field—yet, anyway. However, you'll be an excellent asset here in the office."

I shake my head. "I'd be wasted in the office! We both know that."

Before I know what he's doing, he lightly slaps my gut.

I flinch, but at least I don't cry out.

"You're not ready for the field, Donna."

Angrily, I slap his hand away. "Dirty pool, Ryan! You just caught me off-guard."

"When you left Bellows' office on Wednesday, you drove up the PCH, beyond Malibu. You swam out into the ocean—in your clothes. You floated long enough that the tide pulled you out into deep water—"

"You had me tailed?" I'm just as confused as I am angry. "But...why?"

"Standard procedure. Whenever an operative goes through a traumatic incident, especially one with physical repercussions, we recognize the toll it takes on one's sense of self. For that reason, we'll shadow for however long we feel it is needed." He shrugs. "Better to watch from a distance than to lose a great asset to...depression."

"How comforting," I mutter.

Ryan glances at his watch.

"We want you back, Donna, but for all the right reasons. Putting you back in the field while you're still numbed by your experience not only puts you at risk, but potentially your mission team as well. The office position is there for you if you want it. But if you choose to stay on temporary leave—or for that matter a permanent one—I'll understand." He puts his hand on my shoulder. "Come back to us, Donna, as soon as you can. We need you."

I shrug. "I'll think about it."

He smiles. "That's all I ask."

I'VE JUST GOTTEN BACK TO MY CAR WHEN JACK TEXTS ME:

*Picking up the kids now. XOXO J*

Ah, I get it. They'd prefer to carpool with him as opposed to me. Ha! I guess they're afraid I'll show up with a trunk filled with body armor.

Yeah, okay: it's on order. Amazon Prime delivers it tomorrow.

I'll need to ease my family into this new world order. I'll start with a peace offering: pie. One for each of them, and their favorites: apple pies for Trisha, Jeff, and Aunt Phyllis, and cherry ones for Jack and Mary.

Maybe by the time they've all graduated from high school, they'll be talking to me again.

~

YES, BAKING PIES IS THE RIGHT THING TO DO.

Kneading and then rolling out the dough is as satisfying as any erotic act of love. In the kinetic process of peeling and then slicing the apples, any doubts I have about my dexterity dissolves like the sugar I sprinkle into the fruit compote.

As the aroma of baking pies fills the air, I feel like "me" again.

Something is scratching at the back door. It's one of our dogs, Lassie. She dances around, excited about the offering in Rin Tin Tin's mouth.

I open the door, but I'm certainly not letting him in with it, especially if it's a rodent:

It's not. It's a pigeon.

"Drop," I command Rin Tin Tin.

His mouth opens and the bird falls to the floor. It's still alive, but something is off:

Its wing is broken.

Rin Tin Tin takes a few steps back. Crouching on all fours, he awaits my next command.

At that moment, my precious time with his former master, Nola, comes back to me:

*There is a pigeon, flying toward us from the west, but it crash-lands in our boat. Its wing is broken.*

*It caws Lee's name.*

*West…*

*Wing, broken…*

*Lee.*

Eric's target is Lee. He's going to strike the West Wing.

I REACH FOR MY PHONE AND HIT RYAN'S NUMBER. IT ROLLS OVER TO voicemail, darn it!

A car pulls into our driveway. Jack is home.

Should I tell him what I know? Of course…

But then it hits me: why would I? He'll call it yet another one of my delusions.

I hear the front door open and then footsteps climbing the stairs—

Only to pause at the mouthwatering scent of freshly baked pies.

I hold my breath and say a prayer that my act of contrition will bring me face to face with my family—

Well, with one of them, anyway. Aunt Phyllis's head pops through the kitchen door. "Yum! Something smells great!"

I reward her with a smile. "Thanks! And here's one hot apple pie with your name on it!" As I cut into her apple pie, I do my best to ask casually, "Where are the others? I've made them pies too."

Aunt Phyllis's grin falters. "Jeff and Mary are still at school—in the, er, library."

*Not good.*

My knife stops. "Oh?"

"You know—high school homework." She rolls her eyes.

In other words, they'd rather be there than here.

"What about Trisha? And since Jack picked them up, he must be done for the day at work—"

"He said he was taking the afternoon to play golf. He took Trisha to…to drop her at a play date."

Aunt Phyllis is cracking her knuckles. She does that during poker games too—when she has a lousy hand.

"At Hilldale Country Club?"

Aunt Phyllis nods furiously.

Now I know something is fishy. First of all, we're not members of the country club. And secondly, why would he take Trisha to a play date without first mentioning it to me?

Unless it's to the Western White House—Lion's Lair—which is here in Hilldale.

To meet with Lee.

Jack is hiding the mission from me. He's using Trisha as his beard.

He doesn't think I can handle it anymore. But I can—and I will.

And I know just what will get me through the door:

Intel.

And pie.

# Believe

Performed by the pop artist Cher on the 1998 album by the same name. The song was written by Brian Higgins, Stuart McLennen, Paul Barry, Steven Torch, Matthew Gray, and Timothy Powell. As a matter of fact, Cher also claimed to have a hand in writing it.

The song was ranked as the #1 song of 1999 both on *Billboard*'s "Hot 100" and "Hot Dance Club Play" charts. It was also Britain's biggest-selling single of 1998.

The song turned out to be the biggest single in Cher's entire career. She was the oldest female artist (at the age of 52) to perform this feat.

*Unbelievable!*

*This expression is overused, for one obvious reason: it's easier to exaggerate than to be exacting. In fact, here are a few of the many things that may be described as unbelievable but aren't necessarily so—except under these circumstances:*

*Catching a ball in sports. They've been caught in the air, against a wall, and from behind. However, if someone were to catch one in their teeth, then yes, "unbelievable" would be a great way to describe it.*

*A horse race. Horses win races all the time—some at great lengths or at record speeds. But only if the horse is riding the jockey when they cross the finish line could the event earn the adjective "unbelievable."*

*Lovemaking. Birds do it, yes, and so do bees. According to another legendary song, even educated fleas (albeit this last one is a stretch) do it. Watching two contortionists go at it may also open eyes to some feats never seen performed before, but let's face it: for it to be unbelievable, it's got to take place under pretty special circumstances. Certainly, skydiving would qualify. But one would hope that the climax would in no way be anticlimactic—say, after the lovers hit the ground.*

IT'S SUCH A BEAUTIFUL DAY THAT I DECIDE TO WALK THROUGH Hilldale and up the gentle hill crowned by Lion's Lair.

I've been there enough times—both as a guest and as part of POTUS's governmental entourage—that the Secret Service detail's check of me is cursory at best.

Lee's secretary, Eve, is summoned to meet me at the front door in order to escort me to the elevator that will take us to Lee's private office, on the mega-mansion's second floor. She is one of the few people in Lee's life whose loyalty goes unquestioned, at least by me. She proved it when she discovered her predecessor's iPad held the key to the Quorum's covert surveillance, both in the West Wing and Lion's Lair.

She is surprised to see me, but gives me a welcoming hug nonetheless. "I'm so glad to see with my own eyes that you're up and about."

"Thank you. And it's great to be back to work." Here's hoping I'm right.

On the way to Lee's office, we pass the library. Babette's biographer, Scarlett, sits at a desk facing a window that affords her a view of all of Hilldale. She is perusing what looks like a photo album.

Before she has a chance to turn around, I zip past the door.

Eve arches a brow.

"I'm, um, late enough as it is," I explain. "If I run into Babette—"

Eve grins. "No worries there. Ms. Packard is the only one here from FLOTUS's staff. She flew in with us in order to do historical research necessary for the biography."

Noting my relief, Eve whispers, "She'll never even know you were here."

I blush at the realization that Eve knows my true feelings about Babette. I would imagine she already knows Babette's about me as well.

THE PING OF THE ELEVATOR ALERTS THE PRESIDENT'S SECOND-FLOOR security detail.

Seeing me with Eve, U.S. Marine Corps Major Gordy Collins looks up and smiles. "Talk about a sight for sore eyes," he exclaims playfully. Noting the pie in my hands, he adds, "Not to mention empty stomachs."

As one of the three rotating military attaches assigned the task of carrying and guarding the satchel holding the nuclear codes with his life, Gordy has the privilege of sitting in a chair right outside the door, unlike the two Secret Service agents who stand on either side of Lee's office. However, he gets up when he sees me.

"We'll save a piece for you," I promise.

He laughs. "I doubt it. POTUS is in bachelor mode. He's got the chef here making all the dishes FLOTUS wouldn't let him eat during her pregnancy. But not even the chef can match your cherry pie."

"The First Lady…she delivered her child already?"

"Yes! It was all over the media—" Suddenly, Gordy's grin fades. "Gee, I'm sorry, Donna! I forgot that you were…" His voice trails off. But of course, he would have been standing right outside my hospital room door while Lee visited me.

Gordy continues, "Harrison's birth was almost a week ago now. It was a big thing for her to give birth to the little guy there in the West Wing. FLOTUS barely made it back to the White House, though. Sadly, we hit turbulence on the ride back to D.C. Everyone felt a bit queasy. As far along as she was, I'm sure it helped to speed things up."

"What day was the blessed event?"

He thinks for a moment. "Wednesday."

It was the same day my family chose to be my last.

I'm sure that the child's real father, Salem would have found irony in that.

As for Lee, the day would have been a bittersweet one.

One of the other agents knocks on the door for me.

"Enter," Lee's deep voice is heard plainly through the thick double doors.

The agent opens it but then steps aside for me to do as Lee commands.

I smile supremely, but I'm not surprised that POTUS is the only one smiling back at me.

Ryan's eyes open wide, but he wears his usual poker face.

Jack's frown makes his feelings all too obvious: he's upset that I am here.

Well, too bad. I've got the best reason possible: I have something they need. And I want something in return.

"Donna? Wow! So glad to see you up and about!" Lee's kind

words are proffered with a warm hug. He looks down at the pie. "And you come bearing gifts."

"Like the Trojans," Jack murmurs.

Ryan's way of ignoring him is to say, "Thank you, Donna. But you didn't need to—"

"Bring homemade pie? Why, it's my pleasure. It's great to be back on my feet." I take the chair next to Lee, which is opposite of the couch on which Jack and Ryan are seated. "What did I miss?"

"Well…" Ryan frowns. My appearance has thrown him off his stride. "We're bringing Lee up to date on the reconnaissance we've gotten thus far."

"I see! So, you've already mentioned that there was the correlation between the ransomware used in attacking the hospitals and utilities and what was used to attack the governmental security systems?"

Ryan's eyes open in surprise. "Yes…"

I add, "But that one of the terrorists' real goals was to cover Eric Weber's escape from Magic Mountain."

"We were just discussing that," Jack declares dryly.

Until now, I don't think he realizes how much I heard while I was unconscious. I guess now he's afraid I'll blurt out how I know it because he shakes his head as a subtle warning to shut up.

*No way, guy. That was only the entr'acte.*

"Good," I smile benignly at him. "And, of course, the leaks of government data to the dark web was just another way for Eric and his patchwork of Quorum contacts to point us in the wrong direction."

Lee grimaces. "We were discussing it now. As you can imagine, it's a sore spot with me—and with the intelligence community. Congress has been slow to release funding for our cyber security infrastructure."

"Lee, Acme has also deduced that the security systems in those outlying government buildings were soft targets used to test the

NSA's response," I reply. "Our latest intel bears out the theory that Eric Weber's mission is much bigger—with greater consequences."

Jack and Ryan stare at me as if I've lost my mind. But before they can rebut anything I say, I give Lee the punch line: "Mr. President, you are the real target. And the Quorum wants to take you down *inside* the White House."

Lee is as stunned as Ryan and Jack. Finally, he murmurs, "Do we know when? Or how?"

"We're still…"—Gee, how do I put this?—"deciphering those pieces of the riddle."

"You mean intel, don't you?" Jack retorts.

"Babette is in the West Wing now, alone…with Harrison." Lee paces the floor. "I'd planned to stay here for a few days to take the spotlight off of her for a while. I arranged a series of diplomatic meetings and photo ops to happen here at Lion's Lair. But if the terrorists have broken through the White House security platform, I should head back as quickly as possible."

"Understandable," Ryan murmurs. "While our ciphering team works around the clock with the clues we have"—he glares at me —"perhaps we should shadow the White House security detail for any anomalies that don't fit the usual pattern."

"Of course, Acme will be the onsite point team. After all, you detected this problem. I'll let the White House's Director of Security, Dirk Rappaport, know he can expect you there within the next thirty-six hours." Lee rises. Turning to me, he adds, "Babette was concerned enough about your plight that she visited you in the hospital. I'm sure that she'll be grateful to see how well you're doing—and enjoy showing off little Harrison to you."

Jack says, "But Donna shouldn't—"

"Intrude? Nonsense! It's a direct order." Lee's tone dares him to push the matter. "So far as Babette and I are concerned, you're both family. You know us better than anyone. We can't keep secrets from the Craigs." To make his point, Lee pulls me in for a good-bye hug.

His lips linger on my cheek.

By the time I've pulled away, Jack has stalked out.

"Lee is so full of shit!" At least Jack has waited until Ryan's car is beyond the ornate gates of Lion's Lair before declaring this out loud.

I took the passenger seat so that I didn't have to look him in the eye. But even from the back seat, I imagine the anger I'd find there is just as bitter as I hear in his voice when he says, "And by the way, despite President Chiffray's personal invitation for you to join us in DC, you're staying put right here until you're completely healed."

"It wasn't a 'personal invitation,'" I counter. "It was a direct order from our Commander in Chief."

"No—you're wrong," Jack retorts. "It was yet another one of his flirtatious come-ons to you—"

"Children, please!" Ryan slams on the brakes so hard that we're all jerked forward. I bite my lip to keep from yelping when my seatbelt presses against my wound.

When Ryan is assured that he has our silence, he declares, "Donna, you don't get to decide who goes on this mission." Realizing I'm about to protest, he adds, "I'm not through, Agent Craig." He shifts the rearview mirror so that he can look Jack in the eye. "And you, Agent Craig, have no say in it either."

Leaning forward, Jack sputters, "In other words, you're going to kowtow to POTUS's whim to get a little eye candy while we're saving his ass yet again?"

"I'm certainly going to take it into consideration," Ryan proclaims. "But first and foremost comes Donna's health and wellbeing—"

"Oh. Well, good then." Jack grins as he eases back into his seat. "Sorry, Donna, but you heard the Man."

Ryan growls, "'The Man' hasn't finished speaking."

Jack grimaces, but he keeps his mouth shut.

"I'll get an update from Jonah on Donna's stamina, and from Dr. Friedman on her physical wellbeing," Ryan continues, "as well as a report from Dr. Bellows on whether he feels Donna has demonstrated PTSD or lapses in her mental capability."

Jack shifts his gaze to me. Softly, he says, "Donna, are you going to say anything to Ryan, or should I?"

I feel myself blushing.

But before I can tell him myself, Ryan responds, "Jack, if you're referring to Donna's visions while she was in a coma, she has already made me aware of them." He sighs. "Frankly, as spot on as the first one was, I pray she'll remember more of them."

Jack turns to Ryan. "But…that thing about Varick singing her some sort of clue—"

"Turned out to be true," Ryan reminds him. "Eric is our suspect." His eyes shift in my direction. "Right before you walked in, we'd mentioned to POTUS that we have evidence that ties Eric to the hacker who initiated the ransomware: a Bitcoin payment made from a still-active Quorum account."

"Ryan, that still doesn't justify sending Acme on a wild goose chase because of some riddles in Donna's dream state."

"We'd be remiss if something did happen to POTUS and we did nothing to stop it," I point out.

"Exactly what 'vision' sent you traipsing into Lion's Lair?" Jack asks.

"Nola was in it. Her clues were odd, but they do make sense," I insist.

"Tell us," Ryan replies.

"Okay but…hear me out before you say anything."

Jack's answer is to stare out the window. Ryan's nod is all the assurance I need.

"Nola gave me the riddle. I'd just won a fight with Sebastian Gillingham in the ocean." I shudder again at the thought. "She pulled up in a sailboat. When I asked her where Eric's act of terror would take place, she mentioned that there 'wasn't much time since the sun is setting in the west.' At that moment, a pigeon flew overhead. It landed in the boat because its wing was broken."

Jack leans forward in his seat. "I don't get it."

"The sun setting in the west, and a broken wing," Ryan murmurs.

"Exactly!" I exclaim.

"And what did she say would happen there?" Jack asks.

"She didn't say it. The pigeon…" I'm so excited that for a moment I forget the other thing about the bird…

*Heck! What was it?*

Jack smirks, "The pigeon said something to you?"

"Yes. It cawed out Lee's name." It's my turn to look away. At the time, I thought it was telling me that Lee was in my hospital room—but now is not the time to get into that with Jack.

"What prodded your memory about this particular adventure?" Ryan asks.

"Rin Tin Tin. He came into the kitchen with a live pigeon between his jaws. The bird's wing was broken."

Jack shakes his head in disbelief. "Now I've heard everything!"

"You've got to admit, Jack, that it's quite a coincidence." Ryan counters.

"Yes—but that's all! Look, Donna—you got what you came for: Acme is following up on your paranormal intel. That still doesn't mean you're well enough to tag along."

"Tag along?" I sputter. "How dare you, Jack Craig!"

"The only reason Lee wants you there is so that he can ask you to…" His voice breaks from despair.

Ryan's bushy brows rise almost to his non-existent hairline. "So that President Chiffray can ask her what?"

Jack must be thinking about Lee's proposal to me while I was comatose. I don't know what he's so worried about. Whether I'd been awake or unconscious, I would have said no.

Still, I bat my eyes at him innocently.

Angrily, he turns to Ryan. "Okay, if you're going to let Donna's hunch play out, then as her husband and—I'm still the mission's leader, I assume—"

"For now, yes."

Ryan's answer doesn't deter Jack from making his point. He smiles grandly. "Good to hear it. As I was saying, even if Jonah and Dr. Bellows' assessments clear her for duty, as both her husband and her mission leader, I retain the right to personally assess her physical and emotional stamina."

"Sounds kinky," I purr.

"This isn't a joke, Donna," Jack retorts. "The lives of my mission team are on the line."

I can barely hear Carl's whisper: *Shoot the messenger…*

"And yours," I murmur sadly.

"Thanks for your acknowledgment of that." Jack's statement is cold and crisp.

Ryan looks over at me. "Are you okay with Jack's parameters?"

"Yes," I reply.

Jack is silent the rest of the way home.

WHEN IT COMES TO THEIR MOM AND DAD, OUR KIDS HAVE built-in radar.

When one parent (Jack) gives the other (Me) short, barbed, or pointed answers, all roughhousing stops. This happened when Ryan called Jack and me to say that Jonah gave me a clean bill of health. In fact, Jonah's exact words were, "I've never seen someone work so hard, or get results so quickly."

When one parent (Me) either ignores the other (Jack) or only speaks to him in frosty overtones, chatter comes to a standstill. This happened after Ryan texted Dr. Bellows' assessment that "Donna's trauma is typical of most coma patients. She accepts that her psychotic experiences were, in fact, delusions exacerbated by the guilt she feels for those who died on her watch. On the other hand, her near-death experience has given her clear purpose as to how to make the most of her new lease on life. My assessment is that her participation in the mission will give her closure on her recent subconscious activity."

When their dad stomps off to sleep in the guest room, it's time to duck and cover—like when Jack asked me, once more, to stay home for my own sake.

I said no.

At least, from the guest room, he can't hear me cry.

---

18

# I Don't Wanna Fight

---

Sung by Tina Turner on the 1993 soundtrack album for her autobiographical movie, "What's Love Got to Do with It." Written by British songbird Lulu, Billy Lawrie (Lulu's brother), and Steve DuBerry.

It remains Turner's last single to chart in the Top Ten of *Billboard*'s "Top 100," where it reached #9, as well as #1 on *Billboard*'s "Adult Contemporary" chart.

*Love means never having to say you're sorry? As if!*

*Couples argue. It's inevitable. So, how can you keep your silly little tiff from escalating into a full-scale nuclear war?*

- *Tip #1: Try to reach a compromise. By that, I don't mean you choke him unless he says, "I'm sorry," or by suggesting dueling pistols at five paces instead of ten.*
- *Tip #2: Take a walk around the block to cool off. And yes, you should not stop off at the local gun shop while you're out. Our anger should not lead us to temptation.*

193

- *Tip #3: Never go to bed angry. In fact, if you don't kiss and make up before midnight, try to sleep with one eye open in case your spouse "accidentally" drops an anvil on your head.*

*I mean, let's be honest: no one wants to die while asleep.*

Jack says nothing on the drive to Acme.

When we get there, he leads me into the basement and down a long hallway to the very last door. Beyond it is what Acme euphemistically calls "the Box," a tiny windowless room, where hostile witnesses are interrogated.

I go in first. When he closes the door behind us, it clicks ominously.

The room barely fits one desk and three chairs. Arnie sits behind the desk. He's playing with the buttons on a polygraph machine. When he sees me, he turns red but points to the chair next to his. He clears his throat. "I'm, er, going to have to hook you up."

*Hmmm.*

Okay, I get it. Jack is doing his best to intimidate me. What does he expect me to confess to—that I indeed made a pact with the devil who has allowed me to live in order to carry out some diabolical plot to end all of mankind?

Dammit, I wish I could remember what Carl told me…

I plop down in the designated chair and purr, "Hook me up, Buttercup."

Reluctantly, Arnie places my arm flat on the desk and attaches wired bands on my index and ring fingers. Next, he wraps a heartbeat monitor cuff around the bicep of my other arm. He then puts a belt around my abdomen. It holds six tiny straps, attached to suction cups.

Arnie picks up one of the suction cups. "Um… I'm supposed to attach these doohickies to your, er, chest."

"Let me make it easy for you," I murmur as I unbutton my blouse, exposing my black lace push-up bra.

Arnie stares down, entranced.

"Ah, hell, give that to me!" Jack snatches it out of Arnie's hand.

The whole time he's adhering them to my flesh, his eyes never meet mine.

"State your name," Jack demands.

"Donna Craig," I respond.

"Don't you mean Donna Stone?" he retorts.

I pause just a second before responding: "No. Donna *Craig*."

Arnie winces. I don't take this as a good sign.

"Were you recently in a coma?" Jack asks.

"Yes."

"While in the coma, did you have delusions?"

"No. I heard the conversations of those around me, including those of my mission team, discussing recent hacking of governmental security agencies."

"You're now saying you had no delusions? But didn't you tell me that you had a conversation with the Grim Reaper?"

I hesitate before answering: "Yes," I say emphatically.

"Didn't you also tell me that you made a pact with him in order to come back to the living?"

Ah, heck. In for a dime, in for a dollar. "Yes."

"While in Hell, did you happen to run into one of your hits—an operative named Varick, who had once worked with Eric Weber?"

"Yes."

"And he was starring in some Satanic version of a Gilbert and Sullivan musical?"

"Not starring in it. He sang a clue using the lyrics from one of their shows, *The Mikado*—"

"Ah, I see." Jack tamps down a smirk. "And did your visit to Hades include fighting again with others whom you'd previously killed?"

"Yes. Six of my hits." I shrug. "It was supposed to be seven, but the seventh fight got botched—"

"Thank you," Jack declares. "That ends this session."

"Huh?... That's it?" I glare at him.

"Yes. You passed."

"Oh!" I yank the suction cups off my breast. "Good! Let's tell Ryan."

"Agreed. The sooner he realizes you truly believe you've been to Hell and back, the sooner he'll order you to take the time you need to rest. It's the first step for getting back in the field after suffering Post Traumatic Stress Disorder."

"But the fact that I passed the polygraph means I was telling the truth!"

"You're wrong, Donna. All it means is that you really *believe* these paranormal delusions." I'd like to smack that smug grin off his face. "But I was impressed with the depth of your conviction. In fact"—Jack looks down at Arnie's scribbling—"only one answer was false: when you answered 'no' when I asked you if your name was Donna Stone."

"I hesitated only because of how you asked it," I insist.

Jack shrugs. "Not buying it. The machine never lies, but people do." He turns to Arnie. "Get the recording to Ryan. Tell him we're moving on to the physical fitness portion of Donna's assessment."

Arnie nods at him. But when he sees how upset I am, all he can do is shrug helplessly and turn away.

Jack smiles down at me but points to my chest. "You may want to button up."

True. And I may want to *beat* you up, I think.

I'm about to get my chance. I pray I don't bust my stitches trying.

～

"OKAY, LET'S GET THIS OVER WITH." JACK'S COCKINESS IS SUPPOSED TO throw me off my game.

I'll be honest; I'm a bit nervous. He doesn't know the full extent of my pain, and I'm not going to show it to him now.

We're both dressed for battle, which means the kind of clothing that allows for movement and flexibility—nothing that your opponent can hang onto or use against you. For me, it's a one-piece black catsuit. Underneath it, I've wrapped my wound tightly so that there is no indication that I was ever injured. No need to remind Jack why we're here in the first place.

For him, it's a black wrestling singlet, except it's got the full-length coverage of a surfing wetsuit. In other words, if he keeps taunting me, I'll have to figure out a way to strangle my husband without yanking his belt out of his pants and putting it around his neck like a noose.

That won't be too hard since we're standing in Acme's tactical warrior gym. I've got all sorts of goodies to choose from. The four padded walls of this sixty-by-sixty-foot windowless room are intermittently lined with ropes of varying sizes, garden tools, an assortment of cutlery with blades in varying widths, and a wide collection of home accessories.

We are alone except for the webcams that hang in the top corners of the ceiling. I'm sure Ryan will be monitoring the action, and not just to verify my readiness.

He wants to make sure we don't kill each other.

From the look in Jack's eye, it may happen—

Which is why I'm the first to come out swinging.

～

Jack and I are standing side by side. Still, I'm far enough away to hit him with a sidekick that takes him off balance.

He lands on the floor with a grunt. And yet, he's smiling.

"Clever," he acknowledges. "But not as cunning as all the salt you put in my scrambled eggs this morning." He hops back up. Crouching low, he runs at me.

As I back away, I scan the walls. Ah, I see what I need. "Consider this payback for my freezing shower this morning. I thought you said you were going to fix the thermometer in the water tank." Jack ducks at the cheap ceramic bric-a-brac I hurl at him.

He's not so lucky with the round metal platter that comes flying his way. When it glances off his shoulder, he grimaces. "I thought I had fixed it. *It was supposed to scald you.*" He shrugs. "My bad."

He charges at me again.

I've got just enough time to grab a machete. Jack sidesteps my first jab and dodges when I swing it at his chest. "That would have done some damage," he mutters, crouching low.

I circle him, the blade ready to strike again. "Glad you think so. I want to leave no doubt that I'm up for this mission."

Jack's hand reaches back toward the wall behind him, grabbing hold of a bamboo pole, which he swings in my direction.

It strikes my wrist. I yelp as I drop the machete.

Jack laughs. "I disagree with Jonah. Your reflexes aren't yet up to par." To prove his theory, he comes at me, swinging the pole at my neck.

It's my turn to duck and tuck into a roll, just out of his reach.

When I leap up, I'm close enough to a wall holding an axe. One quick swing and I've chopped his pole in half.

He can't help but nod admiringly, even as he comes at me again. "I hope that's not some sort of metaphor."

I toss the axe far away and grab the fallen half of the pole, which has rolled just a foot away from me. "You men! Why does everything revolve around your—"

I don't have time to finish the sentence because Jack takes a swing at me.

I brace his pole with mine.

The blows keep coming, but each one is blocked high or low, or deflected on one side of me or the other.

But Jack keeps getting closer and closer until, finally, he's close enough that my only defense is to brace my pole against his.

For what seems like forever, we stand there, practically nose to nose—

But he's stronger. He shoves the pole against me—

Slamming me back up to the wall. His pole, held against my shoulders, makes it difficult for me to move my arms—

But not my head. When my noggin slams into his, he folds.

Stunned by the pain, I fall beside him.

We lie there, side by side.

Jack gasps, "Nice head butt. Did one of your ghostly ghouls teach it to you?"

I'm breathing heavy too because my head hurts. However, I force a smile on my face. "Nah. Although I did crack a few skulls when I was in Hell." So that we're eye-to-eye, I roll on top of him. "Frankly, I prefer some of Babette's moves—like this."

I kiss him, long and hard.

When our lips part, Jack sputters, "How did you know that? You heard us kiss?"

"You can't hear a kiss. I already told you I was conscious during my coma," I point out. "I *saw* it."

"You…what?"

He wants me to set the scene? Sure, okay. "You. Babette. My hospital room. Remember? She wanted to 'comfort you.'" I make smooching sounds.

Then I do more than that: I reach for his groin.

He's a man so, yeah, it hardens at my touch.

Did it also stiffen when she touched him?

"Cut it out," he growls.

But he doesn't move. And he certainly doesn't push away my hand.

Like he did when she reached for him.

"Thanks for putting her in her place," I murmur.

His eyes widen at the thought that, yes, I also saw him shove her away.

My eyes soften as a come-hither smile rises on my lips.

But as he leans in to take advantage of my invitation, Carl comes into my mind. His warning plays again and again in my head:

*You must kill Jack…It's the only way to stop Eric…*

By all means, I've got to stop Eric—

Jack gasps, "Donna—stop…*choking me!*"

I must have closed my eyes because when I open them, I see that I'm holding one of the poles against Jack's throat.

When I loosen my grip, Jack jerks the pole out of my hands and throws it as far away as possible. He barely has time to roll out from under me before dry-heaving onto the floor.

Ryan shouts through the room's intercom, "Donna, I think you've proven your point."

His footsteps can be heard as he walks away from the microphone.

I crawl over to Jack. "Look…I'm sorry! I guess I got carried away! Let me see if there's a bruise."

But when I try to examine his throat, he swats away my hand. "Just…don't touch me."

"Jack, I didn't mean to hurt you. Please, believe me!"

"You could have fooled me," he retorts. He rises to his feet. I guess I can't expect him to be a gentleman and help me up since I nearly crushed his larynx.

The door opens. Ryan sticks his head through. Gruffly, he warns, "Thank you, Agents Craig. I think we now have validation."

"I'll say we do," Jack mutters.

Ryan nods. "I'm glad we're in agreement. Okay, Donna, you're mission-ready."

"Are you kidding me?" Jack shakes his head in disbelief. "Didn't you see what happened here? Donna almost killed me, Ryan! It was as if…as if she lost her mind or something!"

"Do you think it might have something to do with all the jibes you've thrown her way all morning?" Ryan jabs a finger in my direction. "Your wife came back from the dead—and somehow she had intel that has already panned out on our suspect. Even if she's just in the vicinity, one of her premonitions may prove useful."

"Great. Now we're Ghostbusters," Jack mutters.

Ryan heads for the door. "Both of you: clean up and grab your gear. The plane leaves in an hour." As he passes Jack, he adds, "Next time, you'll know better than to taunt a woman scorned."

*A woman scorned…*

The vision of Midge Kelsey in the cemetery destroying everything in her path comes to mind, sending a shiver down my spine.

The thought is interrupted by noises coming from the intercom. Apparently, Ryan forgot to turn it off before he left because Arnie can be heard saying, "Darn it! Okay, Emma, I owe you five. But, hey, Dominic is in for ten, so I guess I got off easy."

Emma snorts, "Ha! Yeah, well, I guess I can whistle *Dixie* before I see *that* Hamilton…"

# 19

# You're Gonna Get Rocked

RECORDED BY LA TOYA JACKSON. WRITTEN BY FULL FORCE. RELEASED in March 1988. This single peaked at #103, barely missing the *Billboard* "Hot 100." It also peaked at #66 on the *Billboard* "Hot R&B/Hip-Hop Singles & Tracks" chart, and #90 in the United Kingdom.

*Wanna rock his world? Well, of course, you do! Here's how:*

- *Rockin' Him Trick #1: Put on a sexy negligee! (Tip: It should not be see-through, but opaque, to hide your ever-present Flashbang Bra Holster.)*
- *Rockin' Him Trick #2: Spritz perfume behind your ears and knees. (And if he gets too frisky too fast, you can spritz him in the eye too, which will immediately calm him down—as soon as he gets back from the emergency room.)*
- *Rockin' Him Trick #3: Try something in bed that you've never done before (wink, wink). Word of caution: depending on how*

*much perfume you're wearing, stay away from fire. You want to rock his world—not blow it up, and you along with it.*

THE SEARCH OF THE WHITE HOUSE WILL TAKE ALL NIGHT.

Each member of my mission team has been shadowing a specific White House security detail, which includes bomb-sniffing dogs.

Lucky me, I'm in Detail A, which is charged with securing the First Family's private residence on the second and third floors of the White House.

We were only allowed to search after ten in the evening. The aide who greets us, Candace Forster, warns us to stay out of the master bedroom, Harrison's nursery, and Janie's room.

"The Chiffrays have retired for the evening. The First Lady just delivered her baby," Candace reminds us. "A healthy boy! But needless to say, she's exhausted, so please be as quiet as possible."

We nod as we continue to swarm through the residence but we find nothing out of the ordinary: no incendiary devices, no cache of unauthorized arms, let alone anyone with a fake clearance badge. No people without proper clearance in places they should not be; no doors that shouldn't be unlocked but should now give free access; and no rooms that are locked by those who shouldn't have access to them at all.

One of the unlocked doors leads to the personal library in the First Family's quarters. We know Lee must be in there now because two of Lee's Secret Service detail stand at either side of the door, and Gordy has taken his position as well.

Lee is sitting in one of the room's two easy chairs next to the room's large palladium window. It looks out over the ornate Eisenhower Executive Office Building. He looks up when he hears us enter. His eyes widen the moment he realizes that I'm part of the security detail.

He stands up and walks over to me. When he leans in too close, I take a step back in order to hold out my hand. "Sorry for the intrusion, Mr. President. We'll be quick and quiet so as not to disturb the rest of the household. We'll leave the bedrooms alone."

He grimaces at my pivot, but he knows better than to say anything in front of the others. Instead, he shrugs it off. "Not to worry. The First Lady has already retired. And Janie never wakes up. Harrison is in his nursery with his nanny." He points to one of the two easy chairs facing the large palladium window. Folders are stacked on the table beside it. "I'll keep working there. Feel free to do what you have to do in this room as well."

Two members of the detail, one leading the detection dog, follow Candace down the hall. I'm about to go into another room when Lee asks, "Mrs. Craig, might I have a word with you?"

I nod and follow as he walks back to the window so that we are far enough away from Rappaport and anyone else who may over-hear him. Then, in a soft voice, he murmurs, "I don't know if anyone mentioned it already to you, but I took the liberty of visiting you in the hospital."

I feel my cheeks warming up. "I know."

Lee looks up, sharply. "So, Jack did mention it?"

*Ha! Hardly.* I shake my head. "No…but I—"

I did what—hovered ethereally over him as he kissed me? Watched helplessly as my husband almost punched him out?

Think fast…

"I heard it from one of the nurses. She was quite thrilled."

Lee's smile is hard to resist. When I chuckle, he laughs along with me.

But there is no happiness in his eyes.

Only longing.

As much as it breaks my heart to do so, I say the one thing I know should extinguish the embers of desire that never seem to burn out: "I wish I had been awake to tell you how much I appreciate your friendship and…Babette's."

His way of hiding his disappointment is to shift his gaze to the Eisenhower Executive Office Building, which sits across the White House lawn from the West Wing.

I do the same. I've never taken a good look at the EEOB from this angle. By night, with most of its lights out, it gives its ornately embellished French Second Empire façade the feel of a long-deserted hotel.

Out of the corner of my eye, I catch a flicker in a window directly across from us on the fourth floor.

*Spooks. Ghosts. The building is filled with them.*

Where have I heard that before? Oh, yes, Catherine Martin. She said something else too. It had to do with Lee…

Damn it! If only I could remember.

"Babette has never been your friend," Lee admits. "But you already knew that, didn't you?"

"Yes, I know." My response, faint though it might be, sounds sad even to my ears.

Impulsively, I kiss his cheek.

I turn to find Director Rappaport looking at us with a raised brow. Quickly, he turns and busies himself by running a security wand in a far corner of the room.

My search team is in and out in ten minutes.

By the time we leave, Lee is back in his easy chair.

THE SEARCH HAS BEEN A BUST.

In fact, the most egregious breach was a couple of interns caught in a supply closet, going at it.

Dominic accompanied the detail that found them. Supposedly distressed that both are now to be let go, he slipped the female intern a business card with the promise of "helping you secure other interesting work—er, after I view the security feed of your little liaison here. Perhaps your true talents have yet to be uncovered."

She blushes red at his suggestion. Good for her. Hopefully, she's smart enough to stay away from anything Dominic offers— unless he takes an STD test first.

Director Rappaport's declaration is tired, but firm: "Sorry, Acme folks, but it looks as if this has been a wild goose chase."

"I couldn't agree more." Jack's murmur is low enough that only our mission team hears him.

Miffed, I hiss, "Thus far, my tips have worked out."

"You mean your 'intuition,' don't you?" he counters. "And stop me if I'm wrong, but just like this one, you've misinterpreted all of them."

"Give her credit," Abu says. "One panned out."

"But when it did, it was too late," Jack reminds him.

"Children, let's not air our dirty laundry in public. We can discuss this on your ride home." Ryan's sigh roars through our earbuds. "Donna, admit it: you struck out. For God's sake, it's one in the morning, Eastern Time."

"'Struck out'?" I grumble. "That's rich! Who cares how late it is…"

*Struck. One.*

Salem's words ring in my head: *The clock struck one, and Lee was done.*

"Thank Director Rappaport for indulging us, but wrap this up," Ryan warns me. "He's got an early morning tomorrow. He's testifying in front of the Senate Armed Services Subcommittee Cybersecurity. They're looking for a fall guy for all the recent security breaches. Unfortunately, he may be taking a bullet for the president."

One of Catherine's declarations is just as loud:

*Lee is clueless about the power that is wielded in Washington. I mean, let's face it: He's no Eisenhower. That man knew how to dodge a bullet, literally and figuratively…*

Once again, my eyes are drawn to the window. The Eisenhower Executive Office Building, outlined in the three-quarter moon, looks ominous.

"Dodge a bullet…" I whisper.

"I beg your pardon?" Irritated, Director Rappaport frowns down at me.

"Um—nothing. Sorry, but"—I tap my earbud—"Mr. Clancy asks that you indulge us a bit more. He reminds me that our search didn't cover the Eisenhower Executive Office Building."

Ryan growls, "Donna, I gave you a direct order!"

"The EEOB?" Rappaport sighs, but nods. "Sure, what the hey? Better safe than sorry," he reasons. "We'll go via the tunnel between the buildings. Unit A search the north side, top to bottom. So that this goes quickly, Units B, C, and D will meet us there. B, take the west side. C, take the south. D will cover the east portion."

Jack is with D Unit. Considering the building takes up ten acres of prime D.C. real estate, we shouldn't run into each other. With how he feels about this task, that's fine with me.

Ryan is still yelling in my ear when I pull out my ear bud. What hurts even more is Jack's retort, "Ah hell! Here we go again."

Hell is right.

No, *I'd* better be right.

God, I hope I'm wrong.

WE ARE HALFWAY THROUGH THE TUNNEL WHEN OUR K9 LURCHES forward, almost pulling his handler off his feet. They end up in front of an electrical panel on the right wall. The dog is now on his hindquarters, scratching at it.

One of our detail's IED experts motions for the K9 handler and everyone else to back away. Instead of placing his fingers on the handle of the panel, the IED expert takes out a tiny drill and gets to work on the panel's hinges. When the screws are loosened enough for him to peel back the panel, he peeks in. "It's attached to a bomb alright."

Director Rappaport commands. "Everyone, back up and let the man do his job." He motions to another of the security detail. "Secure every safety door on both sides of this tunnel segment."

We do as he says, making our way back toward the White House. Rappaport follows us through the closest door. It shuts with a tight gasp, signaling that it is hydraulically sealed off from any blast.

ON HIS IPAD, RAPPAPORT IS ABLE TO TAP INTO THE SECURITY CAMERAS that line the tunnel. We sweat it out as the IED expert cuts a wire—

The correct one.

Our detail cheers.

As I raise my voice in solidarity, I hear Nola's voice in my head. My mind's eye sees her again as she pointed to the dove flying over our boat: *Look there—to the west…its wing is broken…*

West. Wing.

The homing pigeon was squawking Lee's name.

My mind flashes back to just a few moments ago, when, as I was standing in the West Wing with Lee, I saw a quick flash of light on the fourth floor of the EEOB…

Catherine's whisper tickles my ear:

*Spooks. Ghosts. The building is filled with them…Carl knows that better than anyone…*

In a flash, it hits me:

Eric is here—

And I'm on the wrong side of the building.

The security door unlocks with a gasp.

I'm through it in no time.

It's now Ryan's voice I hear, shouting, "Donna, where the hell are you going?"

"To the east side of the building! It faces the West Wing!"

"Jack's detail has it covered. Stay with your own!"

Like hell I will.

I run toward the east entrance lobby.

---

20

# Fallin' for You

---

PERFORMED BY COLBIE CAILLAT. RELEASED ON JUNE 26, 2009, IT HIT #12 on the *Billboard* "Hot 100" and #2 on the *Billboard* "Top 40" charts.

*How do you know when you've fallen in love? Here are three telltale signs:*

1. *You're giddy whenever he's around.*
2. *Passion surges through you whenever you feel his touch.*
3. *You never want to let him out of your sight.*

*How do you know if he doesn't feel the same way?*

1. *He frowns whenever he sees you.*
2. *Revulsion makes him shudder when you try to touch him.*
3. *Whenever you're in sight, he runs the other way.*

*So what's a gal to do?*

211

1. *Don't chase. Show some pride!*
2. *Don't cry. He ain't worth the tears!*
3. *Most importantly: DON'T SHOOT. He ain't worth the bullet!*

"HEY—WHERE ARE YOU GOING?" LEONARD, D UNIT'S LEADER, shouts when he sees me.

"Top floor!" I yell back.

"No need. Craig already has it covered," he replies. He shrugs as I fly past him to the elevator.

After pushing the button, my eyes are drawn to the EEOB's celebrated grand staircase. I pause just a moment to peer up at the domed stained-glass skylight five stories above me. With the way in which each of its floors are suspended on elegant white columns, it resembles an exquisite nautilus.

The elevator opens soundlessly. I glance down at my watch. It's two minutes until one.

Each second of the ride is agony.

THE ONLY LIGHT REACHING THE EEOB'S FOURTH FLOOR COMES FROM the full moon's glow streaming in through the skylight. I take off my shoes so that no one can hear me as I run down the marble checkerboard hall to the office suite that faces the West Wing of the White House.

The office's lights are off, but the door is cracked open. I pull out my Sig Sauer P229, holding it low and ready, walking heel-toe to avoid detection or tripping.

As I approach, Arnie murmurs through my earbud, "There's no cam feed in there, but I can send a flying spider drone to the window and take a peek inside."

"Go for it," Ryan commands him.

It feels good to have him onboard, finally.

"Feed is live…" Suddenly, Arnie whistles. "Donna called it! The shooter is at the window and in position—and from the looks of things, he's got a clear shot of POTUS!"

Crouching low, I nudge open the door.

I wait for my eyes to adjust. Yes, I see someone sitting on a chair.

Scarlett Hancock.

Her hair is slicked back. She holds a Heckler and Koch MR556A1 carbine, all tidy with a bipod and suppressor attached. She even sprang for Swarovski glass on top, how fancy.

It's aimed directly at the palladium window of Lee's study—

Where he sits. Babette stands to his side. She has her arms lovingly around his neck.


VARICK'S DITTY PLAYS IN MY HEAD:

*Three little maids in attendance come*
*To one little maid is a bride, Yum-Yum*
*Nobody's safe, for ONE cares for none…*

So, Scarlett is the operative who Eric has on the inside.

Scarlett murmurs. "Shouldn't you have taken off? It's just a few seconds to one." She smirks but she doesn't look up. "Don't they make a cozy picture? Like Jack and Jackie just before Oswald's second hit. Blood splatters on the peignoir will be a wonderful touch, don't you think?"

A bloody nightgown—like the one Valentina wore. It was her second clue to me.

"It was her idea to wear it," she continues. "I even helped her pick it out. I made her model it first, though." She giggles. "I'll bet you wish you'd been there, eh?"

When I don't answer, instinctively, Scarlett turns to see why.

My shot, to her forehead, sends her toppling backward.

"Cleanup on the fourth floor," Arnie declares.

"I'm on my way," Abu assures him.

Who was Scarlett expecting…

Eric, of course. So, he's here too?

That thought sends a shiver through me.

I run out the door. Where is Jack? He should have been here by now.

I head toward the elevator. After punching its button, my eyes are drawn to the stairwell. Each floor below mirrors this one: a mesmerizing checkerboard pattern, framed by an intricate banister that coils its way to the ground floor.

I see Jack two floors below me. Just then, he glances up. Seeing me, his eyes grow big. He frowns.

Because he's looking up at me, he's taken off guard as someone slams his fist into his face.

The elevator pings. I run in and shove my thumb against the button to the third floor and pray I make it before it's too late.

As the elevator door opens, Jack's assailant is splayed faced down, unconscious but groaning. Like Scarlett, Jack, and me, he's dressed all in black.

Catherine was right. This building is filled with spooks.

Jack's gun is pointed at the man. He's about to shoot but stops at the sight of me. Instead, he lowers his arm.

"Thank goodness," I exclaim fervently. "I saw you struggling with him! Are you—"

Before I finish my sentence, he says, "Fine? Yeah, no problem." His voice is hoarse and his grin comes with a shrug. "Saved this too."

Jack's other hand holds a black satchel.

I stare at it. "Is that the president's—"

"Yeah—the nuclear football. Somehow, he stole it," he mutters and then coughs.

Edwina Doyle comes to mind. She's tossing me the football: *Here—catch! But don't drop it!*

When I do, it explodes…

*Nuclear football.*

When I left the White House just now, Gordy was sitting just outside the West Wing library. The satchel—which holds an aluminum briefcase nicknamed the "nuclear football"—was by his feet.

The "Gold Codes" within the briefcase—the numeric sequences the president would use to launch a nuclear attack—are changed daily. However, should anyone gain access to them along with the other items in the briefcase—the Major Attack Options placards and the gold phone tied to a secure transmission channel—our country's nuclear options could be hacked.

Suddenly, Carl's voice comes to me just as clearly as if he's standing next to me:

*He's not Jack.*

But… What?

*Kill Eric—now.*

I stare at the face I've come to know and love. The features are the same: the shape of his cheekbone, the dent in the chin, the curling forelock—

And yes, his eyes are the right color: deep green.

Except that they are too cold—

Too deadly.

They are not Jack's.

Despite the bile seeping into my throat, I manage a smile as I move beside him. I sigh, as if relieved for his safety.

"Thank goodness"—I lean in seductively. When we're nose-to-nose, I whisper—"Eric."

It takes only a moment for him to realize the jig is up. When he does, his smile sours into a grimace. He raises his gun—

But I'm too quick for him. I slap it out of his hand. It flies high before falling over the rail.

Instinctively, his eyes follow it as it falls three stories below.

Even before it clatters onto the checkerboard marble floor, I've wrenched the satchel from his other hand and taken a step back. A high kick, squarely to his chest, sends him over the railing.

As he falls, his scream echoes up through the stairwell.

Through my earbud, I hear the collective gasp of my mission team.

Ryan yells, "Donna—what the hell did you just do?"

Oh, my God! What if…

The man sprawled out on the floor stares up at me.

He, too, is Jack.

Had I not shown up, Eric would have shot him.

Apparently, Jack doesn't see it that way because he's glaring at me as he lifts himself off the floor.

"Here, let me help." I hold out my hand.

"Why? So that you can throw me over—again?"

His words startle me. "What do you mean by that?"

"You shoved that man—a man who looks like me—over a railing three stories up," Jack retorts.

"As you just pointed out, he isn't you," I counter hotly.

"But how did you know that? Donna, when I saw him, I thought I was looking in the mirror! When he turned around, you didn't even give him a chance to speak."

The only thing I can do now is shrug helplessly. The truth is too fantastical—or at least, that's what he'll think. "A wife always knows," I insist.

"Bullshit. You didn't even hesitate." He stares at me as if he's now seeing the ghost I once was. "It wasn't as if you saw me—the *real* me—first before you shoved him, for God's sake!"

"Jack, you'll have to trust me that I knew he wasn't you—that I knew he was…Eric!"

"Eric? But—it doesn't make sense!"

He doubts me. Worse yet, he doesn't trust me.

Abu yells up the staircase from the ground floor. "Whoever the hell he is, I've got a pulse—but barely."

Through our earbuds, Ryan declares, "An ambulance is on its way. Abu, clean up the shooter. You'll find her on the fourth floor: room 467, which faces the West Wing of the White House."

"Right, Chief," Abu answers.

The elevator opens. Rappaport rushes out with two security guards. I hand him the satchel. "If this is indeed what we think it is, then great work," he says jubilantly.

"Dominic, you'll accompany our prisoner to Bethesda Naval Hospital," Ryan commands. "You'll work in eight-hour shifts with Jack and Donna until the suspect wakes up—or expires."

I remember I have a stop to make first. "I'll get there as quickly as I can. Unfortunately, I have to go to back to the West Wing."

"Why?" Jack smirks. "Did you suddenly remember Lee's kiss and his proposal?"

"What are you talking about?" I deny hotly. But my blush tells him he's guessed right.

Angered that he may be right, Jack throws up his hands. "I'm going with the ambulance. Dominic can ride with Donna." He takes the elevator down. The doors close before I can get in too.

I stare down into the lobby, where his twin lies on the floor in a twisted heap. Dominic is kneeling beside him.

When the elevator reaches the lobby, Jack gets out and Abu gets in. He's headed to the fourth floor to see my handiwork.

Dominic stares up at me. I've never seen a more pitying expression.

I guess I've earned it.

# 21

# Back Off Bitch

Performed by Guns & Roses on the band's album, *Use Your Illusion I*. It was written by Axl Rose and Paul Tobias.

Does the song have a backstory? You betcha! In 1982, Axl moved to Los Angeles with his then-girlfriend Gina Siler. They broke up because of his anger issues.

Whereas the lyrics of the song didn't exactly lend itself to airplay back in the day, it helped take the album to #2 on the *Billboard 200* chart, perhaps because it was a crowd favorite with concertgoers, even before the release of the band's debut 1987 album, *Appetite for Destruction*. (Gee, I wonder why?)

*Should some frenemy take it upon herself to be a constant pain in your arse, here are a few things you can do to encourage her to reconsider this aggravating role in your already harried life:*

*First, ask her nicely to check her attitude at the door. If she laughs at the suggestion, smack her head into said door. When she comes to, something tells me she'll duck the next time she crosses your threshold.*

*Next: Reaffirm the adage that she'll "catch more flies with honey than vinegar." To prove this, tie her up and then roll her body in honey so that she can see how many flies show up. If this still doesn't convince her, waterboard her in vinegar. When she comes to, I guess she'll no longer complain about the flies.*

*Finally, have a true heart-to-heart talk with her—literally—by demonstrating how perfectly the shiv you now have in your hand fits between the second and third ribs of her chest. She may whimper as you explain why this would put an end to your friendship (not to mention her life), but one way or another she'll get the point.*

I MAKE DOMINIC STOP OFF AT A 24-HOUR SUPERMARKET BEFORE WE head over to the White House. I come out with two-dozen long-stemmed white roses, tied together with a small blue teddy bear. "For the First Lady," I explain.

He smirks. "You're a cheeky monkey! Are you barmy? I've gotten the distinct impression that she can't be arsed by you."

I laugh. "It's that obvious, eh?" I shouldn't take pride in getting under her skin, but I do. "Who told you that, Narcissa? Chantal?"

"If you must know, both have mentioned it at one time or another—perhaps in unison."

"Speaking out of school, are they?" I bat my eyes. "What else have they told you?"

He puffs up. "Other than I'm a consummate cocksman?"

"I mean, after *that* topic was finally exhausted."

He pouts at the thought. "My dear, 'exhausted'? I can't imagine that is even possible!"

I count to three before starting over. "Surely, their conversation eventually strayed onto other topics! For example, I can imagine that they're quite aware that Babette is still in mourning over Salem."

"Personally, I abhor pillow talk," he grumbles. "But I'm hardly no mouth and all trousers. One must at least attempt some modicum of chitchat between rousing bouts of rumpy-pumpy." His forehead creases as he searches his memory for one of these times. "Ah, yes! Chantal let on that Babette had given Scarlett the heave-ho just yesterday. The saucy redhead stormed out of the West Wing in a huff." He sighs mightily. "Ah, well, there goes my *Charlie's Angels* fantasy: satisfying a blonde, a brunette, and a redhead all at the same time."

"Why was she fired?" I ask.

"According to Narcissa, Scarlett insisted on tagging along to every function on Babette's calendar."

"You just said it was Chantal who told you about Scarlett monopolizing Babette's time."

Dominic cocks a brow. "I say, old girl—it's hard to tell them apart, especially when they're chattering in unison! But the long and the short of it was that she was intrusive. Even in the family's private quarters, Scarlett dominated Babette's time. Now, we know why." He gives me a knowing wink. "That bird was brass monkeys—and it had nothing to do with my prowess—or, that of any other man, for that matter."

"'Brass monkeys'? What do you mean by that?"

"She was cold. Frigid." He looks me up and down as if comparing my temperature with his perception of hers. When he nods sympathetically, I resist the urge to punch him. It can wait, whereas getting to the White House is a priority.

"Obviously, she had an unreciprocated crush on the beautiful Babette," he continues. "Why else would she be driven to kill her?"

I snort. "Who said she was aiming at Babette? She and Eric were trying to assassinate Lee!"

"Such a naïve little fool you are." He chucks me under the chin. "Don't you remember all that blather about Babette's blood spattering on her negligee? What was it the illustrious Ms. Packard said? ...Oh, yes! 'I even helped her pick it out. I made her model it first, though...'" Dominic grins lasciviously. "Sounds to me as if her unrequited love got Eric a bonus hit—well, almost. Babette may owe you her life."

As he chatters on, Scarlett's final words rise in my ear:

*Like Jack and Jackie just before Oswald's second hit. Blood splatters on the peignoir will be a wonderful touch, don't you think? It was her idea to wear it...*

Babette's idea.

Valentina's declaration tickles my memory like a feather: *The wife knows everything.*

Eric was after the nuclear football, whereas Lee's assassination was Babette's idea.

I nod as I fiddle with the teddy bear in my lap, but I'm not just feigning interest. My fingernail has loosened enough threads in the bear's plush belly to slip in a tiny disk that transmits the sound of the softest murmur to one of Acme's many satellites hovering beyond Earth's stratosphere.

Before knotting the seam tightly again, I activate the disk.

A second later, Emma murmurs, "Reading you loud and clear."

Good. Time to clear the air between Babette and me once and for all.

Despite it now being the early hours of the morning, the White House is roused and fully staffed. Word of the attempt on the President's life has put his staff on full alert.

I'll soon find out if Babette is also awake. My guess is yes, if only for the sake of appearances.

Chantal and Narcissa aren't the only White House minions susceptible to Dominic's obvious charms. The night receptionist now guarding the First Family's quarters practically melts under the come-hither gaze emitting from Dominic's baby blue peepers. She barely glances at my bouquet and me as she waves me onto the next gauntlet, Narcissa's desk.

Narcissa must keep her eyes peeled to the lobby's security feed whenever Dominic is in town. Why else would she be practically running down the hall toward him? Make that hopping, because at the same time she's changing into a pair of five-inch Pigalle Plato pumps. This gives me just enough time to slip into a supply closet. If she sees me, she may shoo me away.

When the coast is clear, I walk swiftly to the First Lady's bedroom suite. As always, Lurch and another Secret Service agent are standing close by. Lurch's brow rises when he sees me.

I smile sweetly. After juggling my flowers in one hand, I hold out the other. If he takes it to put me in an arm lock, I'll know that my status with Babette is persona non grata.

To my relief, Lurch shakes my hand warmly. "So happy to see you up and about again. And I'm sure The First Lady will be pleased to see you too." His wink is proof we both know that this is not the case. Still, he knocks on the door.

"Enter," Babette declares. "What took you so long, Narcissa? My God, I need to put out a statement on the assassination attempt immediately…"

Her voice trails off when she sees it's me.

The last vestiges of Babette's baby bump are well hidden under her long-sleeved floor-length silk kimono. Maternity has softened her once sharply etched cheekbones and given her face a healthy natural glow.

Sadly, her puckered pout is the same.

She sits on the living room couch. Her infant son lies in a bassinet beside it.

Chantal sits beside Babette. Seeing me, she almost drops the iPad in her hand. Her frown is practically a snarl.

My way of ignoring it is to murmur, "Dominic and I were just passing by and thought we'd drop this off."

Upon hearing her lover's name, Chantal practically salivates. I wonder which of his many charms elicits this Pavlovian response.

Babette dismisses Chantal with a wave. She doesn't have to ask twice. Chantal is out the door in a flash.

Babette's eyes drill through me. "No need for pretenses. Lee isn't here."

I walk up to her. "I came to see you," I assure her. "May I sit down?"

"Why? Do you plan to stay long? Sorry, but I can't accommodate a social visit at this time. As you know, I just had my son—our son–Harrison."

I sit down anyway and hand her the flowers. "I'm sorry I missed the blessed event."

"Yes, I heard you were predisposed," she replies with a smirk.

"That's one way of putting it." I shrug. "But as you can see, I survived."

Babette pats my hand. "Lucky you."

I put my hand over hers. "Do you mean that? I mean, let's be serious. Wouldn't you rather I'd died?"

She tries to pull away, but I hold on tight. Annoyed, she growls, "Don't be ridiculous! Our girls are inseparable. Janie would have felt morose—for a month, at the very least. And didn't Jack tell you that she and I came to visit?"

"You mean, when you kissed him and told him that you'd always be there to—how did you put it again? Oh, yes! 'To comfort him'."

She wrenches her hand away. "He told you that, did he?" She grins smugly. "Bad boy! What our men won't do or say to see us get into a cat fight."

"Not my style," I assure. "Although, according to Scarlett, you might enjoy a little girl-on-girl action. Isn't that why you invited her to watch as you tried on negligees? Hey, I'm not passing judgment! Your choice in partners—Jonah, Salem—has always shown an exotic bent." I lean in as if I want in on the secret. "Seriously, Babette, is that why you let her go? Or, was it all part of an act to cover up the bigger plan?"

Babette's eyes narrow. "I don't know what you're talking about!" she exclaims hotly.

"Scarlett admitted it." I shrug. "To her credit, she thought she was talking to Eric at the time," I assure her. "As she aimed at Lee from the fourth floor of the EEOB. But you already know she was Eric's shooter, don't you? In fact, you felt comfortable enough with her marksmanship that you offered to distract Lee—in your sexy nightie, no less."

"How dare you insinuate—"

"Sorry, Babette. Her remarks were recorded. Lee will be briefed on them shortly."

She reaches out to slap me—

But I grab her wrist.

"You bitch," she says in a growl. "If you think Lee will take your word over mine—"

"Lee deserves to know the truth."

"He already knows it," she retorts hotly. "He also knows that there is nothing he can do about it. He needed me to get here, and he needs me to stay here."

"You've done everything to undermine his presidency—including conspiracy for treason! For the good of the country, he'll do the right thing," I warn her.

She laughs raucously. "You're such a fool! He's boxed in. Admitting that I tried to kill him will be his political undoing. If I go down, so does he—"

At the sound of Harrison's fearful squalling, we freeze in unison.

I drop her arm.

Big mistake. This time, Babette slap hits its mark. I reel backward.

She stalks over to Harrison and picks him up, nudging aside her robe to put his mouth on an engorged breast. "Shall I ask Lurch to escort you out?" she asks.

"Not necessary. I'm late for a meeting anyway."

I head for the door.

"We got it all," Emma whispers. "What a bitch!"

Before waving goodbye to Lurch, I swing my hair so that it covers the slap mark that still stings my cheek.

Will some foundation cover it up? It's certainly worth a try. I make my way to the nearest ladies' room.

If it didn't hurt so much, I'd laugh at the realization that I was just bitch-slapped by Babette Chiffray.

# He Stopped Loving Her Today

Performed by George Jones. Written by Bobby Braddock and Curly Putnam. Released in March 1980. It reached Number 1 on *Billboard's* "Hot Country Singles."

*Eventually, tumultuous relationships come to an end. Here's how you'll know when the passion you share with your off-and-on-again beloved has finally jumped the shark:*

- *Telltale Sign Number 1: He quits calling. You quit caring.*
- *Telltale Sign Number 2: His lies no longer mean anything to you.*
- *Telltale Sign Number 3: When you're at the target range, you no longer imagine him behind the bulls-eye. He isn't worth the cost of the ammo. It's cheaper to change your locks and move on.*

"Donna! So pleased to see you again." Eve isn't staring at my face, so I guess the makeup did the trick.

She rises to hug me. "And you're right on time! Mr. Clancy presumed you'd be here within the half-hour." She glances at the grandfather clock near the Oval Office door. "I'll buzz the President to let him know you've arrived. He's wrapping up a meeting with Vice President Edmonton, DI Branham, and Mr. Courtland."

I nod as I take a seat.

I'm not in it for long. A few minutes later, the door opens. Lee lingers in the Oval Office's doorway as DI Branham, Todd Courtland, and our new Vice President, Bradley Edmonton, take their leave.

This is my first time seeing Edmonton up close. I suppose Lee chose this former senator and savvy Washington insider as Thomas Drucker's successor—yes, because he was the former Chair of the United States Senate Committee on Armed Services, but also because he's popular in his critical swing state and in the nation as a whole.

Edmonton's Twitter feed profile paints him as an aw-shucks good ol' boy who would "rather be fishing than doing all this politicking." People actually buy into this malarkey, despite his Harvard Law School education, his time as a Rhodes Scholar, and the whip-smart fact-laden soundbites that roll trippingly off his tongue when in front of live cameras. Political pundits have dubbed him, "the silver-haired, golden-tongued fox"—not just because of his full head of salt-and-pepper hair, but because, at forty-five, this once-widowed senior statesman is also one of D.C.'s most eligible bachelors.

In his bespoke Brioni suit and Ferragamo calfskin loafers, he certainly dresses the part.

By the time we're face to face, he's checking me out too. Not that I blame him. I'm just wondering which of my many reputations fascinates him the most. Is it that of the mysterious woman who always has the president's ear? Or maybe he wonders how someone who's been on the *Most Wanted List*—twice—can just waltz into the White House without an invitation.

My guess: he's gawking because, without me, he wouldn't hold the position he now has.

Drucker barely survived an attempt to blow up his motorcade last year, which resulted in the death of his wife, Tilly, and put the vice president in a coma. I was framed for it, but the real culprit was a super soldier whose facial features were altered because her DNA was similar enough that she could pass as my identical twin.

When Drucker woke from his coma, Lee's way of convincing him to resign with a get-out-of-jail-free pardon was to show him the evidence Acme found regarding his act of sabotage: covert surveillance on the President within the White House.

I stand to shake Branham's and Courtland's hands.

"Have you met the Vice President?" Todd asks. "No? Then let me do the honors. Sir, Donna Craig represents one of the Intelligence Community's security contractors, Acme Industries."

When our eyes meet again, Edmonton winks at me.

Cheeky bastard.

His handshake lingers just a moment too long. "After all I've heard about the stunning Mrs. Craig, I can honestly say the pleasure is mine. At least, I hope it will be, very soon." His words flow out as warm and slow as pine sap on a hot afternoon.

Todd and Branham chuckle uncomfortably.

I choose to smile prettily as I lean in and murmur softly, "So sad about Vice President Drucker's accident, isn't it? But I'm sure you'll have no problem following in his footsteps—if not his limo tracks."

Edmonton drops my hand as if it's on fire. He scowls as he strolls out the door.

Well, he can't say he hasn't been duly warned.

Is Bradley Edmonton's allegiance to Lee stronger than Drucker's was? Only time will tell. In the meantime, Lee will have his hands full with a more pressing issue: what to do to a wife willing to commit treason and murder.

As elated as I am to be alive, I don't look forward to briefing him about Babette's role in this latest attempt on his life.

LEE SHOWS ME INTO THE OVAL OFFICE, BUT WAITS UNTIL THE DOOR IS shut before leaning in for a tight hug. "Donna, I didn't elaborate on your situation when we met in Lion's Lair because—well, I didn't want Ryan and Jack to feel uncomfortable. But I have to tell you how great it was to see you…alive. I thought I'd be losing you forever."

"I'm very happy—and very blessed—to be alive," I assure him. It feels good to have someone who cares for you show his joy about it with no remorse.

I wonder if Lee would react as Jack did if I told him that all my intuitions regarding this mission were based on clues I'd received from those in the Afterlife? Would he wince at the madness in my methods, or would he let the outcome speak for itself?

Over Lee's intercom, Eve says, "Mr. Clancy is now on the line."

As I pull away, Lee sighs reluctantly. He walks over to the desk, hits his intercom button, and mutters, "Thanks, Eve. Patch him in."

I'll have my answer soon enough.

"DONNA IS ALREADY THERE, I TAKE IT?" RYAN ASKS THROUGH THE speakerphone.

"Yes, I just walked through the door," I assure him. "I'm ready, at the President's behest." Broad hint: I don't want to be the one to break the news to him.

"Good. Then I'll begin." Ryan takes a deep breath. "So, Sir, I presume that by now you know that the nuclear briefcase that has been in possession of your security detail may, in fact, contain fake or compromised Gold Codes."

Lee winces. "Yes, I was informed of this very disturbing fact. The aides in charge are being investigated now."

Poor Gordy.

Could it have been an inside job? If Eric never regains consciousness, we'll never know. In any event, it's a black mark that now taints the careers of the few who had the privilege to serve in this very important position.

"As for the attempt on my life," Lee continues, "Rappaport divulged that Scarlett Hancock was the shooter, but that she was exterminated by Mrs. Craig. Needless to say, Babette was quite upset."

I'm sure she was, but not for the obvious reasons.

Ryan is quiet before adding: "We have proof that Hancock had co-conspirators."

"By that, you mean Eric Weber?" Lee asks.

"Not just Weber." Ryan clears his throat. "We have reason to believe that Babette also conspired with Scarlett and Eric in your assassination, and in the theft of the Gold Codes."

Lee's eyes meet mine, but neither of us says anything. Finally, I nod.

"Please, explain," he mutters.

Ryan now plays the recording of Scarlett's comments to me as she watched them through the West Wing Window.

My eyes are solely on Lee. He frowns at her sarcastic declaration that they make a cozy picture—"...like Jack and Jackie just before Oswald's second hit."

He frowns when she declares, "Blood splatters on the peignoir will be a wonderful touch, don't you think?"

His eyes widen when she purrs, "It was her idea to wear it. I even helped her pick it out. I made her model it first, though."

And his face becomes a granite mask when she adds, "I'll bet you wish you'd been there, eh?"

Ryan ends the recording.

Lee sits silently for what seems like a lifetime. Finally, he murmurs, "I didn't hear my wife conspiring with an assassin. I heard an assassin laughing about the fact that a kill shot—to me—would spatter Babette with my blood and possibly send her into an emotional tailspin. And I can only imagine what would have happened if Babette were hit instead of me." He closes his eyes at the thought. "In fact, considering Ms. Hancock's professed ardor for her, maybe her target was Babette after all."

"We don't think so." Ryan clears his throat: his tell that more bad news is in the offing. "In fact, we have verification that the First Lady conspired with Ms. Hancock and Eric Weber."

"I beg your pardon?" Lee's shock, leavened by anger, warns Ryan that he's on thin ice.

"I'm sorry to say, Sir, but she admitted as much to Mrs. Craig," Ryan informs him. "Her confession was recorded."

I feel my cheeks redden as Lee turns to stare at me.

If the eyes truly are the windows to the soul, I am looking at a man whose has just lost his.

Not all marriages are grounded in the fertile soil of love. But to learn that your marriage is so fallow that only the seeds of murderous intent are left to sprout is enough to kill one's soul.

I know this first hand.

Ryan adds, "I'll play that conversation for you now."

I shift my hand within Lee's reach.

He looks down at it, but leaves it where it is.

By being the messenger, I may have inadvertently accomplished one of Babette's goals: killed Lee's feelings for me.

Hate truly is the Grim Reaper.

~

I watch Lee as he listens:

My Voice:
Seriously, Babette, is that why you let her go? Or, was it all part of
an act to cover up the bigger plan?

Babette's Voice:
I don't know what' you're talking about!

Me:
Scarlett admitted it. To her credit, she thought she was talking to
Eric at the time while she took aim at Lee from the fourth floor of
the EEOB. But you already know she was his shooter, don't you?
In fact, you felt comfortable enough with her marksmanship that
you offered to distract Lee—in your sexy nightie, no less.

Babette:
How dare you insinuate—

Me:
Sorry, Babette. Her remarks were recorded. Lee will be briefed on
them. shortly.

[Muffled sounds of a struggle]

Babette:
You bitch! If you think Lee will take your word over mine—

Me:
Lee deserves to know the truth.

Babette:
He already knows it! He also knows that there is nothing he can do
about it. He needed me to get here, and he needs me to stay here.

Me:

You've done everything to undermine his presidency—including conspiracy for treason! For the good of the country, he'll do the right thing.

Babette:
You're such a fool! He's boxed in. Admitting that I tried to kill him will be his political undoing. If I go down, so does he—

[Harrison's cries cut her off.]

Lee has sat stoically throughout the conversation but he winces when he hears the slap.

When he turns to me, I look away.

He pushes my hair away from my face. He must see the ghost of her hand mark because he groans softly. He is moved to stroke my cheek lightly.

"Sir?... Are you still there?"

The concern in Ryan's voice is enough to guilt Lee into dropping his hand. Still, he is defensive enough to counter, "Did Babette know she was being recorded?"

"Of course not!" I exclaim.

"Then it is inadmissible as evidence," Lee declares.

"Washington, D.C. has a 'one-party consent' law," Ryan reminds him.

"Covert recordings in the White House are a treasonous offense," Lee insists. "Former Vice President Drucker found this out the hard way—thanks to Acme. I'd hate to ask the DIA to file charges against Mrs. Craig."

Ryan's silence weighs heavy in the room. Finally, he mutters, "Babette committed treason."

"That is still your supposition and yours alone. I don't agree with it in the least," Lee declares darkly. "Unless you have corroboration from one of her supposed co-conspirators. Do you?"

"As you know, Sir, Hancock is dead, and Weber is in a coma," Ryan retorts dryly.

"And if Weber never wakes up, you have nothing other than the ramblings of a new mother suffering from postpartum depression while Mrs. Craig attempts to browbeat a confession from her," Lee points out.

"I did no such thing!" I insist.

"Mrs. Craig, shall we test my theory on the American public, who reveres the First Lady of the United States?"

Ryan and I say nothing.

"Good," Lee says. "And I'm sure that, like me, Acme will do its best to quash any unfounded rumors of the First Lady's involvement."

Ryan's retort is just as steely: "Sir, if you're asking Acme to cover up her crime—"

"I'm not asking Acme to do anything of the sort," Lee counters. "But should such a bizarre story be leaked to the press, needless to say, all branches of U.S. Intelligence would be hard pressed to offer Acme any future contracts."

I'm steaming at Lee's threat. I can only imagine how Ryan feels about it.

His silence speaks volumes. When he finally speaks, it's softer than I'd ever thought possible. "Watch your back, Mr. President. In any event, we will always do our best to keep it covered."

Lee doesn't answer, but by his nod, I know he gets the message loud and clear.

I wait until Ryan hangs up before muttering, "You're an idiot, Lee Chiffray."

He shrugs. "Thanks for your vote of confidence, Mrs. Craig."

I glare at him. "Seriously? You don't feel that Babette should pay for the crime of attempted murder—on you, of all people?"

"I think...I think that my wife has been going through a lot lately, including a difficult pregnancy."

I roll my eyes. "You sound like a lawyer who's testing a defense theory in the hope that it will win your client sympathy votes from the jury."

"If you're saying I shouldn't protect her, well then you don't know me as well as I thought," he replies firmly.

"I'm just saying that it's time Babette quit hiding behind you. Hell, Lee! What I'm saying is that she doesn't deserve you!"

He looks sharply at me. "Even if you're right about that, it doesn't change the fact that I can't have the one woman I want."

I throw up my hands. "I appreciate all you do on my behalf. I—"

In a second, he's at my side. "Don't patronize me, Donna. I'm not asking for your 'appreciation.' I'm asking for your love."

"You have my loyalty. Isn't that enough?"

"Sorry, but no! Look—I almost lost you once. If something should happen to you again, I'd"—the thought stops him cold—"I don't know what I'd do." He sighs. "I once…I asked you to marry me. You were still unconscious—"

"I know." My cheeks heat up at my confession.

Lee frowns. "Jack told you?"

"He didn't have to," I reply. I take a deep breath and then add: "I heard everything."

"Jesus!" Lee shakes his head, awed. "I've heard of cases like that…" His voice trails off as he realizes the consequences of his actions.

"Well, I was one of them." I sit down beside him. "And I appreciated what you said at the time: about loving my honesty, and my strength, and my…my loyalty to you."

"I'm married to a traitor who'd much rather see me dead. At the same time, I'm in love with the one woman who can save me." His wry laughter echoes through the room. "What if she were out of the picture, Donna? Would you reconsider?"

"Don't, Lee! Let's not play the 'What if' game! In real life, there is no what if, only what is." Placing my hand over his, I add, "We have a very odd friendship—more so because neither of the two people with whom we've tied our fate accept the role we play in each other's lives."

Tenderly he strokes my fingers. "What is that role, Donna?"

"We are faithful friends and trusted allies against those who would harm our country."

He tilts my chin so that I can only look him directly in the eyes. "Is that all?"

"What could be more important?" I counter.

"Your love." He takes both my hands in his. "Do you also remember that I told you I loved you, and that should you live, I'd ask you to consider spending your life with me?"

"Yes." My voice is so soft that it sounds a million miles away.

"You're alive, Donna. And I'm asking you."

His eyes won't let go of mine. In their depths I see hope.

But I shatter it when I say: "Lee, I love Jack. And I always will. Forever."

He lets my hand drop in my lap. "I know."

He gets the message loud and clear.

Can you stop someone from loving you? I think you can—with betrayal.

It killed the love I had for Carl.

I wonder if Lee now feels the same way about Babette? If so, would he admit it to me? I think we are close enough that he would.

But now is not the time to ask. I need to leave him on a high note. I try for levity. Slyly, I ask, "Tell the truth, Lee: what if I'd woken up and said yes to your proposal?"

This time, his laugh is genuine. "I'd have been the happiest man alive. Unlike Babette, you wouldn't try to kill me!"

"Don't be so sure. All wives feel like killing their husbands at least once."

He snorts. "And unlike Babette, you'd succeed!" His grin

disappears. "And if not, I'd fight tooth and nail to keep you out of jail."

"Just as you're now fighting for Babette," I reply sadly.

For the longest time, he gazes into my eyes. Then, very slowly, he nods.

*Don't, Lee. She hates you…*

But it's no use. He's made up his mind.

It is said that a dearly departed's loved ones go through five stages of grief: denial, anger, bargaining, depression, and acceptance. Can the same be true for the death of a marriage?

And, if so, surely Lee has been in denial for quite some time.

How long will it take for him to pass through the other stages and accept her role in his attempted murder? For Babette, will his acceptance mean her demise, or will his inaction lead to her resurrection?

"What if she tries it again?" I ask him.

*She will. Lee, you know it too…*

He shakes his head. "She won't. She now realizes that I know the score." His lips rise into a grimace. "We'll soon find out if the adage, 'Hold your friends close and your enemies closer,' rings true." He squeezes my hand. "And if it doesn't, you'll save me—again."

Yes, I will.

And then, I'll kill Babette.

When I rise to take my leave, Lee gets up as well. He hugs me as if he wishes time would stand still.

It won't. We both know it.

I long to go home, but I have one more stop.

# 23

# Let Me Rest in Peace

Sung by James Marsters. Music and lyrics by Joss Whedon.

The song was never released as a single. However, it was part of the 2002 soundtrack album made up of the fourteen songs written for the only musical episode of *Buffy the Vampire Slayer*, "Once More with Feeling." The album reached #49 on the *Billboard* "200" chart; and #3 on the *Billboard* "Top Soundtracks."

The TV episode, celebrated by fans and industry reviewers, was the third-most watched show that week, and is credited with influencing other TV series to "put on a show." Sadly, although the episode was nominated for an Emmy for "Outstanding Musical Direction," the National Academy of Television Arts and Sciences forgot to include it on the ballots sent to its members. And, unfortunately, the make-good postcard to voters did not help it win.

That's okay. For several years after, Buffy's rabid fans flocked to public sing-alongs—until the Screen Actors Guild sued the network for licensing the events. Ah, well. Thank goodness for online clips of the show!

~

*Does a corpse get to rest in peace? Hardly!*

*Decomposition—the breakdown of a dead body—is an ongoing process, especially when it lies a-moulderin' in the grave.*

*To help it along, bacteria, maggots, and other organisms that have used the body as a host while the body was alive are now having a field day in the decay. Talk about a feast!*

*As for the soul, it too goes through a different kind of reckoning. Until we die, we don't really find out if there is a heaven, promised land, Valhalla, etcetera—*

*Which is the best reason to live each day as if it were your last.*

"HAS HE COME TO?" I ASK.

Although Jack's eyes are open and he's seated upright in a chair in Eric's hospital room, he's so exhausted that his head jerks up before he focuses in my direction.

Whereas Acme has the job of interrogating Eric when and if he awakens from his coma, outside the door, two NSA agents are standing guard.

From the look of Eric's medical chart—not to mention his battered body and unconscious state—that's a big if.

Eric's head is wrapped up in bandages. The prosthetic mask he used to pass for Jack is in my husband's hand. Its empty eyes stare up at me like an eerie death mask.

As Jack stretches, he mutters, "No, not yet. How did your 'errand' go?"

"It wasn't fully successful," I admit. "Although I got Babette to admit that she conspired with Scarlett and Eric to murder POTUS, Lee refuses to do anything about it."

"Well, what do you know?" Jack murmurs.

"You sound surprised."

He shrugs. "I guess I am."

"At which part? That she wanted him dead, or that he's letting her skip on it?"

"Personally, I wouldn't mind if he met with an unfortunate incident, so no surprises there."

"I wish you didn't hate him so much!"

"And I wish he wasn't so fucking hot to have you," Jack counters. "As for his being in denial about Babette's true feelings for him, no surprise there, either."

"Why do you say that?"

He shrugs. "She knows he pines after you. That's enough to make any spouse furious."

"But furious enough to kill him?"

"Don't think I haven't thought of it myself," he mutters.

I tap the prosthesis in his hand. "Hey, if she'd had her way, you might have taken the fall, what with Eric masquerading around as you."

Jack nods. "At least now we know why he was able to roam around Capitol Hill without being stopped, let alone arrested." He stuffs the mask into the pocket of his jacket. "Souvenir," he explains gruffly. "I presume you're here to take your shift. I'll leave you to it." He puts on his jacket and heads for the door.

"Jack—wait! Please! We need to…to kiss and make up."

My plea stops him cold. And yes, he laughs at how I put it. But it's a heartless, cold chuckle that implies his total disdain for my request.

He doesn't even turn around as he growls, "Sorry, not this time." He shrugs. "I can't save you from yourself, Donna. I've tried. At the very least, I can save myself from you."

I have no answer to that. After what I almost did to him, he's right.

~

"HOW DISAPPOINTING! I WAS HOPING TO ENJOY YOUR MAKE UP SEX—vicariously, of course." Eric's lustful whisper shocks me awake.

Or am I?

He stands beside me, but he's also in the bed, so I have the answer to my question. The beeps from the monitors surrounding comatose Eric are few and far between.

Eric's soul sees my grimace and shrugs. "It's a shame you weren't successful in enticing Mr. Craig because, as you see, I don't have much time."

"Every act of kindness counts…over there." He knows I mean the Afterlife. "Perhaps, if you answer my questions, the lives saved will count for something—"

His laugh echoes through the room. "Ha! I don't kiss and tell. But if you kiss, I'll tell."

*Ewwww…*

But hey, it's worth it.

I mean, it better be.

He leans in. When his lips touch mine, they are cold with lust and longing.

Our connection allows me to see deep into his soul. I do my best not to pull away, but what I find there repulses me: torturous couplings devised to shred my skin and destroy my soul.

While the stench of his brand on me sears my thigh, he longs to hear me plead for mercy. As he carves his initials in me, I'm to beg for my life. He punches the bullet hole in my gut and laughs when I scream in pain.

He has one fantasy, however, that makes me chuckle: when he rapes me, I'm supposed to enjoy it.

*As if.*

Insulted at my reaction, he pulls back. "I take it I went too far?" he asks stiffly.

"I'm supposed to enjoy it too? *Tsk, tsk,* Eric Weber! You certainly have an over-active imagination!"

One of his monitors hiccups wildly—not a good sign.

"How about we move on to the Q&A portion of the visit?" I ask.

Eric nods.

"So tell me: how and when did you get your hands on the satchel holding the nuclear codes?"

"Not the satchel itself, dear Donna. But the aluminum case within." He shrugs. "Those things all look alike."

"I stand corrected. So, I take it you swapped out one case for another?"

"Go to the head of the class!" He nods admiringly. "Of course, the codes in the fake one won't launch any missiles. However, POTUS would have certainly racked up points in a few MPP games—*Keep Talking, and Nobody Explodes*, for one. I hear it's quite popular."

"You still haven't answered the question of how the case fell into your hands."

"Not exactly the best way to describe it," he retorts. "Like you, Scarlett had numerous talents. One was keeping POTUS's security detail well-hydrated while he slept on Air Force One on his last trip from Lion's Lair to the White House. Some sleight of hand put them to sleep for as long as it took for her to make the slip."

"She would have needed the code to unlock the satchel," I counter.

"Good point! You see, that's where the conniving Mrs. Chiffray came in."

I shake my head in awe. "What was Babette's skin in your game?"

"You mean, besides her usual fifteen percent fee of the proceeds from an auction attended by your country's sworn enemies?" He giggles gleefully. "A more appropriate term would be 'ounce of flesh'." He places his hand over my wound. "Yours."

Now I know: Babette ordered my hit.

"You acted as the middle man with my assassins," I murmur.

"I felt it was a fair trade," he admits.

"Who rigged the bomb in the EEOB's tunnel?"

"Another of Scarlett's specialties. Our IT contact loosened the necessary security precautions that allowed her to do so. It would have added an additional layer of terror to POTUS's hit. Ah, well. Not all great schemes come to fruition."

I shudder when I think of how many innocent people would have been killed.

Time to round up those seeking to do the greatest harm of all. "I suppose the auction's bidders include Russia and China?" I ask. "Can we also expect North Korea? Iran? How about Pakistan?"

"All of the above. A couple of minor players as well, but we anticipated they'd drop out after an initial bid or two."

"Are our enemies still awaiting word on where and when the auction will take place?"

"Yes," he mutters. "Mrs. Craig, you're exacting a high price for that kiss."

"I hope you feel it was worth it."

"I have my doubts," he admits.

"Don't be cruel, Eric. It's *so* not like you... Oh, wait! It is just like you! Now, I'll need the intel on your contacts and your crew."

"So much for my grand resurrection." Eric sighs. "I was staying at the Hay-Adams. The Presidential Suite."

"Under what name?"

He laughs. "Why, Jack's of course!" His monitors are now working overtime. "Anything else, darling Donna?"

"I think that covers it..." I frown. "Eric, I just want to say..."

His eyes soften at my hesitation. I start again: "You'll fit right in."

What else can one say?

He's gone, but I'm sure he heard me.

I make my exit as the crash team rushes in.

------------------------------------

24

# Come Fly with Me

------------------------------------

Performed by Frank Sinatra. Composed by Jimmy Van Heusen, with lyrics by Sammy Cahn. It was the title track of Sinatra's 1958 album, and spent five weeks in the #1 slot on the *Billboard* "200" chart.

Specifically written for Sinatra, the song was a standard in this incomparable singer's concert repertoire, and was prominently featured in at least twelve feature films, including *Catch Me If You Can.*

*When in an airplane's economy class, here is one simple rule of airplane etiquette: have respect for your fellow passengers' personal space.*

*For example:*

*Don't steal another's assigned seat. After all, the seats are all alike (too small for your bum, let alone your legs) and they take off and land at the same time—almost always, anyway. (If not, you've got bigger problems than your seat assignment.)*

*Don't recline your seat. Doing so impinges on the personal space of the person behind you. You may argue, "Well, how am I supposed to relax?" I will counter: "You're not. You're on an airplane." Unless your seat can fully recline—without putting you in the lap of the person behind you—stay awake until you land.*

*(Doing so means you can jump up quickly and get out of that tin can faster than your fellow "bent out of shape" passengers.)*

*Don't fart. Why? you ask. Because everyone who smelt it will know you dealt it. You will become the pariah of the economy class cabin.*

*Suggestion: Consider buying a first class ticket! With the price you paid, in this rarefied air, if you feel a fart coming on, you're free to let it fly. The attendants will pretend they smell roses.*

"More bubbly, Mr. Kahoon?" I smile up at the Pakastani military colonel as I hold out a tray of Baccarat flutes filled with the Moët & Chandon Dom Pérignon White Gold.

Javed Kahoon leans forward from the plush captain's chair in this tricked out Fokker 70 and grabs a glass. He has yet to leave his seat. He was sent by the Pakistan Intelligence Bureau to bid on the nuclear football, and like all the other bidders, he's hoping to end up with the prize to trump all prizes: our country's nuclear codes.

After gulping down his drink, he mutters, "How long before the bidding starts?"

I look at the elegant Calatrava Patek Phillippe watch on my wrist, pretending to gauge his question as it pertains to the reality of this little sting operation. "We just reached cruising altitude five minutes ago, so it should be any moment now," I murmur soothingly.

Apparently, my promise does little to assure him. Still nervous, he turns and stares out the closest porthole.

What Javed is looking at is a looped digital image of Montenegro's skyline projected on a paper-thin vinyl screen. Now and then, Acme's pilot, George Taylor, tilts the wings of the slick private jet just enough to give the impression that we're circling this tiny country's airspace until the last bid has been accepted. Montenegro's lack of extradition agreement with anyone made it an acceptable locale for all the bidders.

In truth, our final destination is a mere forty-five minutes away: the U.S. Army Camp Bondsteel, which is located in Ferizaj, Kosovo. There, our guests will be held as bargaining chips with the countries that sought to ruin our nuclear defense.

Acme had less than a day to come up with a viable plan.

As Eric promised, the list of interested parties was found on a memory card in his room at the Hay Adams. It was taped to the last page of a German-language version of Kafka's *Metamorphosis*.

It took Arnie several hours to decipher it. The card also had the names and contacts of Eric's outside team—yes, Scarlett was among them—as well as the freelancer who released the ransomware and hacked the security systems. He's based in Germany. The BND is already beating the bushes for the guy.

Emma then took the names of the bidding countries and pulled their operatives' bona fides. Along with Kahoon, we're hosting a Russian named Anatoly Popov, who uses his journalistic credentials as a cover for international travel. Also on board is Gong Kwang-Min, a North Korean operative who poses as a South Korean IT student at Cambridge.

China's bidder is the financial industrialist Wen Li, and Iran's Hassan Nouri is his government's senior technology engineer.

It was my idea to hold the auction on an airborne jet. Ryan immediately realized the value in this ploy: no weapons would be allowed onboard, and every inch of the plane is under recorded surveillance to provide the undeniable proof of their participation in the Quorum's scheme.

Dominic is our auctioneer. Abu plays bartender while Arnie acts as the cabin steward, circling our guests with delectable tidbits. While doing so, he's also hacking and scanning the cellular data on their mobile phones.

And I'm the assistant-slash-eye candy to the event's host: the Quorum's CEO, Eric.

Really, it's Jack. I can barely stand to look at him today—not just because it sickens me to know how he feels about me, but because he's now fitted with prostheses that make him look like Eric, whom all parties have met and are expecting to conduct the auction.

When Ryan proposed it, Jack snickered. "Talk about quid pro quo! I only wish I'd known that the Presidential Suite at the Hay Adams was waiting for me."

He would have gone without me. Not that I blame him after my blackout attack on him and the damage I did to his doppelgänger, Eric.

At the moment, Jack is speaking in German to Anatoly. When his eye catches mine, I shift my gaze to Javed so that he too can see that the natives are getting restless.

After giving the Russian's back a firm pat, Jack makes his way to the podium where Dominic stands, gavel in hand. He's still laughing uproariously at Anatoly's request—

Which must have something to do with me because the Russian winks suggestively at me.

Smiling, I wink back.

My role here is to stroke egos. Thank goodness this flight is too short for Mile High hanky-panky—

Did Jack lead Anatoly to believe otherwise? *Why the nerve of him…*

"Welcome, one and all!" Jack's pronouncement, made in English, perfectly mimics Eric's tone and Germanic inflections. "Despite the pleasantries, snacks, and libations, we are here for a bigger purpose." He points to me. "Lola, my beautiful assistant, will hand out the handheld devices from which your anonymous bids will be recorded."

The devices are also registering their fingerprints and scanning for facial recognition: all part of collecting the evidence we'll need to prove their participation in the theft of vital U.S. intelligence.

"As previously discussed, the opening bid begins at a billion dollars," Jack continues. "We anticipate it will rise rapidly from there. All bids will be projected on the monitor to the right of our auctioneer." In a move that was classic Eric, Jack opens his arms wide in a gesture of inclusion. "Gentleman, your bids are now welcomed."

No surprise: thanks to Anatoly and Wen Li, the bids leapfrogged beyond those of Javed and Hassan Nouri.

Gong Kwang-Min hung in there for as long as he could, but even he couldn't keep pace. Seeing his distress, going home may not now be a survivable option. He may actually welcome a long stay at Bonesteel.

The final bid was Anatoly's. Like his Chinese and Iranian counterparts, his blank countenance doesn't give away his status as the victor.

The plane has started its descent. Although the guests have taken their seats, Arnie, Abu, and I are still plying them with their favorite drinks.

When I reach Javed, he waves me away. His dejection is no secret. He slumps down in his chair, glaring out the porthole—

But then something catches his attention. His head swivels up, toward the cabin's interior. Turning back to the porthole, his eyes widen as he scratches at it.

He has etched through the vinyl screen.

I lean beside him, as if offering him a drink. Instead, I flick a catch on my right hand's ring, releasing a tiny syringe with a super dose of Propofol, an instant knockout drug.

He leaps up, perplexed at our duplicity. Still, I'm able to stab him in the neck—

But at the same time, he follows through on his involuntary reflex to fight back, punching me in the gut.

I gasp as I drop into the chair beside him. Though out of breath, I'm able to prop him up without drawing the attention of the others.

I stare down at my abdomen. Blood is seeping through my wound. Thank goodness my dress is the same color.

I'm even more thankful when the plane's wheels hit the tarmac. A moment after, it rolls to a stop. Abu flings open the cabin door and twenty infantrymen rush in to escort our guests out at gunpoint.

But by the time they get to Javed and me, I've already passed out.

# 25

# I'm Sorry

Performed by Brenda Lee. Written by Dub Allbritten and Ronnie Self.

In July 1960, the song made it to #1 on the *Billboard* "Hot 100 Singles" U.S. chart. At the time, Ms. Lee was only fifteen. Her album was released after a debate as to whether someone so young should be singing about unrequited love.

*There is no 'sorry' in relationships? Pshaw!*

*Here are the top three no-no's for couples in love. And since, as we all know, actions speak louder than words, here are the best ways to make amends:*

*No-No Number One: You never say, "I love you."*

*Atonement: Say it loud, proud, and often. Not only that, back it up with a random act of adoration!*

*No-No Number Two: You never take your beloved's drama or trauma seriously.*

*Atonement: Feel his or her pain. By acknowledging your beloved's fear factors, you become her/his super hero.*

*No-No Number Three: Don't lie—because you'll always get caught.*

*Atonement: Hmmm. This is a hard one because it deals with trust— or in your loved one's case, the lack thereof.*

*To resume the lifetime of love you anticipated, devote your waking hours to proving that from now on you'll always live up to your word. Otherwise, you'll spend your sleeping hours with one eye propped open in fear of a bang with a frying pan.*

JACK AND I DRIVE HOME IN A SILENCE SO HEAVY THAT I CAN BARELY breathe. From the way Jack's chest is heaving, I guess he feels the same way.

He's been radio silent since I woke up from my emergency surgery at Camp Bondsteel. The great news: the docs there did a great job of patching me up.

Even better news: the whole time I was out, I had no visitors from the Other Side.

George landed back at LAX's private terminal before dawn. It's early Saturday morning, so the children should sleep for several more hours. Good, because we're both exhausted. I won't be surprised if we don't wake up until Sunday afternoon.

More than likely in separate beds again.

When we get home, Jack trudges up the stairs behind me. Surprisingly, when I turn into the master bedroom, he follows, closing the door behind us.

From the stony frown on his face, it looks as if we're going to have it out here and now.

He seems to be searching for the right words. They come in the form of a question: "Tell me the truth, Donna: did you think it was me you pushed over the banister in the EEOB?"

"No, of course not! I knew…alright, I was told that…that it would be Eric."

"By whom?"

Okay, then, this is our moment of truth: "Carl warned me."

Shock blanches all color from Jack's face. "You saw Carl—at the EEOB? *He's alive?*"

"No." My eyes close as if weighted by my words. Eventually, I mutter, "Like the Reaper, he came to me while I was in a coma—at the same time Nurse Nancy came at you with a syringe! That was when my monitor started beeping like it was the end of the world. *My* world. *Our* world."

Jack's eyes open wide. Incredulously, he murmurs, "So, you saw that too?" He eases himself down onto the bed. "If that's true, I guess I should thank you."

"You're welcome," I say grudgingly.

"So, why didn't you mention Carl before now?"

"Would you have believed me?" I retort.

My hope that my tone convinces Jack to let the topic drop is dashed when he asks, "How did Carl know that Eric would look like me?"

"I don't know! How do the Departed know anything? Maybe they freely roam the space-time continuum." Frustrated, I throw up my hands. "Look, I'm no scientist, and I'm no psychic. But there's no denying that my near-death experience blessed us with some important information throughout this mission."

He stews on that. Finally: "What were Carl's exact words?"

I wince. "You won't like it. He told me that I'd have to kill you —and that, by doing so, I'd kill Eric."

"And you believed him?" Is it disbelief or rage that is causing Jack to shake?

"Yes!" I plop down beside him. "You see, under the circumstances, he had to tell me the truth because we…well, we had a deal. I lived up to my end of it, so he had to as well."

"Talk about a Faustian bargain." Jack scrutinizes me closely. "What did you have to give up in return?"

"My life." I take his hand. "For yours."

"Why, that son of a bitch!" he murmurs.

"Don't you get it, Jack? *Carl knew I'd choose your life over mine.* He gave up even more, just to see me—and to warn us about Eric." I feel my eyes clouding with tears. Exhausted, I close them.

After a million seconds of silence, Jack whispers, "I don't know what I would have done if I'd lost you."

Carl's face appears in my mind. It is how I remember him best: handsome, with a teasing twinkle in his eye, and a sly smile on his face. My eyes open wide when I hear his voice clearly in my ear:

*The letter I left for you—in your recipe book… It explained why I went deep cover. And how I'd never have deserted you—*

His voice fades along with his image—

*—and how I loved you, always.*

Again, he is gone.

My eyes open as I bolt up. "Oh, my God! I forgot!"

Jack's forehead folds in concern. "What now?"

"Carl said he left me a letter in one of my old recipe books! It would explain…why he left when he did." I slap the bed, frustrated. "Damn it! When I was finally ready to move, I dumped a lot of things—including my mother's old recipe books. It's long gone by now."

"No, they're not. Your Aunt Phyllis has those books."

"What? …What is she doing with them?"

"She saw you toss out a box containing a bunch of old mementos. She felt you might want them someday."

"Talk about prescient!" I say, laughing. "Wait—how did you know she had it?"

"I was in charge of vetting you for Acme. As part of the process, I interviewed her."

I frown. "She never said anything about that!"

"She didn't know me at the time. And besides, I was in disguise and I used a standard ploy: that I was investigating the possibility that your father was the beneficiary of a deceased friend's estate, but that I needed proof that he was the legitimate heir."

"My father did inherit something from someone, but he'd long since died. It came to me instead." I frown. "So, the money wasn't part of someone's legacy?"

Jack shakes his head.

"Then where did it come from? Acme?"

"Um…me." His face turns bright red.

"Why? You didn't even know me then."

"Because I…well, the more I knew about you, the more I cared for you."

"As far back as then," I murmur. "Did you find the letter?"

He nods.

"What did Carl write?" I ask excitedly.

"If you're asking me if he came clean about becoming a double-agent to a consortium funding international terrorism, *Hmmm*, let me think," he quips sarcastically. "Gee, nope, nothing like that."

"Please, don't use that tone with me," I warn him. "Tell me, Jack: considering all we've been through together these past three years, why didn't you mention the letter to me?" Suddenly, it hits me. "Don't tell me you're still jealous of Carl!" I can't help but laugh.

"Frankly, I forgot about it," Jack mutters coldly. "Cut me some slack here, Donna. I almost lost you! And now that I have you back, I have to wrap my head around the idea that you interacted with our deceased enemies."

"Some of those souls were our friends too."

"Carl's new address may be Hell, but he's still the smug, conniving asshole he's always been," Jack counters. "Otherwise, he wouldn't be there in the first place. Am I right?"

I shrug because he has a point.

"What if Carl had been lying, Donna? What if you'd killed me and not Eric?"

My eyes tear up at the thought. "I wouldn't have been able to live with myself. The act would have haunted me the rest of my life."

For some reason, that brings a smile to his face. "No. *I* would have haunted you until your dying day."

I snort at the thought.

Hearing me, he laughs outright.

Now, I'm laughing as well. In fact, we're laughing so hard that tears are running down our faces.

I stop first. Or at least I think I have. In fact, Jack isn't laughing.

He's choking back his tears.

Shocked, I shift closer to wipe one away.

He takes my hand and holds it against his face. He turns his head to kiss my palm.

Déjà vu surges over me. Why? ...

Then I remember. "Carl did that too, when we said goodbye," I murmur sadly.

He accepts this revelation with a resigned nod. "I've been in many a situation where I should have contemplated the Afterlife. But to be honest with you, I hadn't. I guess I felt that, in our field, it's always around the corner, so why not live life as if every day matters? And then you came into my life. The last thing I could think of was *you* leaving me." Jack looks down at my palm. He turns it over and stares at my wedding band. Rubbing it with his finger, he says, "I have no right to resent the fact that you made your peace with him."

"Do you mean that?"

"Yes. You were right. Carl knew you'd sacrifice your life to save mine." Jack sighs. "He needed closure with you."

"I wish I could say his unselfish act put him in a better place... but it didn't." I sigh deeply at the thought of Carl's fate.

"He wanted it so badly that he accepted that infernal bargain with Lucifer—Satan, the Devil, or whatever else you want to call him," Jack replies. "And in trusting Carl's clue, not only did you save our lives and that of the President and many others, you proved your faith in the love you once shared with him. Wherever he is, he now realizes that."

"I guess you're right… No—I know you're right." For the first time since returning to the living, serenity eases into my heart. "Jack, thank you for trying to understand."

He shrugs absently. "I think it was Bertrand Russell who said, 'Fools and fanatics are always so certain of themselves, and wiser people are so full of doubts.' Frankly, I'm doing my best to be considered the latter"— Jack points to me—"at least, to the woman I love." He looks down at my hand, which he still holds tightly. "Donna, I couldn't imagine my world without you. You made me whole in a way I never could have been had I not met you."

"Funny," I murmur. "Valentina said that about us."

His jaw drops when he hears this. "Well, she was certainly right about that."

I reach over to hold his hand. I love this man with my whole being.

Jack wipes a tear from my cheek. Suddenly, he laughs. "Hey, just think—you beat the Reaper! Frankly, if you hadn't, I've no doubt you would have given the Devil his due."

"I hope I never get the chance to find out. I have too much to lose." I shudder at the thought.

"You've been given a second chance. It's God's way of saying you're here for a purpose."

Tenderly, he draws me in for a kiss.

We both deserve more than that. I shove him onto the bed and climb onboard.

"Wait! Donna…is it too soon for this?" The concern in his voice is touching.

"Too soon? It was almost too late," I remind him.

The realization that I'm right drives his desire. Jack takes this as an invitation to strip away any and all clothing that stands between us: unzipping my dress, tossing off my heels, peeling down my panties, and flinging off my bra.

As for my bandaged wound, he bows before it, kissing it gently.

Oddly, it's a turn-on. I would not have thought that possible.

His duds take a while longer to shed, but I'm there to help. If he weren't so hard, it would be easier to unzip his pants. Getting his T-shirt over his broad shoulders is also a struggle, but hey, I'm up for it.

He's up for me too.

The collective memory of past intimacies and the shared thrills of our foreplay are the shorthand in our lovemaking. Slowly, gently, he eases into me. In no time, we find our rhythm. Urgency builds with desire. Trauma stokes our frenzy. The emotions swelling within me are matched with each of his thrusts and grunts.

The strain on my abdomen brings both pain—and pleasure. I cry out for all the wrong reasons. But I also gasp for all the right ones.

Our bliss comes in unison.

It is the ultimate celebration of our souls entwined. It is every memory we've ever shared. It's every surge of passion that has ever flowed between us.

It is our undying commitment to love each other for eternity.

By the time we pull away, we've found what was lost in the tragedy of these past days:

Us.

# 26

# One Way or Another

Recorded by Blondie. Released September 1978, the song reached #24 on the greatest hits charts, spending fourteen weeks on it.

*Humans are blessed to have the intelligence to figure out solutions to many problems.*

*Can we solve all the world's ills?*

*Of course not. Certain things are inevitable. As the ironic saying goes, death and taxes are two conundrums that most often come to mind.*

*Okay, perhaps someday, all societies will do away with taxes. (One would hope, right?) As for death, well, that's a long shot. Besides all the problems it would cause (overpopulation, food and water shortages, an endless healthcare crisis) would you want to live forever if you weren't remotely near your physical and mental best?*

*If you answered "Yes," those who felt contrarily would call you selfish and unrealistic.*

*If you answered "No," your critics would assume you could not think outside the box —*

*That box, of course, being your coffin.*
*Until they are proven right, the no's have it.*
*One way or the other, the Grim Reaper is going to get you —*
*Hopefully, later than sooner.*

Home sweet home.

Except for the garage.

Between our two cars is a wall of precariously stacked boxes, four bikes, three skateboards, baseball bats, tennis racquets, Lacrosse sticks, and every ball imaginable.

It's has become an insurmountable obstacle course.

Like the rest of the family, I should already be at Hilldale Park, cheering on Trisha (sans helmet; okay, yes, I caved) and her soccer team in a grudge match with the Newport Beach Nymphs. Apparently, Jack didn't have the heart to rouse me from my deep slumber. The note on his pillow read:

*My Dear Sleeping Beauty,*
  *Walked with the kids and Aunt Phyllis to the game. They're hankering for a post-game pizza, so when you're ready to join us, take the Donna-mobile.*
  *xx forever and through Infinity,*

Jack

Despite my willowy post-coma physique, I can barely squeeze between Jack's car and mine. I'm steps away from the driver's door when my foot lands on something and slips out from under me—

A skateboard sporting a leering skull-and-crossbones on a jet-black background. It's got enough traction to ricochet off a tall plastic bin containing old toys—

Which topples over onto a tower of boxes—

Which lean sideways into another tower, which tilts into another—

Only to be stopped when I leap over an old tricycle and lean against the boxes.

When I'm convinced that they are finally braced against the wall, I sigh with relief. "This is insanity," I mutter.

It's time to clean up this mess, once and for all. I look around for the ladder and find a skateboard instead.

I pick it up: CHEEVER BING is written on the board's underside.

Figures.

My first instinct is to toss it into the trash. But then I calculate the odds of Cheever falling and breaking his neck, and suddenly I realize they're greater if the board was involved, so I toss it into my SUV. He'll retrieve it on Monday when I go back into carpool rotation—lucky me.

Hey, sure beats making pacts with the Devil.

I need to sort through these boxes. To do that, I'll need a ladder to disassemble the stacks.

At least the ladder is where it should be: hanging on a wall with the rest of the yard and hardware tools. As per Jack's nature, it is the one wall that doesn't need tidying. Before he moved in with us, I'd wince when I passed this wall. Do-it-yourself projects and yard work were Carl's release. Despite being told he had died, I set up the wall as an altar to his memory now some eight years ago.

In hindsight, I wonder if his expertise with hatchets, hammers, saws, and chainsaws was part of his wetwork training? My guess is yes.

I open the garage door in order to move my car into the driveway. That way, I'll have the room to sort the discarded stuff into piles. If something doesn't merit a trip to the GoodWill store or isn't anything to hand down to Nicky or any other tot, it'll go to the local dump.

I start with the shortest stack of boxes, which is closest to the door. Most are filled with clothing. I lay out anything worth keeping—adult male, adult female, girl, and boy—on an old tablecloth.

Fifteen minutes later, I'm ready to move onto the next tower of boxes.

The top box isn't as dusty as the others. Only when I open it do I realize why. It contains a lot of Carl's clothing, along with other things of his I'd packed away.

At that moment, I see it: my old recipe book is crammed into the corner of the box.

Ah, now I remember! When Aunt Phyllis cleaned out her garage last year, she came traipsing back with a bunch of boxes she claimed were my mementos. She was right. My old diary was in one of them. I was so taken with it that I stopped to read it, cramming the rest of the stuff in here as well.

I'm shaking as I reach for the recipe book. But just as I grab it, a large garden spider crawls out from under it. I'm so startled that I lose my footing—

And I topple off the ladder.

WHEN I OPEN MY EYES, HE'S STANDING THERE:

Death.

"Oh, heck," I grumble. "Not you again!"

As I stumble to my feet, I stare down at my body: No aches or pains, let alone broken bones. And yes, all appendages accounted for. I turn toward the driveway. Are flames flaring above a hellish abyss?

Not at all. Instead, a pair of robins swoop playfully in the azure sky, so I guess my eyes, ears, and other senses are in fine working order.

Then it hits me: It's my brain. I'm going mad.

"Don't be so paranoid," Death admonishes me. "Okay, granted, in your line of work, you have to be crazy to a certain degree. But you're certainly not *certifiable*."

"Thanks. I think." I sigh. "I notice you're not carrying your little notebook. Can I take that as a good sign?"

"Not to worry. You're in the clear."

"You're too gracious." I bat my eyes. "So, to what do I owe this honor?"

"I'm fulfilling my promise. I said I owed you one. Well, it's payback time." He leans in.

"Much appreciated. Shoot—I don't mean that literally, of course."

He rolls his eyes. "Just a heads-up, milady: within the next twelve months, someone near and dear to you will meet an untimely death."

My heart drops into my stomach. "Who?"

Death wags a finger at me. "Only one favor. A name is TMI."

Too much information? Not if every person in your life is precious to you!

The faces of those near and dear to me flash through my mind: my coworkers; Aunt Phyllis; my children;

And Jack.

Slowly, I nod. "You're right. You've fulfilled your promise to me. Thank you for that."

He holds out a hand to shake.

As I take it, I resist the urge to shudder.

On purpose, he pulls a Macron, holding on longer and tighter than I'd like. There is a lot of pain in his grip: not his or mine, but that of the poor anguished souls who are his most recent victims.

As I pull away, he chuckles wistfully, "Ah, sweet Donna Craig, your *joie de vivre* is infectious! You are so—WOKE! You'll always be the one who got away." He winks as he warns me, "For now. You won't live forever."

"Frankly, I wouldn't want to. Still, when I go, I'll do so on my terms," I assure him.

"You'll leave your legion of fans bereft." His lips twist into a Cheshire cat grin wide enough for me to glimpse inside his mouth. What I see are stars being sucked into an abyss of dark matter.

My way to hide my shock at this revelation is to shrug. "My only hope is that I'll leave those who love me with fond memories," I insist. "I hope that they'll remember the adventures we shared and that they had a laugh or two on me. My goal has always been a well-lived life with purpose."

"Time will tell," he replies. His left wing spreads just wide enough to stroke my cheek.

Instinctively, I close my eyes. I can't say I feel anything much: just the uptick of a slight breeze.

When I open my eyes, he is already gone.

In a year, I'll lose someone I love.

At this realization, my heart plunges into a dark pool of sadness.

It's replaced by a daring thought:

Maybe Death will let me trade places with whoever it is.

I grab my recipe book and flip the pages until I come to my beef stew recipe: Carl's favorite.

Yes, there it is: an envelope, addressed to me in Carl's handwriting.

I open it and read:

*Dear Donna,*

*If you're reading this, it's because I couldn't come home to you, as I planned.*

*Please don't think it's because I didn't want to, or that I didn't try my damnedest. My intention was and has always been to be the best husband in the world, and the best father to our sweet, wonderful children. My leaving was the only way in which I could guarantee your safety, and theirs.*

*I have no doubt that somewhere—hopefully on this Earth, and soon— we'll be reunited. When we are, I'll make good on the promise I made on our wedding day: to spend the rest of eternity with the woman I love.*

*Yours, always,*

Carl

He wanted it all. Instead, he lost everything.

There was a time in which I loved Carl with all my heart. Smitten with Carl, in love with him, and hated him enough to want to kill him.

May he rest in peace.

I DON'T KNOW HOW LONG I'VE BEEN STARING OFF INTO SPACE— thankfully, not Death's Hellmouth—when Aunt Phyllis's cackle admonishes me: "Wake up, Missy! The gang's all here!"

My children gather around me. At the same time, Jeff plants a kiss on my cheek, Mary's lips brush my forehead, and Trisha snuggles into my lap.

But the haze of desolation left in Death's wake dissipates completely when I feel Jack's arms go around me. "Hey, kids, give your mom some breathing room. We have all the time in the world to show her how much we love her."

I scan each of their faces. As always, Aunt Phyllis rewards my gaze with an impish grin. Trisha's eyes are filled with adoration, whereas Jeff's pat on my hand assures us both that we will always have each other's back. Mary's eyes are glazed with sweet tears of relief. As if reading her mind, Evan nods resolutely.

But it is Jack's sweet kiss that gives me the assurance I need that, whatever the future holds, we will get through it together.

I am back.

For good.

For now.

## THE END

Performed by The Doors. Released in March 1967.

"The End" was ranked at number 336 on 2010 *Rolling Stone*'s list of "The 500 Greatest Songs of All Time." It was also ranked number 26 on *Blender*'s list of "The 50 Worst Songs Ever."

That's life. You decide.

<hr>

## Listen to the Chapter Titles'
## Music

<hr>

Part of my process for writing this novel was to choose a song title that best exemplified the action to take place in each chapter. I didn't limit myself to any one genre of music. Instead, I let the lyrics set the tone.

I'd play the song as I wrote. Often, I was surprised how well the words matched up perfectly with the chapter. It set the mood for me. I hope it does the same for you.

While you'll find all of these on YouTube, this page on my website makes it easy to find them all in one place:

https://josiebrown.com/HA16GH-SONGS

Some were created and uploaded by the bands, artists, or their producers for promotional purposes. Others are a fan's homage to the band or the song. A few were from archival televised performances.

Like most free websites, ads may appear on the screen courtesy of YouTube or the uploading source.

Still, I hope these songs inspire you or tweak a few great

memories. If so, I'm sure the musicians would love you to pluck down the small price for these single songs from your favorite streaming site. It's part of spreading the love.

Also, regarding the Ungrateful Deads who fight Donna in her Hellish trials and the helpful souls gave her tips, you'll find her initial meetings with them these novels, although sometimes they appear in subsequent books too:

*Trial 1 (Chapter 4)*

Opponent: Gunter, Book 12, *Husband Hunting Hints.*

Tipster: Varick Velasco, also Book 12, *Husband Hunting Hints*

*Trial 2 (Chapter 5)*

Opponent: Ratko Zoran, Book 3: *Killer Christmas Tips.*

Tipster: Edwina Doyle, Book 2: *Guide to Gracious Killing*

*Trial 3 (Chapter 6)*

Opponent: Salem Rahmin al-Sadah. Book 11, *Weddings, Weapons, & Warfare.* Tipster: Robert Martin, Book 6, *Recipes for Disaster*

*Trial 4 (Chapter 7)*

Opponent: Sebastian Gillingham, Book 7, *Hollywood Scream Play.*

Tipster: Nola Janoff, Book 1, *The Housewife Assassin's Handbook*; and Book 15, *Deadly Dossier.*

*Trial 5 (Chapter 8)*

Opponent: Liang Xia, Book 10, *Garden of Deadly Delights.*

Tipster: Catherine Martin, Book 6, *Recipes for Disaster*

*Trial 6 (Chapter 9)*

Opponent: Midge and Dave Kelsey, Book 1, *The Housewife Assassin's Handbook.*

Tipster: Valentina Petrescu Craig, Book 3, *Killer Christmas Tips.*

*Trial 7 (Chapter 10)*

Opponent: Tatyana Zakharov, Book 9, *Hostage Hosting Tips*; and Book 15, *Deadly Dossier.*

Tipsters: Mara Portnoy, Book 9, *Hostage Hosting Tips*;

**(Chapter 12)**

And, of course, Carl Stone played tipster. You'll find him first in, Book 1 *The Housewife Assassin's Handbook,* and up through Book 8, *Killer App.*

—*Josie*

Next Up for Donna!


**The Housewife Assassin's Fourth Estate Sale**

**(Book 17)**


Donna and Jack must infiltrate a major media conglomerate's newspaper,
television, and radio divisions in order to stop a foreign state's covert
attempt to initiate a global war.

Other Books by Josie Brown

**The True Hollywood Lies Series**

Hollywood Hunk

Hollywood Whore

**The Totlandia Series**

The Onesies - Book 1 (Fall)

The Onesies - Book 2 (Winter)

The Onesies - Book 3 (Spring)

The Onesies - Book 4 (Summer)

The Twosies - Book 5 (Fall)

The Twosies – Book 6 (Winter)

The Twosies - Book 7 (Spring)

The Twosies - Book 8 (Summer)

**More Josie Brown Novels**

The Candidate

Secret Lives of Husbands and Wives

The Baby Planner

# How to Reach Josie


To write Josie, go to:
mailfromjosie@gmail.com

To find out more about Josie, or to get on her eLetter list for book
launch announcements, go to her website:
www.JosieBrown.com

You can also find her at:

www.AuthorProvocateur.com

twitter.com/JosieBrownCA

facebook.com/josiebrownauthor

pinterest.com/josiebrownca

instagram.com/josiebrownnovels